CHERYL ST. JOHN

The Wedding Journey

Love Inspired

Special thanks and acknowledgment to Cheryl St.John for her contribution to the Irish Brides miniseries.

Recycling programs for this product may not exist in your area.

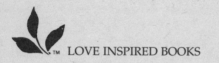 LOVE INSPIRED BOOKS

ISBN-13: 978-0-373-82911-8

THE WEDDING JOURNEY

Copyright © 2012 by Harlequin Books S.A.

www.LoveInspiredBooks.com

Printed in U.S.A.

"I'd like to hire you for the position of my assistant."

"But I have no formal training."

"Experience and quick thinking are often worth more than book learning, Miss Murphy. You've already proven yourself more than competent."

Maeve thought of all those she'd treated and seen worsen and eventually die. Less than two weeks ago, she hadn't been able to save her own da. But right now, her sisters needed her to agree to this. Their welfare depended on someone earning a wage.

"We accept your kind offer," Maeve said. She prayed her abilities were enough that she would be a help.

"Very well then. The three of you should go get settled. Afterward, you can return and help me store the supplies."

"We're indebted to you, Dr. Gallagher," she replied.

Gathering their things, the sisters made their way back out to the corridor. Once the door closed behind them, Bridget grasped Maeve's arm through her sleeve. "I think he likes you."

IRISH BRIDES: Adventure—and love— await these Irish sisters on the way to America....

Books by Cheryl St.John

Love Inspired Historical

The Preacher's Wife
To Be a Mother
  "Mountain Rose"
Marrying the Preacher's Daughter
The Wedding Journey

CHERYL ST.JOHN's

love for reading started as a child. She wrote her own stories, designed covers and stapled them into books. She credits many hours of creating scenarios for her paper dolls and Barbies as the start of her fascination with fictional characters. At one time, Westerns were her preferred reading—until she happened upon LaVyrle Spencer's *Hummingbird* in her local store. After that, she couldn't read enough romance, and the desire to create stories of hope and forgiveness was born.

Cheryl loves hearing from readers. Visit her website, http://www.cherylstjohn.net, or email her at SaintJohn@aol.com.

For a selection of collectable mini-bookcover cards, send a SASE to: BOX 390995, Omaha, NE 68139.

God resists the proud, but gives grace to the humble.
Therefore humble yourselves under the mighty hand
of God, that He may exalt you in due time, casting
all your care upon Him, for He cares for you.
—*1 Peter 5–7*

"My dream is of a place and a time
where America will once again be seen
as the last best hope of earth."
—Abraham Lincoln

Chapter One

June 1850, Castleville, Ireland

Lilting over the roar of the ocean, the haunting notes of a flute raised goose bumps on Maeve's arms. There were no men in the Murphy family to carry the plain wooden box holding the remains of their father on their shoulders, so she and her two older sisters followed behind as the men of the village proceeded from the small stone church up a grassy incline to the cemetery.

The gathering reached the crest. Here the sound of thundering waves far below the cliffs grew to a crescendo, nature's hymn as familiar as the expansive sky and the salty tang of the ocean.

Beside Maeve, her sister Bridget wept into her handkerchief. She'd worn a somber secondhand brown bonnet, fashionable some ten years ago, yet still serviceable. "What's going to become of us without Da?"

Maeve comforted Bridget with an arm around her shoulders. "Shush now, *ma milis,*" she said, calling her sister *my sweet* in their native Gaelic tongue.

"We'll come up with a plan." The eldest of the three, Nora, always had a plan. The sisters were stair steps in height and age, Nora being tall, Bridget in between and Maeve petite.

Most of the simple graves were marked with stones, others with weathered wooden crosses. Goat's-beard grew in thick patches throughout the grass, the yellow blooms a cheerful contrast to the mood. A hole had been dug in the rich black soil, and Maeve had only to glance about the crowd to note which of the young men's hair was damp from exertion. She spotted two familiar heads of curly red hair. She would thank the Donnelly brothers later.

Reverend Larkin had prayed over members from every household represented at the graveside today. The famine that had taken its toll on their countrymen had spared no family. Hunger, sickness and poverty were all these people knew, but the believers of Castleville clung to their faith. Now the reverend stretched his hand toward the pine box as six farmers dressed in their Sunday clothing lowered it by ropes down into the earth.

"Jack Murphy, your daughters long for one more day spent at your side. When we lose someone we love, it seems that time stands still. What moves through us is a silence, a quiet sadness, a longing for one more day, one more word, one more touch."

The ache in Maeve's chest threatened to cut off her breath. Security had been whipped out from beneath her with the death of her father. The pain of never seeing him again, of never hearing his thick brogue, was almost more than she could bear. She worked to hold back the grief and fear bearing down on her—and to steady Bridget, who swayed on her feet.

Their female friends and neighbors wept softly into their handkerchiefs and shawls. The men stared at the ground and worried the brims of their hats as a red-billed chough flew in a lazy circle overhead.

"We may not understand why you left this earth so soon," the reverend continued. "Or why you left before we were ready to say goodbye, but little by little we shall begin to remember not just that you died, but all the days that you lived. We will see you again some day, in a heavenly place where there is no hunger or sickness. No rocks in the fields. Now, Lord, bless the daughters of Jack Murphy. Keep them safe from harm and provide for them by Your bounteous grace and mercy."

Reverend Larkin turned and nodded at Nora. "You first, dear."

Maeve's oldest sister seemed taller than her already admirable height while she kept her back straight and stepped forward. She wore her chestnut-brown hair fashioned as she always did, in a practical bun, so not even a single strand of hair caught in the breeze. Kneeling, she picked up a handful of earth and dropped it into the grave. The clods hit the coffin with a dull thump. Bridget followed, her dark wavy hair hidden by her bonnet, with Maeve going last.

She performed the task quickly, without thinking, without gazing upon the pine box, but still she imagined her father laid out in his frayed suit. He wasn't in that lifeless body, she reminded herself again. He'd gone onto glory and was right this moment looking down from beside her dear mother. They were together now in a place where there were no potatoes to dig or mouths to feed.

Scully and Vaughan Donnelly rolled back their sleeves over beefy forearms and shoveled dirt upon the casket.

Maeve watched for a few minutes until Mrs. Donovan, who'd been a dear friend of her mother's, pressed a coin into Maeve's hand and hugged her soundly. "I'll be prayin' for ye, I will."

Maeve swallowed the sob rising in her chest and pressed her fisted hands to her midriff. She accepted condolences and pennies from her neighbors. Her fellow countrymen were poor, so these modest offerings were sacrifices they couldn't afford. Their gifts humbled her. The fact that so many had come to the funeral at all was enough to touch her heart.

It was a workday, as was every day in County Beary, except the Sabbath, and the landlord didn't take kindly to a day off.

"I still be missin' your beautiful mother," a long-time friend told her and enveloped her in a warm hug. "Colleen and I were dreamers, we were, as girls, but these times steal a woman's dreams. Don't let anythin' or anyone take your dreams, lassie."

The woman joined her daughter and together they walked through the knee-high grass.

After extending their sympathies one at a time, the rest of the mourners headed back down the green hillside toward their homes and fields.

With the ocean pounding below, the Murphy sisters stood on the lush green crest above the village until they were the only ones remaining.

"Mr. Bantry already has someone waiting to move into the cottage, he does." Nora spoke of their landlord. "We'd better go pack and clean."

Maeve set her jaw. "I'll not be cleanin' the house that ill-mannered tyrant's forcing us out of."

"Our mother kept that cottage clean all the years she lived within its walls, and we'll not be shaming her by leaving so much as a speck of dust."

Nora was right, of course. She was always right.

"What's to become of us, then?" Bridget asked.

"Mrs. Ennis said we could board with them temporarily." Nora showed them the wrapped bundle she held. "She gave us a loaf of bread."

"They have seven mouths to feed as it is." Maeve took off down the hill and her sisters followed. A startled grouse flew out of the tall grass.

"Our neighbors gave me coins." Bridget extended her hand.

The three of them compared what they'd received. The total was pathetically insufficient and would barely purchase a week's food. Their cupboards were empty. That morning they'd shared two partridge eggs Maeve had found.

Maeve led the way around a field bordered by a low rock wall. They crossed a stone bridge over a creek and continued toward the only home they'd ever known. The stone cottage greeted them with a lifetime of memories. Their mother had died here ten years previous, during the worst of the influenza epidemic. Their father had repaired the thatched roof numerous times, and the newest foliage showed up distinctly against the old.

Inside, Nora set the bread on the scarred cutting table. Bridget removed her bonnet. The three of them gathered around and studied the golden brown loaf reverently. "The Ennises couldn't afford to part with this," Maeve said.

"Our neighbors are a generous lot, they are," Nora agreed. "The Macrees brought bramble jam earlier. We could each have a slice with it now."

Bridget shook her head. "We should save it. I'm not very hungry."

"My stomach is tied in knots, as well," Maeve agreed. "We'll want it later. It will last us through tomorrow."

Nora wrapped the bread in a clean square of toweling. She brushed her hands together. "Very well. We'll pack."

"Pack. Where shall we go?" Bridget asked.

Nora placed her hands on her hips. "We must each find a husband immediately."

"And not marry for love?" Bridget asked with a horrified expression. She placed her hat on a hook by the bed they shared. "We should stay with the Ennises. We'd still be near the village and the young men we know."

"No proposals have been forthcoming yet," Nora reminded her. "All the men here are as poor as we are. None can afford to take a wife and work a piece of land on his own. Honora Monaghan married one of the Kenny brothers, and now she has to live with his whole family."

"Perhaps Mr. Bantry will allow us to work this land ourselves," Bridget suggested. "We've worked it alongside Da all these years. We're as capable as any man."

"Mr. Bantry has his own kinsmen waiting to occupy the land," Nora replied.

Maeve picked up her mother's Bible and touched the worn cover. "May God turn Bantry's heart, and if He doesn't turn his heart, may He turn Bantry's ankle, so we'll know him by his limping!"

"Mind your tongue, Maeve Eileen Murphy," her eldest sister admonished. "And spoken while you're holding our dear departed mother's Holy Bible."

"I learned the saying from her, I did." Maeve laughed, the first sound of merriment in this house for many weeks. "We'll simply have to find work," she told them logically. "And you know as well as I there's not a job to be had in all of County Beary. We must travel to County Galway."

"We can use Mother's trunk." Nora removed an oil lamp from the top and pulled the trunk into the center of the room that served as their kitchen and living space. "We'll have to sort out all the things we can't take."

They found a few neatly pressed and folded aprons, a piece each of their baby clothing, a bundle of letters and a few daguerreotypes, one in an aged frame.

Nora picked up the likeness of their beautiful mother and caressed the frame with farm-roughened fingers. "What would Mother have done? She was practical above all else."

"Where did practicality get her?" Bridget asked. "She never had a day's happiness."

"Romantic notions won't put food on the table." Holding the frame too tightly, Nora's fingers poked through the fabric backing. She turned over the frame and examined the hole. Peering more closely, she worked three folded pieces of paper from inside. "Whatever are these?"

The younger sisters crowded in close for a better look. The first paper Nora unfolded was a letter, the second some type of legal document and the last a pencil drawing of a house. "How odd."

"Read the letter," Bridget coaxed and reached to take the drawing.

"'May 1824,'" Nora began. "'My dearest Colleen, I know you have made your choice. My heart is broken, but I understand your decision. I've gone to America, to Faith Glen, the village in Massachusetts we spoke of so often. The town was founded by an Irishman. It is just ten miles from Boston, yet I have heard it is so much like

Castleville, though, of course it is another world. I have purchased a small home for you—'"

"Who's the letter from?" Maeve stepped in closer to have a better look at the handwriting.

Nora waved her away. "Let me finish. 'I have purchased a small home for you on the water's edge. Should you or your kin ever be in need of a place to go, know this house is yours. With undying love, Laird.'"

The three sisters stood in stunned silence for a full minute.

"I told you she whispered the name *Laird* with her last dyin' breath." Bridget looked up from the letter to Nora's tense expression. "But the two of you insisted she was just trying to say *love*."

"We didn't know any Laird," Maeve said.

"Until now." Bridget gave a satisfied nod.

"What's this mention of undying love?" Maeve asked.

"Dated a year before I was born, 'tis." Nora turned her attention to the pencil drawing Bridget held, and the three of them studied the depiction of a home near the ocean. The artist had even drawn flowers blooming in gardens on two sides.

"Mother was in love with this man!" Bridget's expression showed her shock. "He bought her a house in America, but she stayed and married Da? I can't conceive of it."

"There must be a logical explanation," Nora said.

Bridget's hazel eyes were bright with excitement. "The cottage sounds ideal. We should go there."

"They say there's so much land in America that anyone can own a share." Maeve took the deed from Nora's fingers and examined it. "The soil is rich and there's plenty of rain. There are schools and jobs. Western men are hungry for wives."

"That may be so, but it takes more than we have to purchase ship's fare and travel there. Fanny Clellan sold both her cow and her mother's brooch to buy a ticket. We don't even *have* a cow." Nora snatched the paper back. She pointed to the date. "This deed is over twenty-five years old, 'tis. The house is most likely occupied—or it could have been destroyed."

Maeve went to the coffee tin and dumped out the contents on the kitchen table. Bridget added the coins they'd received that morning, and the two of them tallied the amount.

"This could get us to Galway," Nora pointed out.

"But we'd have no food or lodging," Maeve argued. "We have something we can sell to buy tickets to America."

"Don't even speak of it." Nora gave Maeve a cautionary glare.

Maeve went back to the trunk. "Once we land we could find an inn and secure jobs. We can look for this house in Faith Glen and learn if it's still there. Think of it! We might have a comfortable place to live just waitin' for us." She knelt and took out several objects that had been packed in fabric at the bottom.

Bridget unwrapped one and held up a silver sugar bowl, followed by the teapot. "I never saw Mama use these."

"I never did, either." Maeve unwrapped a creamer. "They've always been in the trunk."

"They've been there as long as I can remember," Nora said. "Da once told me Mama got them from a woman she worked for. He said she had saved them for a rainy day. Even when times were the worst, she held on to them."

"This is the rainiest day I can think of," Bridget commented.

Maeve gave her eldest sister a pleading look. "It would be a fresh start, Nora. We have nothing left here."

Nora looked about the barren room, her concern clear, but her resolve crumbling. "Even selling that, the tickets would take every last penny."

"Perhaps there are positions aboard one of the sailing vessels. None of us minds a good day's work." Excitement laced Bridget's tone.

Nora refolded the papers and carefully tucked them inside the Bible. "I suppose it can't hurt to go see how much the tickets actually cost and learn if it's even possible for us to hire on."

Bridget shot a delighted bright-eyed gaze to Maeve. A broad smile lit her sweet face. Reaching for Maeve's hands, she squeezed them until Maeve winced. "We're going to America! Can you conceive of it?"

"Only if we can afford to buy fare," Nora reminded.

Maeve tried to hide the jitters weakening her knees. If they didn't have enough, they'd have to find a way by the end of the week. They couldn't remain here. Butterflies fluttered in her stomach. What did three simple village girls know about traveling aboard a sailing ship? What if the deed truly was worthless and there was no place for them once they arrived?

The sense of hopelessness she'd lived with for months had lifted, however. They were taking action to change their situation. Even if the house was gone, anything was better than this. God had already seen them through difficult times. All they had to do now was trust Him.

"Into Your care we place ourselves, Lord," she prayed

aloud. "Show us the path You would have us take and bless us as we seek a new home and a new start. Thank You for hope."

Chapter Two

Two weeks later, Minot's Ledge, Port of Galway, Ireland

"Move aside!" A barrel-chested man carrying an enormous crate on his shoulder jostled passengers awaiting their turns to board the *Annie McGee*. Overhead, gulls with black-tipped wings cawed and swooped.

Maeve and her sisters backed out of the way. All of their earthly possessions had been whittled down to the trunk, which had been stored aboard earlier, a few crates, a donated bandbox and a battered satchel. The pungent smells of fish and brine burned Maeve's nose.

The rude man set down his burden at the foot of the gangplank and headed back to a wooden cart, which interrupted the line of waiting passengers. The harnessed mule jumped nervously at the man's approach, and the fellow picked up a switch and waved it in a threat.

The mule sidestepped, rocking the cart precariously.

"Stand still, you good for nothin' bag o' bones!" His accent plainly emphasized a lack of Irish heritage.

With a loud bray, the frightened animal kicked out with his hind feet, solidly connecting with the cart and tipping the entire thing backward.

Crates toppled onto the ground as a piercing cry rose.

"There's a lad beneath the cart!" someone called.

High-pitched screams raised the hair on Maeve's neck.

The burly man grumbled and, together with several bystanders, righted the cart back onto its wheels.

"Aren't you the doctor's assistant?" a gentleman in a black suit asked the grumbling bear of a man. His face showed noticeable concern. "The lad here's bleeding."

"Filthy urchin shouldn't have been beggin' on the wharf," the big man snarled. He picked up one of the spilled crates and headed for the gangplank without a backward glance.

Maeve didn't hesitate to set the satchel she held at Nora's feet and rush to the fallen boy's side. She'd seen more than her share of sickness and injuries over the past few years, and the lack of a proper village doctor had given her plenty of opportunities to pick up numerous nursing skills. She didn't know if she could help, but she'd do whatever she could.

The scene was alarming. Blood flowed from the boy's thigh at a steady rate. Thinking quickly, she untied the scarf from around her shoulders, twisted it into a rope and tied it about his leg.

"I have need of a stick," she called.

"Will this do?" A nearby woman shoved an ivory comb into her hand.

Maeve tied the tails of the scarf around the comb and twisted until the makeshift tourniquet cinched tight and the flow of blood ceased. Certain the bleeding was stopped, she lifted her gaze to the frightened boy's dirty face. Tears streaked the grime on his pale cheeks, and wide frightened brown eyes appealed to her.

"You're going to be all right," she assured him. She

glanced into the crowd. "Has someone sent for the doctor?"

"Yes, miss," a female bystander replied. "My husband alerted the sailors on the gangplank. One of 'em rushed aboard."

"It won't be long now," Maeve assured the boy. "What's your name, laddie?"

"Sean," he replied, his lower lip trembling. "Sean McCorkle."

"Is your family nearby?" she asked.

"Aye. Me two brothers. Emmett be right over there."

Maeve glanced about and spotted the younger boy he'd indicated standing several feet away, wearing a terrified expression. Both of them appeared dirty and uncared for.

"'Tis the doctor comin' now," the woman called to Maeve.

Stepping around passengers, a tall man hurried forward. His chocolate-brown gaze analyzed the scene, taking in the patient, the improvised tourniquet and lastly Maeve. He leaned over the lad, looking into each eye, and then pressing long fingers to the boy's sockless ankle above his battered shoe. The doctor's black hair glistened in the morning sun as he bent to examine the wound.

The scent of sandalwood clung to his clothing and drifted to Maeve's nostrils. His efficiency impressed her.

He raised his head, piercing Maeve with an unsmiling, yet admiring look. "That was mighty quick thinking, miss."

"I did what I could."

He knelt and effortlessly picked up the boy. Maeve stood as he did, keeping her grip on the twisted scarf and comb secure. "I'll take him to the dispensary, where I can treat him."

"His name is Sean McCorkle. Says he has brothers, but he didn't mention parents."

"It will be helpful if you hold the tourniquet in place while I carry him aboard." He called to one of the sailors. "Find this lad's family! McCorkle's the name."

As dirty as he was, Maeve couldn't imagine his family or home. "Where's your mother, Sean?"

"She be with Jesus, miss. Don't have a da, neither."

She exchanged a significant look with the doctor.

His contemptible assistant chose that moment to return for another armload. The doctor stabbed him with an angry dark gaze. "What happened here, Hegarty?"

"Filthy beggar got in the way. Shouldn't be underfoot, that one."

A man with coal-black hair sticking out from beneath his cap stepped forward. "Takin' a switch to the mule, Hegarty was," the man supplied. "Frightened the poor beast into tippin' goods all about the wharf and spilt the cart right atop the laddie here."

"Cruelty to animals and children isn't acceptable behavior under my employ," the doctor proclaimed, already walking away with the boy. "Pack your belongings and leave the ship immediately. You no longer have a job."

Hegarty dropped the crate with a resounding crash and brushed his beefy hands together. "You can keep your measly wages. Too many smelly Irishmen aboard this vessel for my taste, anyhow."

The doctor directed an undiscernable look at Maeve. It was apparent from his speech, he was every bit as Irish as she, though obviously from a higher social class and far more educated. In those brief seconds it didn't matter.

The obnoxious man had insulted the majority of people on the wharf.

"Are you boarding the *Annie McGee?*" At her nod, the doctor asked, "Can someone see to carrying your belongings?"

"Aye, my sisters."

"Call to them, if you will, please. All of you can come aboard with me."

Quickly, she turned and called out before the crowd had time to close in behind them. "Nora! Bridget! Bring everything and follow us!" She addressed the doctor again. "You're taking him aboard the sailing vessel?"

"Can't very well leave him here unattended, can I? We've no other choice."

"He said he was with two brothers, but I saw only one, I did. A lad younger than this boy."

"The crewman will search them out," he replied. "I suspect if there are brothers, they've either sneaked on the ship already or will board as soon as they have the opportunity."

Maeve left her last footprint on the soil of her native land and stepped onto the wooden gangplank.

Reaching the deck, she kept pace with the long-legged doctor, and they made their way to the companion ladder. He descended ahead of her, and she leaned as far forward as she dared without toppling over to keep hold of the tourniquet.

Once below deck, he led the way along a corridor until they reached a closed door. She had a free hand, so she opened it and stood back. The doctor was so tall, he had to bend to enter the room, but Maeve walked through upright. Her sisters followed, with Nora bending to fit under the doorway.

"Set your belongings inside the door," he instructed.

"I apologize for my lack of manners, ladies. I'm Dr. Flynn Gallagher."

"Oh, goodness, no," Nora objected. "You were involved with an emergency situation and could hardly have been expected to tip your hat."

"He isn't wearing a hat," Bridget said with a grin.

Nora ignored her. "I'm Nora Murphy. This is Bridget, and your capable helper there is Maeve."

He had already laid down the boy and was now washing his own hands in a basin. Beside it was a stack of folded towels and linens. The dispensary was impeccably clean.

"Will you assist me?" he asked Maeve.

Clearly he had no one else to help now. She couldn't have imagined that Hegarty fellow would have been of much use anyway. The doctor took hold of the comb while she washed her hands as thoroughly as he had.

Dr. Gallagher's brows rose in obvious appreciation for the care she took. On her return, he handed her a small brown bottle and a cloth folded into a square.

"What will happen if his brothers aren't found?" she asked. She didn't want to see this lad separated from his family.

"Where do you suppose your brothers are right now?" Dr. Gallagher asked Sean.

Sean didn't meet his eyes. He was sweating from the pain.

"They're stowing aboard, aren't they? Was that what the three of you cooked up?"

"What would happen to them if they did?" he asked.

The doctor nodded at Maeve. "We'll see them eventually. Go ahead."

She uncapped the bottle, held it well away from her nose and caught a whiff to test its contents. Knowing full well what it was and what he intended it for, she poured a small amount on the cloth, capped the bottle and held the fabric over the child's nose. "Close your eyes now, laddie. The doctor's going to fix you up as good as new, he is."

Dr. Gallagher cut away Sean's trousers, covered him with toweling and doused the area with alcohol. The boy's eyes were peacefully closed as he proceeded.

"I'll need a good helper for this voyage. I'd like to hire you for the position of my assistant."

"But…" Caught off guard, she looked up. His diligent attention was fastened on his task. "I have no formal training."

"Experience and quick thinking are often worth more than book learning, Miss Murphy. You've already proven yourself more than competent."

Maeve thought of all their neighbors and her own parents whom she'd treated and seen worsen and eventually die. Two weeks ago she hadn't been able to save her own da. She didn't know if she had the courage to take care of any more sick people. "I don't know."

The handsome doctor glanced toward Nora and Bridget as he took instruments from a small metal box and threaded a needle. "How shall I convince your sister to become my assistant?"

"May I step closer to speak with her?" Nora asked.

"Have you a weak stomach?"

"I'll be averting my eyes, if that's what you ask."

He gestured for her to come forward. "Yes, come speak to her."

Nora shot Bridget a glance and hurried to Maeve's side, deliberately keeping her eyes averted from the surgery.

"This is a divine opportunity," she whispered in

Maeve's ear. "Think on it. We spent nearly every last penny on tickets and have nothing left for emergencies or even lodging when we get to Boston, should our plans fall through. We tried in vain to seek positions before the ship sailed. And now this perfect opportunity is presented to you and you want to refuse it?"

"If it aids your decision," the doctor interrupted. "I'll secure positions for the three of you. The cook always needs help preparing meals for the crew, and only an hour ago one of the passenger families was inquiring about a governess."

Maeve looked up into Nora's pleading blue eyes. Her sisters needed her to agree to this. Previously they'd been turned away each time they'd sought work on the ship. They'd risked the voyage anyway, but their welfare depended on someone earning a wage.

"We accept your kind offer," Maeve said with a surprising sense of anticipation. She prayed her abilities were enough that she would be a help. The thought of learning from a skilled physician buoyed her enthusiasm.

"Very well, then." Within minutes, he had neatly sutured a punctured vein as well as the flesh on Sean's leg. "Your quick thinking spared the lad's life. He might have bled to death if you hadn't fashioned that tourniquet."

"I knew what to do and I did it."

"I can finish up from here. The three of you should go get settled. Afterward, you can return and help me store the supplies. We'll have plenty of time to discuss working arrangements once the ship is underway."

He glanced at Nora. "Is one of you better with children than the other?"

"That would be Bridget," Nora replied. "I've had more experience in a kitchen."

"The family I spoke of are the Atwaters," he said to

Bridget. "They have three daughters with whom they need help on the voyage. Mr. Atwater believed he had a governess, but at the last moment, she disappeared with their silver spoons and the cobbler's son. I'll send a note of recommendation with you. You can inquire above about his present whereabouts."

The doctor cut away the remainder of Sean's trousers and rolled them into a ball for the rubbish bin. "And I'll let Mr. Mathers know he can expect you in the galley tomorrow bright and early," he said to Nora.

"We're indebted to you, Dr. Gallagher," she replied.

"Not at all. I'm sure you'll each make a valuable contribution to the voyage." He inquired about their cabin number and gave them simple directions.

Gathering their things, the sisters made their way back out to the corridor. Once the door closed behind them, Bridget grasped Maeve's arm through her sleeve. "The angels surely blessed that man with staggering good looks." She gave Maeve a grin. "I think he likes you."

"What a nonsensical dreamer you are," Maeve replied. "He was as staid and solemn as a grave digger."

Perhaps that comparison had been thoughtless, so soon after burying their father, because Bridget got tears in her eyes. Maeve too often spoke without thinking.

Other passengers had begun boarding the ship, carrying their belongings and herding children. Nora led the way, turning a grateful smile on Maeve. "Thank you. This income sets my mind at ease."

"Now we'll all feel more prepared to dock in America," Maeve assured her.

They'd been assigned a small cabin that housed twelve bunks anchored to the walls by chains. On either side of the door were lockers with padlocks. Several other women had already chosen lower bunks and stowed their things, so the sisters chose beds near each other, with Bridget above Nora and Maeve on the next top bunk. This would be the first time they'd slept in separate beds, so the closeness would be a comfort.

Quickly, they stored their clothing and the food they'd brought, so they could hurry above.

Back on deck, Bridget was first to the railing. Maeve and Nora stood on either side. A small crowd stood at the wharf, waving scarves and hats. Maeve didn't recognize any of her countrymen, but she waved back. What a monumental moment this was. A life-changing day. To embed the scene in her memory, she took in every rich detail.

"Weigh the anchor!" came a shout, and she turned to spy a bearded man she assumed was the captain. A tingle of expectancy shimmied up her spine. She held her breath.

The anchor chain had become entangled with the cables of several fishing boats, so the moment lost momentum and her nerves jumped impatiently. At last, with much squeaking and creaking and dripping seaweed, the anchor chain was reeled in. The sound of men's voices rose in a chant as the sailors unreefed the enormous topsails and the bleached canvas billowed against the vivid blue sky. The sails caught the wind and the ship glided into the bay.

Goose bumps rose along Maeve's arms and the thrill of expectancy increased her heart rate.

In a matter of minutes, an expanse of water separated them from land, and the lush green coast with its majestic steplike cliffs came into view. She strained to see far enough to recognize the familiar outcroppings near her village, but of course the Murphy sisters had traveled a far piece to get to the ship, and it couldn't be seen from here. Perhaps when they were farther out in the ocean.

Maeve glanced to find Nora's face somber, her expression tense, as though concerned for their future. Between them, Bridget's soft weeping caught her notice. Always sentimental, a friend to all, Bridget would miss their friends and the people of their village. Her love for their community had been tainted by that despicable Daniel McGrath leaving her brokenhearted at the altar, however. It gave Maeve a sense of satisfaction to know that Bridget was leaving him behind once and for all.

Maeve put her arm around Bridget's shoulders and gave her a comforting hug. "'Tis a brand new start, *ma milis.*"

Bridget dabbed her eyes and nose with her plain white cotton handkerchief and gave her a tremulous smile. "I'm glad to start over. But I shall miss what used to be. Before Mother and Da died. Before the famine. But I know we have much to look forward to. In America we'll solve the mystery of that letter and learn who Laird is. We'll live in the lovely house by the ocean and plant flowers."

Nora moved to stand on the other side of Bridget and wrapped her arm around her waist. "Don't raise your hopes too high, just in case."

"At the very least we can learn who that Laird fellow was to Mother," Maeve said.

She turned from the diminishing view of their homeland as they cleared the breakers and left the lighthouse behind to face her sisters. "We're headed for the land of opportunity."

She didn't know what the trip held in store, but she liked the way it had begun. The doctor had treated her—and her sisters—with dignity and respect. Bridget's teasing comments flashed through her mind, but she quickly set them aside. Yes, Dr. Gallagher did possess startling good looks, no doubt about that. Looking at him nearly took her breath away. She would have to work on composure.

The last person he would ever find of interest was a simple farm girl away from home for the first time. Ignoring her own attraction meant her new job was going to be challenging in more ways than one.

Chapter Three

"Come in," Flynn called at a rap on the closed door.

"Couldn't find any of the boy's kin around Minot's Ledge," a bearded sailor told him, setting down the last of the supply crates. "Inquired along the wharf, and learned he was beggin' handouts from the passengers waitin' in line. Villagers from nearby say he's an orphan."

"That goes along with his story. In which case I doubt anyone's looking for him," Flynn replied. "Soon as he's on his feet, he can be my errand boy."

"Looks mighty scrawny," the man noted with skepticism. "Don't know how much work you'll be gettin' out of 'im."

"You'd be scrawny, too, if you'd never had a mother to put meals on the table."

"I'm supposin' you're right about that, doc. My dear ma, God rest her soul, set out a feast every noon and evenin'. Miss her cooking somethin' fierce, I do."

Flynn thanked him for searching, and the man went back to his tasks.

Before Sean awoke, Flynn washed the boy's grimy face, hands and bony arms. For sure, the lad needed a good scrubbing, so he did the best he could. After removing his ill-fitting shoes and seeing Sean's dirty blistered feet, he got more clean water and soap, scrubbed, then treated and bandaged both.

It was obvious this boy had gone without proper clothing and food for some time. Bones protruded at his wrists and ankles, and his ribs stood out in sharp relief. What was wrong with the world that children starved in the streets? The signs of such clear poverty made him feel shame at the thought of his own life of wealth and privilege.

He thought of the petite little miss he'd hired as his assistant. He was used to ladies who never mussed their elegant dresses and who always had every hair in place. They were at home in drawing rooms and shone seated at elegantly appointed dining tables.

Maeve Murphy, on the other hand, he could picture running barefoot across a meadow or gathering flowers and wearing them in her hair. She was natural. Unaffected.

And he had no business thinking about her. He had no room in his life for complications, not even a beautiful, obviously compassionate and capable distraction.

Sean opened his eyes and blinked. "Am I dead?"

"You're not dead, laddie. You're stitched up and in my dispensary aboard the *Annie McGee*. You'll be good as new in a few days."

The boy's face blanched even paler, and he raised his head off the pillow. "What of me brothers? Am I at sea all alone?"

"I sent someone to search, but he didn't turn up any brothers."

"Gavin and Emmett are surely worried by now." Tears glistened in his eyes.

"I suspect you were planning to board the ship without paying passage." He raised a brow. "Am I correct?"

Sean gave him a sheepish nod.

"It's also my guess that your brothers found their way aboard. That both of them were nowhere to be found on the wharf is a good indication. Did you arrange a meeting place, the three of you?"

"Aye. On the foredeck at sundown."

"I shall be there on your behalf."

The boy's expression turned to one of terror. "Will they be thrown overboard? I heard sharks follow the ships."

"No one will be throwing children overboard," Flynn assured him. "And this isn't one of the coffin ships of years past."

Flynn himself had lobbied for legislation to put an end to the overcrowded and filthy, disease-infested vessels. Now there were passenger limits and a doctor aboard each ship. He was putting in his own time to see that the plan was fulfilled.

"Lie down and rest now. I'm going to get you something to eat so you can build up your strength."

"I have no way to be payin' you for tendin' my leg," Sean said in a thick voice. "Or for food."

Flynn got a knot in his chest. It took him a moment to speak, so he busied himself rolling a clean length of bandage. "If not for my fool assistant, you wouldn't have been injured, so the responsibility lies with me. You owe me nothing."

"Thank you, sir. I'll keep you in me prayers, I will."

Flynn covered him with a blanket and at last met his brown eyes. Young as he was, those eyes had seen the worst side of life and known more misery than any child should. His mention of prayer caught Flynn off guard.

Perhaps the lad had more sway with the Lord of heaven than he. He hoped so, for the boy's sake. "You're welcome. Now sleep."

Bridget had gone off to meet with Mr. Atwater and acquaint herself with the family, so while Nora made up their bunks, Maeve headed up to locate the line for their daily allotment of food.

The topsails snapped in the wind that had swiftly carried the *Annie McGee* out to the ocean. The sharp cliffs of her homeland were still visible, and the sky was vivid blue. She paused at the rail to gaze out over the water and have another look at the receding cliffs. From here they all looked the same, so spotting Castleville was hopeless.

Was anyone she knew back home watching the ocean and seeing this ship on the horizon? She had spotted vessels many times, never dreaming she'd ever be aboard one.

The sun's reflection on the water nearly blinded her. She blinked and refocused on the person beside her.

The tall woman wore a flounced dress and matching capelike jacket, with six inches of lace at her wrists. Requirements for boarding had specified no crinolines or hoops, so her layered skirts hung shapelessly and a little too long on the deck.

Maeve's plain brown dress was far more practical, though poverty had driven her choice, not fashion or even practicality. The woman's dark auburn hair was parted in the middle and severely drawn back. She stood gazing at the horizon, and appeared to be a few years older than Maeve's mother had been when she'd died.

"I'm Maeve Murphy," she said by way of introduction. A good many people were going to dwell in close quarters for the duration of the voyage; she might as well get to know a few of them.

The woman turned and glanced down at her, taking in her long red curls and plain dress.

Maeve felt at a distinct disadvantage, being petite and obviously from a different social station. She resisted the urge to smooth her worn skirts with a calloused hand. They were fellow countrymen, after all, embarking on a journey together. There was no reason they couldn't be friends.

"This is all so exciting. I've never before been away from Castleville. Have you traveled aboard a ship before?"

The woman's chin inched up until she was literally looking down her nose at Maeve. She took a handkerchief from her sleeve and held it over her nose as though she smelled something odiferous. "Someone of your station should not be speaking to a lady, unless first addressed. You've obviously had extremely poor training. Where is your mistress?" She glanced around. "Shouldn't you be seeing to her needs instead of bothering passengers?"

Maeve drew a blank. No words formed, and humiliation burned its way up her neck to her cheeks. She'd never been dressed down in such a rude manner, but then she'd never mingled with anyone other than the people of her village—simple people just like the Murphys. The doctor had been kind and mannerly, so this woman's rude behavior caught her off guard. "I have no mistress. My sisters and I are taking this voyage to Massachusetts together."

"Then it will serve you well to learn your place. Never address a lady unless spoken to. And I certainly have no intention of speaking to you again." The fabric of the woman's skirts swooshed as she gathered them and marched off as though she couldn't get away fast enough.

Maeve stared at the two elaborately braided buns on the back of her head. The deliberate shun pierced her previously buoyant mood.

Maeve was from a poor family. The landowners and their families lived very different lives from hers, but she'd imagined that in a situation like this, the boundaries would be less severe. Apparently there was no escaping the attitudes of those with more money than humanity.

She gave the ocean one last look and made her way across the deck until she found the line for food supplies and stood at the end. The man ahead of her was dressed in a black suit and stylish hat. He glanced at her, but since her previous lesson still stung, she kept her silence.

Minutes later she was joined by a woman in a pretty white-on-tan silk dress with a flounced skirt and long puffed sleeves. Surreptitiously, she admired the woman's pretty dark hair, and the way it gleamed in the sunlight and remained gathered within its confines, but quickly turned away.

The woman spoke from behind her. "Aren't you the young lady who helped that boy on the wharf this morning?"

Surprised, Maeve turned to face her. "Yes, ma'am. The lad's name is Sean McCorkle."

"That was very quick thinking, indeed. I dare say the lad might not have survived had you not gone to his aid when you did."

Pleased by the woman's friendly manner, she warmed to her immediately. "Dr. Gallagher is a fine surgeon," she replied. "Sean should be on his feet in no time."

"Have you chosen a spot on deck for your evening fire yet?" the woman asked.

"Not yet." A brisk gust of wind caught Maeve's hair, and self-consciously, she quickly fashioned it into an unruly fat braid and tucked the end under her collar. She would find a bit of twine when she got back to the cabin.

"I'm Aideen Nolan. I'm traveling with my aunt, Mrs. Kennedy."

"A pleasure to meet you, 'tis. I'm Maeve Murphy. My sisters and I are headed for Boston—well, a small village nearby called Faith Glen, actually."

The woman glanced at the nearby passengers. "I suggest we reserve our spaces next to one another. That way we'll be assured that at least one of our nearby supper companions will be familiar. Unless, of course, you have other plans. I'm probably being presumptuous."

Maeve gave her a bright smile. "No, we hadn't made plans yet. I'd very much like to find a place near yours. I'm confident my sisters will be glad for friendly company, as well. I've already had an encounter with a rather unpleasant woman who put me in my place for speaking to her." Maeve glanced down at her clothing. "Thought I was someone's maid, she did."

"I'd wager that was Mrs. Fitzwilliam," Aideen said. She leaned near and spoke quietly. "The gentleman just ahead is her manservant. I know her from the ladies' league in Galway." She took a brochure from the deep pocket of her skirt and flipped it open. "This list of preparations and rules for the journey instructs us to select the areas where we will be cooking our meals for the next several weeks." She glanced at Maeve. "Are you familiar with cooking procedures?"

"Indeed I am," Maeve replied with a sigh. "My sisters and I have been preparing meals since we were quite young."

"I shall be forever indebted if you will show me how."

Maeve had suspected from her dress and speech that Aideen was well-to-do, and her admission confirmed that thinking. "I'd be happy to tutor you, but you won't be indebted. Communities help one another, and we're going to be a community while we're aboard. Like a village on the sea, wouldn't you say?"

"Yes, I definitely would. My aunt and I had rooms in my grandparents' home until recently, and they always had a cook. Neither of us have ever attempted our own meals."

"My dear da passed on, only twelve days ago, God rest his soul. My mother's been gone ten years now. We've had a lot of experience at creating meals from nearly nothing."

"Next!"

Maeve turned to accept a burlap sack and a piece of chalk from a sailor whose face was coated with smoke and soot. "Daily allotment for three," he said. "Find yer cook spot and mark it with yer name or yer mark. Respect yer neighbor's planks and douse yer fire promptly at eight. Next!"

Maeve accepted a surprisingly heavy bag and a square of chalk, while the man recited the same instructions to Aideen. Together the two women headed away from the line in search of the fireplaces.

Along both sides of the foredeck, sections had been marked off with jagged stripes of black paint. For the most part, the areas were all the same size. The hands had obviously counted rows of deck planks in making the partitions. Each rectangular section held a curved brick cooking pit, partially open to one side, with three iron bars on the other to confine the coals.

They stood planning their strategy, hoping to predict which spot would be most protected from wind and weather. Praying they had it right, Maeve and Aideen wrote their surnames with chalk in side-by-side plots.

Setting down the bag, Maeve looked inside and found half a pound of rice, a small slab of bacon, flour and a tin of peaches. "My sister is a better cook than I am, but these are basic foods and there's not a lot we can do with them. We should take them to our cabins now, and we'll prepare them side by side this evening."

"I look forward to meeting your sisters." Aideen gave her a grateful smile. "I hope we'll become fast friends."

Maeve returned below deck, where she stored the food in their locker and gave Nora the key to wear around her neck. "I met a lovely young woman, and we saved our cooking areas beside each other. You will meet her and her aunt this evening. She was delightful, she was. From a rich family, I'm certain, but she struck up a conversation and wasn't the least pretentious.

"Wait until you see her hair, Nora. It's dark and sleek. I didn't see it without her bonnet, of course, but I could imagine it's nothing like these wild ringlets."

"She sounds very nice, indeed." Nora had finished making their beds in her efficient and tidy manner, with corners tucked and pillows fluffed. "On the doctor's recommendation, I met with Mr. Mathers, and he assured me of a job with his staff. The galley is surprisingly roomy and clean. I'll learn my duties tomorrow," she said. "The others are men, but he said there would be another woman besides myself. The chores don't look like anything I haven't done a thousand times."

"I hope he gives you a chance to show what you can

do and doesn't have you washing all the dishes. The crew would miss out if you couldn't cook for them."

"You're a sweet lass. Biased, of course."

"Dr. Gallagher is expecting me back in the dispensary to help organize supplies." Maeve located a faded apron in her bag and slipped it on over her dress. "This will have to suffice for a uniform."

"It's clean and adequate," Nora assured her. She rested her hand atop Maeve's as her sister reached into her bag for her comb. "Thank you for accepting the doctor's offer, Maeve. I know you worry you're unqualified for a job with so many responsibilities, but you always did your best to help Mother and Da and our neighbors in Castleville. The local women declared you the most knowledgeable and dependable midwife in all of County Beary. I've no doubt you will be a benefit to the doctor."

"I'm hoping to learn from him." Maeve braided her hair as neatly as she could manage and secured it with a length of twine. For the first time she wondered what other passengers like that Fitzwilliam woman would think of her helping the doctor. Maybe they would simply see her as his servant, and find that acceptable. Was that how the doctor saw her? She surely didn't look forward to any more encounters like the one with Mrs. Fitzwilliam.

"The three of us will have an income...all because you so bravely went to that boy's aid."

"Helping him was simply instinctive," she replied. "Not heroic."

"Tell that to the lad who is alive, thanks to you."

"God provided the way for us," Maeve told her eldest sister. "He used what could have been a tragedy to find us jobs and bring the boy onboard. It will be interesting to see what develops next with Sean."

"Only you would find the silver lining in an otherwise cloudy situation."

Maeve stretched to her fullest height to give Nora a peck on the cheek. Nora leaned forward to accept the kiss. She took Maeve's face between her hands and looked into her eyes. "Mother always said you were like a bright star on a dark night. Even as a wee bairn, you saw everything differently than the rest of us. 'Tis a quality I admire."

"Nothing would get done without your practical thinking and logical planning," Maeve reminded her. "Sometimes I wish I was more like you."

"You're perfect just the way you are." She released Maeve. "Now go about your duties at the dispensary."

Maeve turned and headed for the door. For the first time in as long as she could remember, she was looking forward to something.

Chapter Four

A knock sounded on the door. Flynn looked up as Maeve Murphy opened it and peered in. She had bound her wild red hair and donned a plain coarse apron in preparation for her duties. He liked that she was efficient and punctual, adding those qualities to her quick thinking and kind manner with the boy. So far he liked everything about her.

"Come in, Miss Murphy. I've only just opened the first of the supply boxes." He gestured to the wooden crates lining the wall in the rectangular room.

She walked toward him, her bright blue gaze taking in her surroundings. In the morning's confusion he hadn't looked her over, and he did so now. She was a tiny thing, her flaming red hair creating ringlets that framed her cheeks, while the rest had been contained in a braid. Her skin appeared as fragile as porcelain, with healthy pink cheeks and a mouth like a China doll.

If a person judged on appearance, he'd think she was nothing more than a sweetly pretty girl, and overlook her wit and courage. Not many people had the knowledge or the compassion to jump to the McCorkle boy's aid the way she had.

She glanced with keen interest at the sturdy cabinets with chicken wire instead of glass in the doors, where only a few bottles and tins stood. "If you'll be so good as to acquaint me with your system, I'll store the supplies."

"We'll both work on it." He led her to the other room, where Sean lay sleeping on a low cot, a blanket pulled to his chin.

"How is the laddie doing?" she asked softly.

"Very well, indeed," he replied. She smelled good, too, like clean linen and spring heather, and his reaction startled him. He hadn't noticed a woman in that way for a long time. He took an unconscious step away.

Her inquisitive gaze took in her surroundings, fastening on the storage cabinets and workspaces. There were no rimless surfaces in his dispensary. Everything had been designed to accommodate the normal rock and sway of the ship or even a storm. He explained his mortar and pestle for grinding roots and seeds, the scale and weights for measuring ingredients, the piece of marble on which he prepared salves, sets of measures, dosage spoons and a plaster iron. The young woman listened with interest and apparent understanding. She asked surprisingly insightful questions. He was glad now that he'd learned of Hegarty's true nature before the ship sailed. Maeve Murphy looked to be the better choice.

He described the contents of each crate as he carried and opened it. Between each ocean voyage, he spent weeks preparing bottles of saline draughts and barley water, jars of calves' foot jelly and plasters. He saw to it that those who fell sick on a ship he worked received the best care possible. His meager pay didn't begin to cover the cost of medicines, but he drew from his inheritances and vast investments.

He'd left his father's practice over the objection of his family to make a difference and to forget. He truly believed it was his calling to help people so desperate to start new lives that they risked a journey like this. Everyone he encountered had a dream of a new beginning he didn't share. He didn't think about his future, only about the work he had to do today.

"I wish I'd had half as many cures when my friends and neighbors were ailing," she said wistfully. "I may have been able to save more of them." Tears shone in her wide blue eyes as she gazed at a bottle of vitriolic acid.

Uncomfortable with the intimate glimpse at her suffering, he placed the bottles he held inside the chest and withdrew from his pocket the key he carried at all times. "We'll lock the mercury, laudanum and calomel in this chest under the case here." He stood slowly.

"Truth be told I wouldn't have known what to do with half of them." She raised her gaze to his in an earnest plea. "I'd like to learn."

He couldn't ignore her sincerity. "It won't be a bother to share their uses and common dosages," he said. "You have a natural instinct, Miss Murphy. I might even learn a few things from you."

He handed her his checklist and a pencil. As they worked he explained the contents of each bottle and their uses. She knew most of the more common medicines and was fascinated by others. He also took the opportunity to educate her a bit about ship life.

"They're electing the council today," he mentioned.

"What does that mean?"

"Each voyage the male passengers meet and select a group from among them to form a council. When problems arise—and they will—these men govern by representing the passengers."

She couldn't imagine what would come up that would require their government, but she trusted the process.

"Are you ever on the council?"

"No, I'm technically not a passenger. I'm part of the crew."

When Sean woke up, Flynn's new assistant efficiently saw to his needs, inquiring about food supplies and then making the boy a gruel of millet and rye flour. Though Flynn grimaced at the concoction, the boy lapped it up and lay back with a contented smile.

"You're a blessing, you are, Miss Murphy," Sean said to her, his dark eyes adoring. "I be grateful for your care."

"You might well change your mind when I wash that head of hair of yours. It's going to need a good scrubbin'. I'm going to fill a pail now, and you can lie right there with your head over the edge of the table."

"I'll catch me death of cold, I will," the lad howled.

Flynn turned aside to hide a grin. "I have free access to the barrels of rainwater, Miss Murphy. Just ask a sailor for help toting buckets."

Sean's smeared face showed his concern. "I'd just worked up a good skin coverin' afore the doctor began to scrub it away."

"It's June, not December," she argued. "You'll not catch cold. And it's a good thing the doctor got a start on scrubbin' off the filth, otherwise we may have mistaken you for a bit of firewood lying on the wharf. You'll be washin' your face and hands every mornin' while you're here."

As she argued with the boy, her brogue got amusingly thicker. Flynn chuckled.

The room grew silent, and he turned to see the both of them staring at him. Perhaps his laugh had sounded as rusty to them as it had to him. "I don't think you're going to win this one, laddie. We'll find you some clean clothing, as well."

"Aye, sir," Sean said, putting aside his bowl. "Thank you, Miss Murphy. 'Twas a delicious gruel."

"I don't know that it was delicious," she said with a raised brow. "But it will build up your strength. Tomorrow I'll make you a flavorful potato soup that will stick to your ribs."

The boy beamed at her promise. "I'll not fight you on a quick washin' today. The doc's already done me feet."

She'd known just what to do with the meal to make it palatable, and Sean had eaten it as though it was fare fit for a king.

Flynn didn't know Maeve's background, but her clothing, while clean and pressed, indicated a lack of means. Her older sister had whispered how desperate they were to earn a wage. And Sean, an orphan, surviving in the village streets… Flynn had no concept of such poverty.

His privileged life had been glaringly different from the ones these two had lived. His family owned property in three countries, had a home in each and employed servants to do the work and the cooking. There was no such thing as a simple meal where he came from. Four courses served with silver utensils and gold-monogrammed china was the norm.

Even he himself owned land and a house in England and had purchased a home in Boston. His lifestyle was extravagant compared to those of his poor countrymen. But money didn't mean happiness or contentment, he knew for a fact. It was heartwarming that Maeve seemed satisfied with next to nothing. It said a lot about her temperament…and her faith.

Flynn got called away several times that afternoon to

tend passengers unaccustomed to the sea. Many lay on their bunks with heads swimming and stomachs roiling. There was nothing to be done for them, save bathe their heads in cool water. Since they weren't ill or contagious, he assured each one they would feel better in a day or two and advised them to stay on deck, rather than below.

As the day waned, the doctor sent Maeve on her way. She felt good about her day's work and confident she'd earned her wage. She passed a man with an easel set up at a good vantage point and paused to watch him sketch the horizon, with its craggy cliffs and white-crested waves. Minutes later, she joined her sisters on the foredeck. A piece of paper fluttered from beneath the edge of one of the bricks that made up their cooking pit. Nora reached for it and unfolded the note.

Immediately, she handed it to Maeve. "It's for you."

My dearest Miss Murphy, she read silently. *My aunt and I have been invited to dine in the captain's cabin this evening. Please accept our regrets, and we will look forward to meeting with you as soon as possible. Sincerely, Aideen Nolan.*

Bridget, who'd been reading over her shoulder, found a small keg and perched on it. "The Atwaters were invited, as well. After this evening, I'll be eating with them and their daughters most of the time. This dilemma never entered my mind. I don't know the first thing about proper etiquette. I can't let on and make mistakes or they'll think I'm not an appropriate governess."

"Nonsense." Nora paused in piling wood in their brick hearth. "You're a fine young woman, with the common sense God gave you and the convictions of your beliefs. You will make a wonderful role model for the children."

"I'm sorry you didn't get to meet Aideen and Mrs. Kennedy this evening," Maeve added. "They might be a help in teaching you proper etiquette, so you may in turn teach the children. Aideen is the friendliest person I've met so far, she is. Not haughty like some of the others."

"The kitchen help are all quite nice," Nora added. Together, she and Maeve started a fire and put on a pot of water for rice and tea. Nora cut their small ration of bacon into six slices. From the other nearby cooking pits came the mouthwatering smells of frying bacon. Maeve's stomach growled.

She marveled as the heavens changed color. The smells were unfamiliar here. Of course the salty tang of the ocean was predominant, but there were no green scents. Grass, flowering bushes, heather had all been left behind, and she found she missed them. The smell of tar reached them from time to time, and always the smell of cooking food permeated the air.

As the sun set lower in the sky, the wind grew more chill. They bundled themselves in their shawls and unobtrusively glanced at the neighboring passengers.

"Tell us more about the Atwaters," Nora said.

"There are three young daughters," Bridget began. "Laurel is eleven. Hilary and Pamela are younger. When I arrived, Laurel actually looked at my dress and asked if I'd come to clean their stateroom." She smoothed her hand over her skirt, as though the memory still stung.

After her encounter with Mrs. Fitzwilliam, Maeve could certainly understand.

Bridget glanced up. "Not that I wouldn't have, mind you, had that been the duty assigned me."

"They have a stateroom?" Nora asked. She had mixed ingredients and set the dough on a smooth clean brick beside the fire to rise. Once it was baked they would have bread for tomorrow morning.

"Aye. It's well-appointed, with room for the girls to do

lessons. Hilary has brought a canary aboard, and little Pamela has an array of China dolls like I've seen only in catalogues."

"A canary?" Nora set out a small jar. "Our rations contain enough molasses to sweeten our tea. I should think it was unnecessary to bring a bird aboard a ship."

Bridget shrugged. "Perhaps she simply enjoys the songs, and her parents indulge her. I glimpsed a life unfamiliar to anything we know. The girls bicker among themselves and argue over who gets the largest or best portions or whose shoes are prettier."

"Mother would never have allowed us to behave in such a way," Nora said.

"She was strict, but she disciplined us with love," Bridget agreed.

They bowed their heads and held hands in a familiar circle.

"Father God, we come before You, grateful for this opportunity You've given us," Maeve began. "We are thankful that we could buy tickets and amazed at Your provision in giving us jobs so quickly."

"Thank You that we are not going hungry," Nora added. "This is more than adequate food for Your humble servants."

"And thank You," Bridget added softly, "That none of us has the seasickness."

"We ask that You heal Sean McCorkle's leg now," Maeve added. "And watch over his brothers, wherever they are. In Jesus' name we pray…"

"Amen," the sisters chorused and gave each other tired, but joyful smiles.

The wind had come up, so Nora tied a scarf over her hair before dishing the rice onto three tin plates. Bridget divided the bacon equally. This allotment of food was more than they were accustomed to, and Maeve truly did feel blessed. She vividly remembered many times when Nora had told them she'd already eaten and split pitiable amounts of potatoes between the two younger girls.

"There's a can of peaches," Maeve told Bridget, and her sister's eyes lit up.

The boat rocked upon the waves. The wind tossed Bridget's hair. Maeve looked upon each of her sisters with a fond smile, and hope buoyed her spirits. *Thank You, Lord.*

Flynn had been standing in the same spot for nearly half an hour. He'd glimpsed a shaggy-haired boy earlier, but the lad had slipped away before he could speak to him. So he waited.

Finally, a boy sitting on a coil of rope caught his attention. Flynn hurried over. "You Sean McCorkle's brother?"

Smaller and even skinnier than Sean, the boy's frightened brown gaze darted about as though seeking an escape. "Who are you?"

"I'm Dr. Gallagher. I have Sean in my dispensary. If you want to see him, come with me."

The boy shot Flynn a cautious look. "What're ye gonna do to us?"

"Put you to work to earn your passage. How does that suit you?"

"You're not gonna make us walk the plank?"

Flynn chuckled. "I promised Sean I wouldn't feed you to the sharks, and I'm a man of my word. Now get your brother and bring him back here."

The boy scrambled to his feet and ran off, arms pinwheeling as he nearly toppled forward in his haste. A few minutes later, he returned with a young man of about eighteen in tow. "This here's Gavin."

"What've you done with Sean?" The tall lanky boy squinted with skepticism.

"Cleaned and sewed up his leg. The Murphy girl saved his life, you know. Has big plans for washing Sean's hair. Can't wait until she sees the two of you. Fresh water is rationed, but I get a larger portion for medical purposes. Come on."

"Where you be takin' us?"

"To the dispensary so you can see your brother. Have you had a meal today?"

"We ain't hungry."

"I doubt that's true."

"How do we know you won't get us down there and put us in stocks?"

"No stocks aboard the ship," he replied. "Are you coming?"

The boy glanced at his little brother. "Aye."

They followed Flynn down the ladder and along the passageway. Flynn opened the door and stood aside for them to enter. "He's in the side room over there."

The tall young man inspected his surroundings before moving to the door and peering into the other small room.

"Gavin!" came Sean's gleeful shout. "Is Emmett with ye?"

"Aye, he's right here, he is."

The two boys crowded at Sean's side and gave him awkward hugs. Emmett, the littlest one, pulled back with tears streaking his dirty cheeks. "We was afeared you be dead."

"No, the redheaded Miss Murphy saved me life for sure. Her and the doctor here. They been real good to me, they 'ave. The doc said he'd give us jobs, so we can earn our fare."

Flynn moved to stand closer. "You two will have to take baths. And we'll find you clean clothes. Can't have the captain catch you looking like that."

"Can they sleep 'ere with me?" Sean asked. His desperate expression threatened to open a crack in the barrier around Flynn's heart.

"I have a stateroom," Flynn replied. "There's plenty of room for pallets, so the three of you can be together." He pinned Gavin with a probing look. "I'd appreciate your telling me why you were planning to stow aboard."

It was plain Gavin didn't fancy sharing his business. "We been stayin' in the back room at Ferguson's Livery. Old Mr. Ferguson left the door unlocked 'til we was in at night. But he died, and his missus sold the livery. The new owner shooed us out, so we was sleepin' under wagons and in back o' the millhouse. Sean here overheard stories of America. We came up with a plan to make our way there. I'm gonna find work and Sean and Emmett can go to school."

"Well, that sounds like a fine plan. I admire men with foresight. What happened to your parents?" Flynn asked.

"We ain't seen our da since Emmett was a wee babe. He just up and left, he did. Ma took care of us best she could, but then she took sick an' died."

Flynn wasn't surprised to hear their story. Death and hunger had been part of everyone's story over the past several years. The plight of the Irish had been grim for anyone not born into a wealthy family. "First things first," Flynn said. "Let's get you bathed."

"Why are ye and Miss Murphy so firmly set on bath takin'?" Sean asked.

"Because cleanliness is important. You should bathe and wash your hands often to prevent disease."

"What kind o' disease gets on yer hands?" Gavin asked.

"I've studied epidemiology for most of my career."

"Epi— What?" Gavin asked.

"Germs. Bacteria. Skeptics will say something you can't see can't hurt you, but that's not true. And in truth you *can* see germs, just not with the naked eye. In fact, I'm sure I can show you something that will convince you to wash your hands."

"What's that?"

"Before we get you in the tub, I want both of you to scrape under one or two fingernails, and place the dirt on a glass slide. Then I'll show you through my microscope what is living there."

"Living?" Sean asked, with a squeak.

Flynn grinned. "But not for long. Let's heat water." Instinctively, he knew his new assistant was going to be pleased when she saw the McCorkle boys clean. He looked forward to her reaction.

Chapter Five

The following morning, the Murphy sisters shared bread in their cabin before going their separate ways. Maeve arrived just as Dr. Gallagher peered out from the dispensary.

"Thank you for being punctual. I'm going to go above deck to boil water and then carry it back."

"I could do that for you," she offered.

"I spent the night here with Sean. I'd like a few minutes of sun and fresh air, if you don't mind. I'll probably eat before I return."

"Yes, of course! Take all the time you need. How is young Sean this morning?"

"Already talking about that potato soup you promised him. The galley help will provide you with anything you need for our patients. Simply introduce yourself as my assistant. You can make a trip to the galley after I return. I won't be long."

He headed away from the dispensary.

Maeve found Sean awake and obviously listening for her. "Mornin', Miss Murphy!"

"Good morning, Sean. Did you sleep well?"

"Yes'm. Didn't much notice the ship's sway. This 'ere cot is comfortable and the doc found me brothers."

"He did? My sisters and I prayed for them. And for you, too."

"Yes, he did. He made 'em take baths and then he put 'em up in his stateroom. He stayed here with me all night, he did. He told me after I eat, he will carry me to lie on his very own bunk."

She was glad to hear that the doctor was looking out for them. It was bad enough that Maeve and her sisters had been left with no family, but at least they were adults. The McCorkle lads were little more than babies. "Are you boys alone in the world?"

"Yes'm. We're headed to America so Gavin can work and me an' Emmett can go to school."

"You look well today. How are your brothers faring?"

"They're clean for sure. An' the doc showed us germs what was *livin'* under their fingernails!"

She wrinkled her nose. "That's disgusting."

"Yes'm, 'tis. You can be sure I'll be washin' me hands afore I eat from now on."

"Well, it was an effective lesson, to be sure."

A rap sounded at the door.

"I have to see to the caller," she told Sean.

Two women stood in the corridor. The younger woman's ebony hair had been brushed to a sheen and fashioned stylishly upon her head. She was strikingly lovely, with aristocratic cheekbones and dark winged brows over deep blue eyes. Her dress had been designed to fit her tall slender frame in the most flattering way, and she carried herself with confidence. Maeve had never laid eyes upon a more beautiful woman.

Maeve stepped back and gestured for the two to enter. Immediately, she hid her work-roughened hands behind her back and wished she'd had something nicer to wear, even though she was only coming to work. After the up-braiding she'd received the previous day, she said nothing.

The shorter woman was older, and obviously the younger one's mother. She had the same black hair, though silver strands laced her temples and a shock of silver had been artfully drawn back from her face. Maeve had never seen a woman of her age without creases or lines in her face. Her hair and a few nearly imperceptible crow's-feet at the corners of her eyes were the only subtle clues to her age.

The older woman considered Maeve with disdain and dismissed her as though she wasn't there. She guided the one Maeve assumed was her daughter into the dispensary.

Now Maeve was faced with a dilemma. She hadn't intended to speak until spoken to, but she couldn't very well let these two stand there without telling them Dr. Gallagher wasn't in. She took a breath.

"Flynn?" the younger one called and glanced expectantly toward the back room.

Maeve released the air in her lungs. *Flynn?* "The doctor's not here at the moment." She glanced at the younger woman and then away. "He should arrive soon."

The woman's glance traveled from Maeve's face and hair to her shoes and back up. She towered over Maeve by a good eight inches. She narrowed her eyes. "Don't devise any designs for the doctor's attentions."

Maeve couldn't have been more startled. No words came to her.

"Flynn's family and mine are close. He and I are cut from the same cloth." She let her gaze fall again, as though pointing out the world of difference in weaves of cloth.

Maeve resisted touching her skirt with a self-conscious hand.

"Our fathers have made arrangements, and Flynn and I have an *understanding*. So don't imagine your undeveloped charms will hold any appeal to him when he has someone like me."

Maeve remained speechless. What might she have said to that?

The dark-haired young woman turned her back and faced the other direction.

Perturbed at their rudeness, she tamped down growing irritation and went about her chores.

Several minutes later and not a second too soon, the doctor returned.

"It's a pleasure to see you this morning, Kathleen. Mrs. Boyd, how are you faring?"

"I am well, thank you," Mrs. Boyd replied.

"What brings you to the dispensary so early?"

"It's Kathleen," the older woman said. "She barely slept a wink last night. Her ears hurt severely."

"Did you meet Miss Murphy?" he asked.

The two Boyd women didn't look at Maeve.

"They only just got here," Maeve answered. "We didn't have an opportunity to chat." She offered Mrs. Boyd a sweetly antagonizing smile, and immediately regretted it.

The woman's nostrils fared.

"Miss Murphy has filled a position as my assistant. She's as efficient and capable as they come. I can already tell she's going to be my right hand during this voyage."

Kathleen shot Maeve daggers. "How unfortunate for

you, Flynn. I heard you had no choice but to hire someone off the dock."

"And she's already proven herself. Look how Hegarty turned out, and he had references. I wouldn't have selected her if I hadn't thought she possessed the skill required for the job. Miss Murphy, this is Miss Kathleen Boyd and her mother, Mrs. Estelle Boyd."

Maeve gave a polite nod. "'Tis a pleasure to meet you both."

"Let's have a look at those ears," he said and reached for Kathleen's hand to help her up the wooden step to the examining table.

She stretched her long pretty neck to accommodate him and batted her thick lashes.

"You've traveled by sea before." His words reiterated what Kathleen had revealed about their relationship. "Have you had problems in the past?"

"Yes, I felt this same way last time."

"Are you experiencing any vertigo?"

"Why yes. Yes, I am."

"That should go away in a day or so as your body grows accustomed to the ocean. Any queasiness or vomiting?"

"A little."

"Excessive tiredness?"

"Yes, now that you mention it. But I can't sleep."

"How about a tingling in your feet?"

"Yes, the tingling definitely kept me awake most of the night."

"I suggest you spend as much time above deck as possible. It helps. There's nothing I can do for you. You might want to place a cold cloth on your forehead. Don't drink any alcohol or eat apples."

"Shall I bring her back for another consultation?" Mrs. Boyd asked.

"It's always a pleasure to see you both," he answered politely.

At a knock, Maeve crossed to usher in another young woman.

"I'm not feeling well," she told Maeve. "I'd like to see the doctor."

"He'll be right with you."

With his smile in place, Flynn ushered Kathleen and her mother out of the dispensary. In passing, Kathleen inspected the incoming patient with a frown of concern.

Once the door was closed, Dr. Flynn whispered to Maeve, "I made up the tingling feet part."

Maeve raised her eyebrows in surprise. Kathleen had gone right along with his list of symptoms, making it obvious she'd only come to see the handsome young doctor—and perhaps to warn away his new assistant.

"What can I do for you this morning?" he asked the young woman who'd just arrived. Maeve already had a nagging suspicion that no matter what the complaint, this case would have a similar outcome.

"I fell against a doorpost when the ship tossed. I believe I've injured my shoulder."

"Miss Murphy will help you slip one arm free, so I can examine your shoulder." He turned away and washed his hands.

The young woman gave Maeve a disapproving glance.

Maeve gestured for her to sit upon the examining table. "What's your name?"

She unfastened the back of the other woman's rust-colored satin dress. The fabric was like nothing she'd ever felt, and the buttons were tiny carved ivory disks. Beneath it she wore a fine silk chemise.

Flynn dried his hands and joined them.

"I am Miss Ellnora Coulter. Having just finished school in London, I'm traveling to the States with my parents. My father has investments in Boston."

Her English was proper with no hint of a brogue. Maeve glanced at Dr. Gallagher to gauge his reaction to the pretty young miss. He didn't seem interested in anything but her shoulder as he moved close. "I don't see any bruising. Help her back into her sleeve, Miss Murphy."

Once her dress was in place, he probed the area with his fingertips. "Does this hurt?"

"Yes."

"This?"

"Yes, indeed. It's quite painful."

Without a warning knock, the cabin door opened and Nora entered, stooping to accommodate her height. Her face was flushed, and she wore an expression of worry and concern Maeve had seen far too often. The surprising thing was that she cradled a bundled apron against her breast.

"Nora?" Maeve said, turning to meet her. "Whatever is...?"

"I was in the storage apartment, searching for a bag of salt, when I moved aside a sack and heard the oddest sound, like a mewling. I thought perhaps a kitten had been closed into the depot of provisions. Just look now what I discovered lying between the sacks of oatmeal, Maeve."

Her sister lowered the apron to reveal what lay within its folds. Maeve stepped close, and her heart caught in her throat.

An infant, obviously no older than a few hours or possibly a day at most, lay with eyes pinched shut, fists at its face, turning its head this way and that with mouth wide open.

Maeve stared in astonishment.

Chapter Six

"A baby? Nora, you found a *baby* in a storage bin?"

"Not in a bin. Between bags of oatmeal, almost right out in the open and near the entrance to the apartment. Is the little *grah mo chee* all right?" After referring to the infant as *sweetheart,* she handed off the bundle to Maeve.

Maeve took the baby just as Dr. Gallagher joined them. Nora explained again where she'd found the child. "Someone had wrapped a flour sack around her and left her like that."

He peeled the apron all the way back, revealing the pink infant's froglike legs and several inches of umbilical cord still attached. Her skin still bore streaks of mucus and blood.

"She's a newborn," he said unnecessarily. He glanced at Maeve. She hadn't seen him wear this look of discomfort before. "I haven't had much experience with infants." And he stepped away. "I'll get a basin of warm water so you can bathe her, and then I'll listen to her heart and lungs."

"What about my shoulder?" Miss Coulter called from the examining table.

"Your shoulder will be fine," Flynn told her. "I think it's just a little bruising."

"Perhaps you could call on me tomorrow to make sure I've improved."

"Certainly," he replied and saw her to the door.

Maeve exchanged a glance with her sister. "An unending stream of young ladies have sought medical attention since yesterday," Maeve whispered. "The good doctor is obviously prime husband material."

Nora only had eyes for the baby in Maeve's arms. "Will she live, Maeve? She's puny, is she not? You've seen a lot of babies born. What do you make of this one?"

"Let's clean her up and look her over." Maeve asked Nora to spread out towels on the examining table and proceeded to sponge the infant with clear warm water.

"All babies this young look puny," she told her sister. "She's average from what I can tell. She seems perfectly healthy and quite obviously hungry, the poor dear."

Once the baby's skin was clean and dry, Maeve made a diaper from the cotton bandages Flynn kept stacked nearby. Flynn opened a drawer on the other side of the room and offered a folded shirt.

Nora accepted the garment. She studied the intricate embroidery and monogram and asked a question with her expressive blue eyes.

"It's just a shirt," he said. "Cut it up to make her gowns. I have plenty more."

Nora used his bandage scissors to cut off the collar, sleeves and buttons and crudely fashion a garment.

"She appears fine," Maeve told her. "But we need to feed her."

"Rice water?" Nora asked.

"No, milk is best."

"It will have to be goat's milk." Flynn took a small tin container from inside a cabinet and headed for the door. "The sailors have a nanny aboard. I'll be back with milk."

Nora glanced about. "How will we feed it to her?"

Maeve handed her the now-squalling baby and searched in earnest for a feeding method. "We could soak towels…or gauze."

She opened a cabinet and picked up a length of rubber tubing. "Better yet. We'll use this."

"That?" Nora asked, cuddling the infant.

"Aye. It's pliable, see. We'll puncture a couple of needle holes in it for the milk to come through and bend it like so. The baby will suck on it."

"Are you sure?"

"Stick your finger in her mouth and see if she doesn't latch onto anything."

"I've just washed all the sailor's breakfast dishes, so I expect my finger's clean enough." Nora offered the baby the tip of her index finger, and the crying stopped immediately. Nora got tears in her eyes. "The poor *grah mo chee* is so hungry."

"We'll have her fed in no time." Maeve placed the tubing in a kettle of water. "I'm going on deck to boil this."

Nora's eyes widened. "And leave me here alone with her?"

"You'll be fine," Maeve assured her. "Just cuddle her, as you're doing. She likes your warmth and the beat of your heart. If you'd like conversation, Sean McCorkle is lying in the next room."

"Who would leave their newborn baby on sacks of meal, Maeve?" Nora looked into her sister's eyes with a look of concern and disbelief. "She's only just been born, wouldn't you think? Aboard the ship…maybe right there in that storage apartment?"

"Seems likely, it does. But why her mother abandoned her is a mystery. If she'd died, someone would have found her body—or at the very least we'd have heard of a death."

"Maybe her mother couldn't care for her," Nora suggested.

"Her mother was the one with milk to nourish her," Maeve reminded her. "She could have cared for her better than we."

"Perhaps something happened to her and she was unable to return. If she was a stowaway, like those boys, she may have been hiding in that storage depot."

"We'll do everything we can. Have a seat. I'll be right back."

The situation did puzzle Maeve. Perhaps the woman would show up. Perhaps the infant had been left there by accident. Maybe she'd been taken from the mother. There were too many questions to think about, without any facts, so she set about doing what she could to help.

Flynn explained the situation to a couple of the sailors seated near their pens of chickens and only several feet from the goat's enclosure. The men generously gave him a cup of milk and told him to come back any time he needed more.

The newborn's presence knocked him a little off-kilter. Returning to the dispensary, he regarded the situation. He'd cared for children aboard ship, of course, but he hadn't been in close proximity to a baby only hours old since his own son had been born. The thought caused him more pain than he could deal with now.

Two years ago he'd lost his young wife and tiny son to

the deadly cholera that had spread through Galway and so much of Ireland. His countrymen referred to potato blight and epidemics as *an Drochshaol,* the bad times, which were still prevalent and still a threat to lives and livelihoods. He'd read that after thousands had died, nearly a quarter of the remaining people had fled to other countries.

An Drochshaol was personal to Flynn. Unbearable. He'd studied to learn how to treat people and heal them. He'd devoted his life to medicine and research...but when the shadow of death had come to his own door, he'd been unable to do anything to save his wife and child.

He'd cared for them feverishly, night and day for weeks. Jonathon had gone first. Sturdy and strapping though the boy had been, his eventual dehydration caused by vomiting and diarrhea had been more than Flynn could stave off.

Grief-stricken, he'd buried his son and turned his attention to his wife, only to lose the same battle. Once they were gone, he had avoided people—even his family. He hadn't wanted to practice medicine, turning instead to research in an all-consuming drive to understand and eliminate the contamination that caused so many deaths.

He rarely let himself think about Jonathon or his failure to save him, but the memories of all he'd lost stalked him in the night, haunting his dreams and stealing any peace he hoped to find.

The risks to a newborn on this ship terrified him. And the dilemma of caring for a baby posed a problem, as well. Perhaps, if no mother was found, they could find a family to take in the infant for the duration of the journey.

He approached Maeve and Nora. "Boil everything

that touches this baby," he told them. "Boil the cups in which we carry the milk." He glanced at the tubing. "You're using that to feed her? Did you boil it? Good. Wash your hands thoroughly." He handed Maeve the half-full cup. "Throw out any she doesn't take and get fresh each feeding. I'll notify the captain that she's been found. A search to turn up her mother will come next, I have no doubt. Shall we find someone to care for her?"

Nora appeared stricken at the idea. "I can take care of her!"

"Nora, what about your kitchen duties?" Maeve asked.

"You and Bridget can help. We'll share her care and feeding." She gave her younger sister a pleading glance. "Please. She's so tiny and alone. We know she'll be safe with us—and under the doctor's supervision. With someone else we can't be sure they'll care for her properly or give her the attention she needs."

Maeve looked at the fragile little human being in Nora's arms, now frantically sucking at the pinpricks they'd made in the tubing and swallowing in noisy gulps. "I have helped care for a good many newborns. 'Tis not such a hardship."

She glanced at Flynn, and her compassionate blue gaze shot him through, touching a tiny crevice in his hardened heart. Thoroughly impractical though it may be to have an infant strapped to his assistant or a kitchen worker, the warm burst of admiration he felt at their earnest concern and willingness to take on this task couldn't be denied.

He didn't let himself look at the baby, but the sound of her sucking speared his heart. He gave Nora a stern look. "Clear your intent with Mr. Mathers. Assure me you have his approval and promise you'll take no safety risks in the galley. If you're to be near fire or water, you will give your turn over to one of your sisters."

"Yes, of course," Nora acknowledged quickly. "Thank you, Dr. Gallagher. God bless you."

"I'm going to assign one of the McCorkle boys to run errands for you part of the day. Emmett is the youngest and most agile, so he will run for milk and carry messages between the three of you." He looked at Maeve. "Thoroughly instruct him on sanitation."

She nodded her understanding. "Certainly, doctor. I'm relatively sure he already comprehends hand washing. Sean filled me in on their lesson. It made quite an impression."

Flynn asked Nora to place the baby on the examining table once she'd burped. "Let's have a listen now." He glanced up and then away. "The two of you may call me Flynn when there are no patients or other passengers present."

Maeve gave him one of her stunning smiles. "Thank you, Flynn."

A soot-faced cabin boy appeared then, extending a piece of paper. Flynn took it and read the hastily scrawled note. Seemed the captain had invited him to dinner in his cabin that evening. "Tell Captain Conley I'd be happy to join him and his wife."

The lad nodded and hurried off.

Once Flynn had listened to the baby's heart and lungs, he left Nora to diaper and dress her as best she could.

"Are we going to try to find the baby's mother?" Maeve asked in a near whisper.

He gestured for her to follow him into the smaller room. "One of us can go to the captain while the other stays here."

"I'll go," she offered.

He nodded his approval.

Maeve told Nora what she was doing and left to find the captain in the chart house. "May I have a moment to speak with you?" she asked.

Once she'd explained the situation, he removed his cap and scratched his head. "Never had this happen b'fore. Plenty o' babies been born aboard, but none have been deserted."

"I was thinking you could go over the ship's manifest," Maeve suggested. "See how many women of childbearing age are aboard and then question them."

"Sounds like a logical plan. Come with me."

She joined him in his cabin, where Mrs. Conley was cheerfully humming and scrubbing potatoes. Their cabin had a tiny kitchen area with hanging pots and pans that swayed with the ship's movement.

The captain set the heavy manifest on the scarred table with a thump and opened to the last pages.

After hearing Maeve's story, Martha Conley joined their efforts. She got a paper, pen and ink to make a list, then pushed them toward Maeve. "Your writin's probably better'n mine, dearie."

They came up with thirty-nine possibilities for someone who might have given birth.

Martha took a knife from a crock and slit the paper in half, handing half to Maeve. "We'll each take half. Do you think you can talk to nineteen women today?"

Maeve nodded. "I'll do as many as I can this morning and the rest after I'm finished in the dispensary."

"We'll compare this evening, then," Martha said.

After visiting with fifteen women, Maeve determined all of them unlikely to have given birth to a baby and abandoned it. Five were pregnant and three had new babies. The rest were widows. With four remaining on her list. Maeve went about her duties. She didn't hold much remaining hope for finding the baby's mother.

At noon she carried a meal to Sean, who had been moved to the doctor's quarters and made comfortable. She looked about the physician's neat room, noting rolled pallets where the three McCorkle brothers had slept. Books lined specially made shelves with brass bars to hold the volumes in place, and more were stacked here and there, where Flynn had left them. The doctor had a private cabin, with more space than she and twelve others shared each night.

She pictured him here, poring over his books. It was curious that a man of his age, especially one so handsome and intelligent, didn't seem to be married. But he must be single. If he wasn't, he wouldn't have taken a position like this.

Sean was glad for company, so she stayed while he ate his potato soup. "Dr. Gallagher said in America boys like me learn numbers and words. He said he'll help find us a family to stay with, where we can do chores an' go to school."

He talked her ear off before she could get away. Half of his sentences started with *Dr. Gallagher.*

Upon returning to the dispensary, she gathered containers and went to the foredeck to boil more water. While it cooled, she absorbed the warmth of the glorious sun and gazed across the vast Atlantic. The water's surface was crowded with slimy-looking objects of varying size, form and color, some of them resembling a lemon cut in half. In the distance two ships on the horizon kept the *Annie McGee* company. Were those ships as laden with immigrants escaping lives of poverty as this one?

Nearby, male passengers in three-piece suits and ladies in finely made dresses strolled the deck or sat upon wooden folding chairs. The women held parasols over their heads to protect their skin from the sun, reminding Maeve that she'd been standing there too long. She covered the pots of water and carried them back to the dispensary.

"It's a beautiful, sunny day."

Dr. Gallagher had been seated at his small writing desk making notes since she'd left. He didn't look up.

"Did you stop for a meal?" she asked.

"Lost track of time," he replied distractedly.

A commotion sounded in the corridor, and the door burst open. A woman's screams raised the hair on Maeve's neck. A sailor leaned in and spotted her. "The doctor in?"

"He's right here. Is someone sick?"

"We got her right here." He backed into the room, carrying one end of a blanket, upon which a woman lay, writhing in pain.

Flynn shot up and ran to meet them as the second man, a passenger dressed in plain clothing, entered with the other end of the blanket.

The reason for the woman's distress was immediately obvious. Her skirts were blackened, with much of the fabric burned away, right down to her pantaloons. The sickening smell of scorched wool reached Maeve.

Chapter Seven

Maeve swallowed and took a deep breath to stay calm.

"Caught her skirts on a cook fire, she did," the passenger said.

"Are you family?" Flynn asked.

"Aye, she's m'wife," he replied.

Maeve had treated burns before, and she knew how much pain the woman suffered. "Laudanum?" she asked automatically.

"Chloroform first," Flynn answered. "Bring her over here to the table," he instructed.

Maeve doused a square of gauze. "What's her name?" she asked the husband.

"Goldie," he replied in a thick voice. "Goldie McHugh." He cleared his throat, but didn't tear his stricken gaze from his wife.

"The doctor's going to take good care of you, Goldie." Maeve smoothed the woman's hair at the same time she placed the gauze over her nose and mouth. "Just take a few deeps breaths now. You'll sleep."

The woman's eyes, filled with pain and fear, met Maeve's in those torturous few moments before her lids drifted closed and she lay blessedly still.

"Now prepare a dose of laudanum," Flynn instructed. He turned to the husband. "Miss Murphy and I are going to have to cut the remainder of her skirts away to see how severe her injuries are. I understand your concern for your wife, sir, but the fewer people in here while we treat her, the better her chances."

"I'm not leavin' my Goldie like this," the man argued.

"Understand now, she is at risk for serious infection, and until we can see how badly she's burned, your presence places her in jeopardy."

His words were severe, but Maeve comprehended his concern to keep the room and the wounds as clean as possible.

Goldie's husband seemed taken aback by that information and stood with his mouth clamped shut.

"Every second I spend with you is a second I'm not attending to your wife," Flynn added.

Maeve watched their interaction with deep compassion for the man and appreciation for the physician's wisdom.

At last a look of resignation crossed the big man's face. "I'll be in the corridor."

As soon as the door had closed, Flynn was all business, cutting away the remaining skirts as close to the burned area as possible. Maeve removed the woman's shoes and cut the remaining portions of Goldie's wool stockings away. Maeve assisted him as he used a large pair of tweezers and removed bits of fabric seared to the lower portions of Goldie's legs.

Each time flesh was revealed, Maeve marveled that there was skin intact beneath the scorched fabric.

"I don't want to peel away skin, but I can't leave this fabric stuck to the burns," he said as though thinking aloud.

Maeve studied the patches. "We could soak rags in vinegar and lie them over the wounds to keep it all wet while you work."

"That's a sound idea." He gathered rags and a basin of vinegar and plunged the fabric down in the liquid.

"I honestly expected to see much worse," Maeve confessed.

"As did I. She's extremely fortunate. Seems whoever doused the flames did so quickly enough to spare her." He draped the wet rags over her shins. "How would you have treated this patient back home?"

"With whatever was available. Potato peels work well. I once made a liniment of turpentine and yellow basilion. But I most appreciate the properties of cotton ash paste."

"That's my first choice, as well. How did you make yours?"

"Burned cotton wool and mixed it with any oil available. Usually linseed or olive."

"Cotton wool ashes are in the big jar in the base of that cabinet." He gestured with a nod as he lifted the corner of the rag and loosened a bit of fabric from their patient's leg. "This is coming right off. Go ahead and mix the ashes with peppermint oil to make a paste."

She did as directed, stirring the blackened concoction that smelled better than it looked. She placed the container and a wooden spatula at the ready.

To their amazement, once Flynn was finished removing fabric, there were only half a dozen small patches of seriously burned skin and a few blisters. Goldie would definitely be in pain, but she would heal.

Flynn took the container and carefully smeared black paste on the woman's shins. "We want to keep this dressing fresh and the skin completely covered for a few days."

Maeve nodded.

"How did you learn all you know about methods of healing?" he asked. Her instincts were impressive.

"My mother had a good many home remedies," she answered. "I was always interested in her methods, and she was eager to teach." The stick he used became too glommed with paste, so she handed him a clean one.

"I have always found it fascinating how our ancestors used home remedies—roots, flowers, herbs—with excellent healing properties," Flynn commented. "I have often wondered about the first people who tried such a remedy. Where did they get their ideas?"

Maeve shook her head in reply. "There was an elderly woman in our village who tended the sick for many years, until she grew too old and feeble. It was then her nephew and his family took her in. She sat in a chair just outside their front door the last years of her life. Sharp as a tack, she was. Anything I needed to know, I went to her. Plus, much of my education came by accident and necessity."

"You have a natural instinct," he told her. "I saw physicians graduating with less skill than you. What is it you plan to do when you get to America?"

"Have you heard of a place called Faith Glen?"

"Indeed. It's not far from Boston."

"Is it pretty there?"

He glanced at her and then back down at his work. "It's on the coast, so the countryside is green and lush. A welcoming little village, much like those in Ireland. Without the lava beneath or the eroded cliffs, of course."

"I can see it now," she breathed.

"How did you learn of Faith Glen?"

"After my father's death, my sisters and I found a letter written to my mother many years ago. In it, the writer explained he had bought her a cottage in Faith Glen. We had nowhere to go, because the land we farmed had been given to the landlord's family…so we decided to set about learning if this deed is legal and if the house is still there. Have you ever heard of a man named Laird O'Malley?"

He finished the task and draped clean cloth over Goldie's legs. "Can't say I have, no. Is he family?"

"We're not sure who he is—or was. But he thought enough of our mother to buy a house and deed it to her." After checking that Goldie still slept soundly, she cleaned up supplies and put away containers. "We've left behind everything we ever knew on the chance that there's a new beginning for us in that village. We spent all we had on fare and food to last this journey. Working on the ship will give us a little money to live off, but once we reach our destination, we'll need jobs."

Flynn covered Goldie with a crisp clean sheet. "No doubt the wondering is a burden to the three of you. Will you find this house? Does this O'Malley fellow exist?"

His perception warmed her even more to the man. "We've had to turn the worry over to the good Lord," she told him. "He tells us not to be afraid, because He is with us and takes care of us no matter what. I believe that."

The doctor rolled the scraps of burned fabric and Goldie's ruined skirts into a compact ball. "I'll burn these on deck later."

"I can do it."

He listened to Goldie's heart and tested her pulse before looking up at Maeve. "She's doing well. I want to keep her dosed and unconscious for the rest of the day."

"It will be the kindest thing to do."

"And it will prevent movement and dislodging of the dressings."

"I will stay with her."

"Maeve," he said, "if the house in Faith Glen isn't there or is occupied—if you can't find this O'Malley fellow or anyone to recognize the deed, I'll make certain you find quarters in a good boardinghouse. You and your sisters won't be left with nowhere to go. I give you my word."

Maeve's eyes filled with tears she rapidly blinked away. "Thank you. My sisters will be as relieved as I am to hear that." She chanced a direct look at his face. "You're a kind and generous man, Flynn."

He dropped his gaze to the patient. "I'd like to think someone would do the same for my sisters."

"You have sisters?"

"Two of them. Spoiled and pampered. One is getting married next month."

"Where is your family?"

"Galway," he replied. "That's where I lived before..."

"Before?"

"Before I researched and traveled. I'll be talking to Goldie's husband now. I'm grateful I have good news for him."

He strode to the door and ushered the man inside.

The entire time he spoke with the man about his wife's injury and fortunate circumstance, Maeve counted her blessings. Their future was still uncertain as far as the house in Faith Glen went, but at least Flynn's assurance they wouldn't be on the streets set her mind at ease.

She couldn't wait to tell Nora and Bridget, but first she had another four women to locate.

His capable—and undeniably beautiful—assistant had generously offered to check on Goldie that evening while Flynn enjoyed a leisurely supper in Captain Conley's cabin.

Flynn had sailed the *Annie McGee* on several occasions and had previously sampled a delicious and hearty lobscouse, unsurpassed by any other stew he'd ever tasted, prepared by the captain's missus. This one was tender lamb with chunks of potato and turnip. Her biscuits were gold and flaky, and he was grateful to Maeve for the opportunity to enjoy this meal without having any fear for his patients' well-being.

He had to wonder, however, what she and her sisters dined on this evening. The daily allotment consisted of meal and usually another staple, sometimes ham or bacon because it could be stored in salt. Perhaps he could beg a dish of lobscouse from Martha Conley to carry back for her.

From across the opposite side of the table, Kathleen gave him a generous smile, while her mother chatted with Martha. Martha Conley had apparently invited the Boyds because she'd known Flynn for years and knew his family and hers were close. His father had suggested Flynn marry her, but Flynn didn't have those kind of feelings for her.

He could never look at Kathleen with love or passion. She was indeed lovely, educated and brought up to run a household. Any man would be fortunate to gain her attentions. Her social status made her appealing to a man, and her family was wealthy, qualities that would make her a good match one day soon.

Flynn couldn't think of marrying again. He did not feel at ease with the idea—and especially not with some-one he considered a friend.

Currently, he divided his time between Boston and Galway, with lengthy trips to Edinburgh, where medi-cine was beginning to advance and he had opportunities to work with colleagues and study the groundbreaking practices of Joseph Lister.

There would come a day when he wanted a family and a home, but he couldn't work on it now, even if he did become a bookish recluse. Perhaps one day he'd find a woman content with his overzealous commitment to medicine, but it wouldn't be Kathleen.

He couldn't marry for love: love hurt too much. Nor could he marry someone he didn't love, even though that sort of marriage might neatly and efficiently preclude any chance of additional hurt or grief. It was plain he couldn't marry for any reason.

"How is the McHugh woman?" the captain asked.

"She's doing very well. I confide I didn't have a good feeling when I first saw her, but her husband and sev-eral sailors put out the flames before her skin was badly damaged."

"The good Lord was watching over her, He was." Martha placed a bowl of golden brown custard on the table.

"I agree, Mrs. Conley. There's no other way she could have been spared from a worse fate, but by divine inter-vention."

"Is that dwarfish person still assisting you?" Estelle Boyd asked.

Flynn blinked in consternation. "Who?"

"The girl with the blinding red hair."

"You must mean Miss Murphy," Martha said. "I think

she's a lovely little thing, and her hair is as bright and pretty as can be. 'Tis a true Irishwoman who has skin and hair like that."

Estelle's caustic comments about Maeve didn't sit well with Flynn.

Kathleen gave him an apologetic smile.

"Did you notice the ships to the south this day?" Captain Conley asked, changing the subject.

"I didn't see them myself, but I heard they were in sight."

The captain nodded. "By tomorrow we should be able to make them out and recognize the vessels."

"Will you be staying in Boston for any length of time after this voyage?" Estelle asked. "Kathleen and I are planning to host a celebration once we find a suitable home."

"What will you be celebrating?" Martha asked.

"Our move to America," Estelle replied. "So many of our friends and acquaintances have moved to London or New York or Boston that we've been sorely alone. The merchants haven't been stocking items we require, and even the sempstresses have taken other employ."

"*Sempstress* sounds so primitive, Mother," Kathleen chided. "In America they use the word *seamstress*."

Estelle rolled her eyes. "*Seam*stress, rather."

"Aye, these tryin' times have been hard on Irish in all walks of life," Martha agreed. "Shipping or sailing seems to hold the most promise."

"They say the cities along the coast of America are brimming with jobs, and merchants are doing well," Captain Conley said. "Immigrants are heading west, and they need supplies for travel."

"I should warn you we're not considered the cream of society in America," Flynn told Estelle. "The English have been there for quite some time, and they've already set the standards."

Estelle didn't appear pleased by his pronouncement, but he thought it better she be forewarned to the snobbery that prevailed.

"We are people of means," she informed him. "We shall buy a home and prove ourselves in the community."

He hoped she was right, but he felt no assurance of that.

Flynn was enjoying a bowl of custard when there was a hard knock at the door. "Cap'n, sir!"

"What is it? Come in."

The sailor entered and stepped to the captain's chair, where he leaned to say something in his ear.

Conley shot his gaze to Flynn. "Excuse us, ladies. The doctor and I are needed."

"Thank you for the exceptional meal, Mrs. Conley," Flynn said, standing. "Excuse me, Kathleen, Mrs. Boyd."

Outside in the corridor the captain turned to Flynn. "Seems someone's found a young woman's body. Do you know who it is?" he asked the sailor ahead of them.

"No, sir."

On deck, the crew had considerately rigged canvas to hide the girl's body from the eyes of the passengers. She lay in what would have been plain view where she'd fallen. This wasn't the area where the passengers had their fires, so only a few passengers who'd been strolling the deck stood nearby.

Flynn glanced up. "Looks like she fell from the forecastle onto the deck."

"Passengers aren't allowed up near the crew's quarters," Captain Conley said.

"Nobody saw her or knows what she was doin' there," the nearest crew member told him.

Flynn stepped closer. It had been obvious even from a distance that the girl was dead, but gathering all the details was part of his job. Her curly mane of dark wavy hair was matted with blood. He brushed a skein from her neck and pressed his fingers against her vein. No pulse, as he'd expected.

"She's dead."

"Does anyone know this girl?" Captain Conley asked.

A young woman of maybe sixteen or seventeen who clung to her mother's hand, raised stricken eyes. "I—I have talked to her before."

"Do you know her name?"

"She told me her name is Bridget."

Flynn's heart stopped for half a minute. Maeve's sister? The one working for the Atwaters? His chest felt as though someone had rested a weight upon it. Maeve would be devastated.

How was he going to tell her?

Chapter Eight

A knot formed in Flynn's throat. "Bridget is the name of one of the Murphy sisters."

"We'll lay her out before you get the others," the captain said. "This isn't a pretty sight for her kin."

Flynn waited with the captain while several men brought a coffin with holes drilled in the side and sand in the bottom. He'd seen burials before, but the box was still a shock. He helped place the body in the coffin, and waited while the deck was scrubbed clean.

When all was presentable, he went in search of Maeve.

"I'll be fine sittin' here, Miss Murphy. You go eat your supper."

"She's had another dose of laudanum, so she will sleep a couple of hours," Maeve told him. She left Goldie's husband seated at his wife's side and called on the last women on her list before joining Nora for a meal of stirabout and dried apples beside their firebox. Maeve held the squirming baby while Nora cleaned their dishes. Bridget had gone to have dinner with the Atwaters.

"I called on half the possible women aboard this

vessel today," she told her sister. "To no avail. Mrs. Conley took the other half of the list, so I still need to meet with her."

"She took her milk and slept in her sling most of the day. I even had a few minutes here and there to cut some of this fabric in preparation for sewing her clothing."

"That's what newborns do." Maeve changed the square of flannel the child wore for a diaper. A few of their fellow passengers had generously given them scraps of material and a few pieces of cast-off clothing. "Right now she's easy to care for. Meet her needs and she's happy. Will you have time to wash these tomorrow?"

"I thought I'd wash them out tonight, while we have a fire going. I can hang them in the morning. Laundry days are designated on Mondays and Thursdays, unless someone has a baby. If there are diapers that need to be laundered, we can hang them any time we please."

"I'm sure that rule is in place as a favor to everyone," Maeve replied with a smile. "Isn't she the prettiest little thing? Look at her silky fine hair. I hope it's not curly."

She bundled the infant in a lightweight square of cotton to keep her secure and protect her head from the breeze. It was still light enough to make out her features and her delicate fingernails. Maeve touched her incredibly small, soft hands with wonder.

Nora finished her chore and came to sit beside them. "She is indeed a pretty baby. I've been thinking, Maeve. Our *grah mo chee* needs a name."

"She probably has a name already," Maeve said.

"No one has claimed her, and it looks unlikely that you're going to find her mother or anyone who knows of her existence. For now we're all she has, and we can't go on calling her baby."

"You call her *grah mo chee*," Maeve added.

"Her name isn't *sweetheart.* She needs a real name."

"I suppose you're right." Maeve waited, because she knew Nora had already thought it through.

"I was thinking Grace or Faith."

"I like them both."

"Grace it is, then?"

"Grace is a fine name."

Nora took the baby and nestled her close. "Baby Grace, we are going to take care of you. You have our promise."

Maeve smiled at her sister. She couldn't have anticipated Nora's fascination with the little one. She was quite obviously besotted with the child, as were Maeve and Bridget. No baby ever received so much attention and affection in their first day as this one.

They hadn't been paying attention to their surroundings, so the swift approach of booted feet upon the planks caught Maeve unawares. She glanced up, even more startled to find Flynn, his stark expression serious.

"Dr. Gallagher!" she said. "What brings you here this evening?"

"Please. Stay seated." His forehead was wrinkled with concern at the sight of her and Nora sitting together, and he looked around, as if he'd hoped to see someone else with them. "May I join the two of you?"

"Yes, of course. Have you eaten? I can offer you tea."

"Nothing, thank you. I'm afraid I have some bad news for you."

"What is it?" Maeve asked. "Is it Goldie? She was sedated when I left, and her husband was right at her side."

"No," he answered. "That's not it."

Maeve waited for whatever it was he had come to say.

"This is going to be difficult." He glanced from side to side, as though reconsidering or perhaps not wanting their neighbors to overhear. His expression was decidedly pained. "Perhaps this isn't the best—"

"We have a guest? How delightful!"

The feminine voice caught Flynn's attention, and he turned as Bridget approached. She wore a bright smile, and as usual her hair had escaped its confines and trailed down her back.

"The Atwaters chose to share the evening with their daughters, so I was dismissed after supper. Their cook is traveling with them. We had the most delicious fish and potatoes."

Color drained from Flynn's face. He jumped to his feet and stared at Bridget. "You—you had supper with the Atwaters?"

"Yes. I've just left there."

"Why, I—I don't know what to say." He grasped Bridget's shoulders and tugged her to him, hugging her soundly before releasing her. "I'm so glad to see you."

Even in the semidarkness, Bridget's blush was apparent. She was quiet for a full minute, which plainly showed her astonishment.

Maeve was dumbfounded, as well. His demonstrative behavior was completely out of character.

"Forgive me," Flynn said, his voice low. "That was forward of me, but I believed... Well, I..."

Maeve and Nora were on their feet now. "What did you think?" Nora asked the doctor.

"I was so glad to see your sister alive and well," he explained. "You see, there was an accident earlier. A young woman who looks just like Bridget here fell from the forecastle and was killed."

Bridget gasped, and Nora hugged the baby to her breast.

"How dreadful!" Nora exclaimed.

"And you saw this young woman?" Maeve asked.

"Aye. She had the same hair as your sister. Similar clothing."

"And that's what you'd come here for? Thinking you were going to tell us our sister had fallen to her death?"

He nodded, clearly disturbed.

"Oh, my goodness," Maeve breathed.

"That was kind of you, Dr. Gallagher," Nora said. "And very brave. Thank you. Now I'm believing some other poor girl's family will be grieving her this night. Let's pray."

And just like that, the Murphy sisters joined hands, Maeve and Bridget taking his on either side. Maeve's hand was small, the bones delicate in his palm, though her grasp was strong, and she had small calluses at the padded bases of each finger. He tried to picture her with a pitchfork or behind a plow, but couldn't get the image to gel.

Nora led them in a simple, but heartfelt prayer for the family of the deceased girl.

"And thank You for our friend, Lord," Maeve added, squeezing Flynn's hand. "Bless the good doctor's hands as he treats patients and assists You in healing Your people. Amen."

The sisters chorused their *amens*. Visibly shaken, Flynn sat at their fireplace with them, as much for the tea as to steady his turbulent emotions and jumping nerves. Nora refilled his cup. "I must return and let the captain know we haven't correctly identified the girl."

"As soon as you've finished your tea," Nora insisted. "You had a bad scare."

Flynn experienced broad relief that all three sisters were alive and well. The captain would need to search for someone who knew the identity of the dead girl. The fright he'd had while thinking it was Bridget Murphy was more stress than he needed this night. He sipped his tea and focused on remaining calm.

The weather was appropriately dismal the following morning. Dark clouds hung over the ocean and a fine mist dampened hair and clothing, chilling those who stood on deck. Both Bridget and Maeve had secured their curly hair with nearly an entire tin of pins and wore hats, as well, since their tresses turned into unruly corkscrews in this wet, bleak weather.

There was much ceremony, and faces were somber as Captain Conley and the crew prepared to deliver the coffin into the sea. Those who'd brought instruments along played hymns. Bundled passengers lined the deck in wait. As mostly Irishmen were aboard, the eerie sound of bagpipes floated across the dreary gray ocean.

News had come that an accounting of passengers and crew had turned up the identity of a young woman traveling alone. As coincidence would have it, the dead girl's name had been Bridget Collins. Her belongings had been stored in hopes of finding relatives once the ship docked. No one the captain had spoken to remembered much about her. She stayed to herself and cooked her meals alone, not speaking to the other women in her cabin. Everything about her was a mystery.

Maeve had come above deck with Flynn and the Mc-Corkle brothers. They stood together, watching as the plain coffin was raised with rope and swung out over the water.

"What's them holes for?" Sean asked.

"So the box takes in water and sinks faster," Gavin replied quietly.

Sean's Adam's apple chugged up and down several

times. He reached for Maeve's hand and squeezed it. The sailors maneuvered the ropes so the coffin slid out of the loops and into the water.

A woman passenger with a fair, lilting voice began a hymn, "'Fairest Lord Jesus, ruler of all nature. O thou of God and man the Son.'"

People joined in the singing, Maeve and her sisters included. "'Thee will I cherish. Thee will I honor, Thou, my soul's glory, joy, and crown.'"

Beside her, Flynn's deep baritone joined in. "'Fair are the meadows, fairer still the woodlands, robed in the blooming garb of spring. Jesus is fairer, Jesus is purer, Who makes the woeful heart to sing.'"

Everyone who'd spoken of the dead girl had lamented over the fact that no one had known about her or her circumstances. Some said she'd deliberately jumped to her death; others speculated she'd been dallying with a crew member. In any case, it was a sad and lonely way to die and be buried.

The sound of the bagpipes caused Maeve a healthy pang of homesickness, but she soon recalled the hunger and suffering and reminded herself why they'd cut ties and set sail aboard the *Annie McGee*. It was a harsh fact that not all who had boarded would set foot in Massachusetts. But she'd do her best to assist the doctor in making sure as many arrived safely as it was in their power to help survive.

She made her way through the dispersing crowd to where Martha Conley stood. "I apologize for not coming to see you last night. The day was longer and more exhausting than I could have expected."

"Don't give it another thought, dear. You had your hands full." She tucked a strand of gray hair under her cap. "I didn't have any luck. How about you?"

Maeve shook her head. "Nothing."

"Could be someone's lying," Martha suggested. "Or the baby's mother might not be listed on the manifest."

Maeve met her eyes. "A stowaway?"

Martha shrugged. "We get plenty of 'em. You did your best, child. I'm just thankful you and your sisters are willing to care for the babe."

They parted on that note. Not long after their conversation, she returned to assist Flynn as he changed Goldie's dressings. The woman was staying awake for longer periods with less medicine. "Heard tell a poor girl died," Goldie said.

"Yes, ma'am," Flynn replied.

"Do you think I can go back to my cabin soon?" she asked. "Truth be told, I get more time with my husband here, since we're separated in men's and women's cabins otherwise, but I don't want to be takin' up space someone else could use."

"It's up to you, wherever you're most comfortable," Flynn told her. "As long as you keep the wound clean and covered with the dressing, you'll do fine. If I send along a bottle of medicine for pain, I think we could let you go tomorrow."

"I have little to pay you," Goldie told him with an embarrassed shrug.

"The shipowner pays me by the trip," he told her. "You don't owe me anything."

"I do think I owe you, but I thank you nonetheless."

"Miss Murphy will show you how to get around using crutches, but I want you to stay off your feet as much as possible."

"Anything you say, doctor."

That afternoon, Maeve tended to a gaggle of female patients with questionable complaints. Most were disappointed they didn't get to see the doctor, and two were downright rude, but by now she was accustomed to their behavior and prepared to deal with them. With all this attention, it was a wonder the doctor didn't have an in-flated sense of his own importance, but he seemed to take it all in stride, often exchanging a private look with her that said he was on to these women's tactics.

When she got to the deck later, dark clouds hung low in the sky, making it seem later than it was.

A crewman cried out from the rigging above. "Fire to the east! All hands on deck! All hands on deck!"

Startled, she oriented herself to figure out which way was east. Passengers had already run to the side of the ship.

An odd light burned a quarter of a mile away. One of the ships that had been keeping pace with them was on fire. Alarm spread through the crowd watching the scene on the other ship.

Maeve's heart kicked blood more quickly through her veins. No doubt there were hundreds aboard that vessel, people just like these around her—people just like her.

Sailors climbed the rigging above for better vantage points and called updates to their fellow mates.

Smoke billowed into the night sky, eerily lit by the flames fueling it.

"'Tis a sail ablaze now!" a man called down.

"They're handing buckets up to the riggers," another said.

The water probably added to the amount of smoke. Maeve prayed for the safety of the passengers and crew.

Captain Conley called orders that had something to do with the sails, and the *Annie McGee* bobbed closer to the other ship. His next command was to furl the sails and drop anchor.

Too many passengers had moved in front of Maeve, so she worked her way through them to reach the rail. The others could see over her head.

Objects in the water became visible, but from this distance she wasn't sure what they were.

"Lifeboats and swimmers!" came the call from above.

Swimmers? In these shark-infested waters? Her heart dropped to her stomach.

"Excuse me, please. Excuse me." Flynn worked his way to the rail beside her.

"Man the lifeboats!"

Crew members urged the bystanders away from the side, so the rowboats could be manipulated with ropes and pullies.

"Two men in each boat!" Captain Conley ordered. "Away!"

Flynn hurried forward.

"You're needed here," the captain said to him. They looked at each other for several seconds, and then Flynn backed away.

Two sailors climbed into the boat and were lowered down over the side.

"Go for my bag," he said to Maeve.

Obediently, she turned and ran to do his bidding.

"We'll need an area where anyone injured can lie down and I can treat them. Preferably not too far from a fire."

Maeve designated a place on the deck, added fuel to the fire and spread out blankets in preparation for patients.

It seemed as if an eternity passed before the boats from the *Annie McGee* reached people floundering in the water.

Turning to those standing nearby, she called, "More

blankets! We'll have to get them warm when they get onboard. Bring as many blankets as you have."

The passengers jumped into action, some moving no farther than their fireplaces for a blanket, others disappearing down the ladder to their cabins below. The pile of blankets grew.

The first boat came near, and those paying attention above tossed down ropes, which the sailors hooked. The boat was hoisted upward, dripping water.

Ingenious brackets fit the boat snugly against the side of the ship, so it was held steady.

Maeve had counted eight heads besides those of the sailors as the boat had neared, so she grabbed blankets and passed them out.

"I'll check each person for injuries first," Flynn called to everyone within earshot. "If I deem him well, take the person to your cook fire and get him warm."

Flynn's assessment consisted mostly of asking each dripping-wet and shivering refugee if he or she had been hurt.

One had a long gash on his arm. Flynn wrapped it tightly and sent him with Maeve.

The next boat was full of dry passengers, who had obviously climbed into a boat and not jumped into the water.

A barrel-chested fellow she'd seen a time or two led a dripping-wet, sobbing woman to Maeve. "Doc said she has a bump on her head."

Sure enough swelling over her left eye prompted Maeve to look into the woman's eyes. "We'll get you warm and keep a cold compress on that."

Bridget and Aideen showed up just then. "What can we do to help?" Bridget asked.

"I see the two of you have met."

"We were just getting ready to start supper when all the excitement started," Bridget replied.

"Bridget, I could use a plaster for this woman's head, if you please. I'll tell you exactly where to find it in the dispensary and how to prepare it."

"All right."

Aideen and Bridget ran errands for both Dr. Gallagher and Maeve as the survivors were brought onto the ship. There were very few injuries. Mostly things like contusions and scrapes from the passengers panicking and jumping overboard.

They learned the other ship was the *Wellington,* and it had left a port just west of them within hours of the *Annie McGee*'s departure. Once the initial emergency was over, Bridget and Aideen went back to their cook fires.

"I don't know what will happen," Flynn said to her. "We can't go forward with this many additional people."

Concern and disappointment rolled over Maeve like a wave. They couldn't go back now! Perhaps they could find a port where the additional passengers could await a new ship. She worked hard to place herself in the others' shoes and not think selfishly What if the situation had been reversed? She would want someone to take her and her sisters in and see to their welfare.

"We can't share what we have and go forward?"

"There are laws," he told her. "Set in place to prevent overcrowding and disease. There isn't enough food or water to accommodate this many more people for the duration of the trip. The risk of disease increases with each person who is added. The most likely solution would be to put them off somewhere, but it would take us out of our way."

She didn't even know how to pray, but she silently

asked God to assist these people and help her overcome her selfishness.

As darkness fell, there were no longer flames licking at the other ship. It rested on the waves like a painting she'd once seen. Bobbing at sea lent the ship a different feel. How far would dropping anchor set them back? Where would they go from here?

From where she sat, watching over two resting patients, Maeve observed as yet another boat was stabilized and two men stepped out onto the deck. Captain Conley was there to meet them, and the men walked away together.

"That must be the *Wellington*'s captain. I think I'll go join them to see what's happening on the other ship."

The additional passengers they'd taken on were distributed at the other cook fires around the decks.

A short, round woman with a headscarf over her hair joined Maeve and offered food she'd prepared for the two patients. "All the others are eating meals with our people."

Maeve thanked her. The woman and man, who hadn't met each other before ending up here, sat forward and accepted bowls of rice.

"Everythin' got so confusing," the woman told them. "Fire was licking up the mast and people were screaming and running. I kept thinkin' we'd only just left everything behind to start over, and now we'd be killed at sea."

"The sailors were telling us to remain calm," the man said. "But it's hard t' stay calm when a ship is burning out from under ye in the middle of the ocean."

"I can only imagine how frightening that was," Maeve told them.

Flynn returned less than half an hour later. "Seems

there's not much damage. People panicked, as is their nature, and yet the fire was being brought under control. The sail will be mended overnight, and the captain plans to continue forward come morning."

Relief warmed her heart. "Thank You, Lord."

"There's nothing more we can do," he told her. "Everyone should get a good night's rest. You did an excellent job this evening. I was wise in my decision to hire you. I'm going to go check on Goldie now. Her husband is with her, and I'm sure they're hungry for news of what's been happening."

His praise warmed her cheeks. She was exhausted, but she felt good about how she'd handled herself. She'd had many doubts about her abilities, but if things continued this way, her job would be tiring, but nothing she couldn't handle.

It was late for supper, but that evening the Murphy sisters finally had a chance to help Aideen Nolan and her aunt with their cooking. After the near-panic earlier, it was good to develop a routine and grow familiar with each other. The women shared their histories and how they'd come to be here.

Mrs. Kennedy had been married to a clergyman for only six years before his untimely death. She'd been a widow since the early thirties, and had become a milliner to support herself, but her parents had insisted she come and live with them, so all her earnings went into savings. When Aideen's father, Mrs. Kennedy's brother, had died, Aideen had come to live with them, as well. Aideen had never married and was an accomplished sempstress.

"That explains your beautiful clothing." Bridget fed Baby Grace warm milk with the rubber tubing. "I can't help but notice the soft fabric and the lovely embellishments."

Maeve had admired their beautiful clothing, too. She had a difficult time imagining the luxury of a cook and a housekeeper, though they must have missed the companionship of others their own ages, living with Aideen's aging grandparents. Unlike the other well-dressed passengers, these women didn't turn up their noses at the sisters in their plain browns and grays.

"What is our fare this evening?" Aideen asked.

Maeve showed her the bag of meal. "Stirabout again."

Bridget groaned and shifted Grace to her shoulder.

"We brought additional rice and sugar in our provisions," Nora said. "Why don't we make rice pudding as a treat?"

"Don't you need eggs?" Mrs. Kennedy asked.

"We have eggs," Nora told her.

"However did you preserve them for the trip?"

"Dipped them in paraffin and then packed them in our flour bin," Nora replied.

Bridget glanced at her older sister in surprise. "Nora, your impracticality on the matter of using our eggs just for a treat is astonishing."

"We deserve a celebration," she said simply. "We thought we were witnessing a disaster, but it all turned out just fine."

"Dr. Gallagher predicted we'd have had to make for port somewhere out of our way if the *Wellington* had been badly damaged." Maeve placed her palms together. "Thank You, Lord, that didn't happen and the passengers were all safe."

"All I could think about were the sharks we hear about all the time," Aideen said. "I was sick with dread. It's a miracle that no one was killed in the water."

"I believe you're right about that," Nora agreed.

The women combined their rations and made a pot of stirabout, which simmered over the fire, while Maeve prepared the pudding, covered the pan and set it to bake.

Most families had already finished their meals, and here and there neighbors joined together with wooden flutes and fiddles to liven up the atmosphere.

"'I've traveled about a bit in me time,'" came a clear tenor voice. "'Of troubles I've seen a few. I found it far better in every clime to paddle me own canoe.'"

The ladies looked at each other and grinned.

A man with a deeper voice picked up the next verse. "'Me wants they are small. I care not at all. Me debts they are paid when due. I drive away strife from the ocean of life, and paddle me own canoe.'"

It was just the thing needed to change the mood after the death of Bridget Collins that morning and the emergency this evening. Maeve had never anticipated this much drama aboard ship.

"'I rise with the lark from daylight to dark, I do what I have to do. I'm careless in wealth, I've only me health to paddle me own canoe.'"

Someone got out their union pipes and joined the gaiety. The distinctive sound carried across the ocean, and Maeve was certain those remaining on the *Wellington* could hear the merriment.

The song changed to one less frolicking, but every bit as familiar and more sentimental. This time many voices joined in with the ballad. Even Bridget sang along. "'Tis the last rose of summer, left blooming alone. All her lovely companions are faded and gone.'"

Aideen joined in. "'No flower of her kindred, no rosebud is nigh, to reflect back her blushes, to give sigh for sigh.'"

The song continued, with other passengers picking up the familiar words and joining in.

The next song struck up and Maeve had to laugh. It was an exaggerated tale of a ship's demise, the lyrics listing millions of barrels and bricks among a multitude of supplies on the ill-fated ship. When it came to the last verse she joined in. "'We had sailed seven years when the measles broke out. Our ship lost its way in the fog. Then the whale of the crew was reduced down to two. Just myself and the captain's old dog.'"

The passengers wound up for the finale, singing loudly, and even Mrs. Kennedy joined in.

"'Then the ship struck a rock, O Lord what a shock, the boat was turned right over. Whirled nine times around, then the old dog was drowned. And the last of the *Irish Rover.* Whirled nine times around, then the old dog was drowned. I'm the last of the *Irish Rover.*'"

Laughter changed the somber mood that had prevailed since the poor girl's burial that morning. Around them merry conversations buzzed.

"We're a hardy people." Mrs. Kennedy wiped a tear from her eye. "To survive what we've been through and still have a zest for life."

They prayed together and shared their meal. A feeling of well-being and belonging settled over Maeve. There were many uncertainties ahead, yes, but the love of God and the assurance of His provision was a certainty. Already He'd given them new friends.

Chapter Nine

At daybreak the *Wellington* sent its own lifeboats, and crewmen on the *Annie McGee* filled theirs, and the process of returning all the passengers to their own vessel got underway.

The *Wellington*'s captain sent men back with bags of meal and a barrel of water to replenish provisions and as a sign of goodwill.

The process took a couple of hours, but once all the people had been returned, both ships unreefed their sails and let the wind catch them. Maeve had awakened early to witness the process and to enjoy seeing the ship set sail once again.

She made oatmeal for herself and her sisters and brewed a kettle of strong tea. Breakfast was ready when Bridget and Nora came above deck.

"Did you sleep?" Bridget asked.

"Aye. I don't believe I moved a muscle all the night through. I woke in the same position as I laid down."

Grace emitted a strong cry, and Maeve took her from Nora while Bridget went for milk.

"You're a hungry baby, you are. Do you want me to take her with me this morning?"

"If I need you to take her, I will bring her, but we should be fine."

Maeve brushed the baby's forehead with a kiss and handed her over. "I'm off to work, then."

She arrived at the dispensary just as Flynn was preparing to see Goldie to her cabin.

"Thank you for your kind attention, Miss Murphy," the woman told her.

"You're so welcome. Send for me if you need anything."

While the doctor was gone, Maeve put the dispensary in order, sterilized and organized the instruments. She changed all the linens on the cots and washed down every surface. Humming to herself, she sang and prayed softly as she worked. Her employment afforded her more quiet time than ordinarily available on this crowded ship, and she was grateful. By the time she got to her cabin at night, she was exhausted, and the lights were extinguished.

Cleaning the dispensary had become her quiet time, and she honored it as best she could. She was sure God understood the lack of privacy and honored her faithfulness.

Gavin McCorkle showed up with bleeding blisters on the palms of both hands. Though only eighteen years of age and lanky, he towered over her.

"Whatever have you done to put your hands in this condition?" she asked.

"One o' the mates by the name of Simon asked Dr. Gallagher if I'd be wantin' to apprentice. Seems he needed another lad. I'm not just a swabbie, neither. I'm a rigger."

The pride in his voice touched Maeve.

She gestured for him to sit and carried over a basin of water and a soapy sponge. "And what does a rigger do?"

"I inspect the rigging and report ropes and sails what need fixed."

"The task does sound important." She washed his hands and he hissed between his teeth. She got an uncomfortable feeling from his explanation. "Where do you do this inspecting?"

"Why, on the masts, o' course."

She'd observed the sailors and apprentices who climbed the masts like wiry monkeys, and her heart dropped every time. It sounded like a risky thing to do, especially for one so untested. "The doctor allowed you to take this position?"

"I don't recollect he knows about it just yet."

"Are they feeding you well?"

"Aye, more food than I can eat. Fish at every meal. The captain's wife gives us mackerel she's cured to take with us. As much as we like. I share with Emmett. He don't eat much."

"I don't know that it's a wise idea for an inexperienced young fellow like yourself to be swinging about on the sails." She pierced blisters that hadn't yet broken, dabbed them dry and applied ointment.

"I like me job, Miss Murphy. I'm earnin' money so we don't have to live in the alleys and beg food when we get to Boston."

"I don't believe Dr. Gallagher would let you live in the streets," she assured him. "And neither would I."

"You and Dr. Gallagher are the kindest people I ever did meet. The way this turned out was like God was makin' a way for us to get to America and have a new home."

"God didn't put Sean under that cart. That was that despicable Hegarty fellow."

"I know that, miss. But God used somethin' bad to change our future. A man still has to earn his own way."

She secured a bandage around both hands and looked him square in the face. The hairs on his chin were soft and as yet unshaved. He was a mere lad. But a lad with pride and integrity. She admired that about him. She wondered if she'd ever know how any of these boys fared once they landed. "You have to keep these bandages on and keep those areas clean, so they don't get infected."

"Aye, miss."

"Do you have a pair of gloves?"

He shook his head. "The other apprentices would laugh me right off the rigging."

He was a handsome young fellow, this one, with brown eyes that would someday set some lucky young girl's heart aflutter. He wasn't afraid to work, and he was determined to make a better life for himself and his brothers. The McCorkles' story paralleled that of the Murphy sisters in an uncanny manner.

She sent him on his way, and left the dispensary to have a word with the captain. She found Captain Conley on deck, his slouch cap shading his eyes and an ivory meerschaum stuck between his teeth, smoke curling upward. The area of beard and mustache around his mouth was stained from his habit.

"Gavin McCorkle is climbing the rigging, his first time on a ship," she told him.

"And a fine rigger, he is," Captain Conley replied.

"Is it your habit to place these young boys in dangerous positions?"

"Simon, my first mate, is the best instructor of the

bunch," he assured her. "We've only had one accident in all my days as captain of this ship."

She studied him and noted no deception in his gaze.

"And the lad wants t' learn, Miss Murphy. He's an eager young fellow. 'Tis far safer to have the young ones up there than the others, I assure you. Simon wouldn't have picked him for the job if he hadn't known the lad was capable."

"I've treated his hands for blisters," she said.

He nodded sagely. "'Tis a common malady until their skin is seasoned."

The man was obviously convinced Gavin could handle himself. Without a doubt, hundreds had done the job before him—it just seemed more frightening when the person up there was of one's acquaintance. "I shall hold you responsible for his safety," she said at last. "I want him to sail into Boston Harbor whole and sound."

"As do I, Miss Murphy."

She reached to shake his hand, as though affirming their understanding, then turned and walked away.

Nora arrived at the dispensary midmorning. "I have cooking to do around the fire. Will this be a convenient time for you to take Grace?"

"This will be a fine time." Maeve accepted the improvised sling and adjusted it to fit her much smaller frame to hold the infant close against her, with her hands free. "Grace will be my little helper, won't you, *grah mo chee?*"

The baby blinked sleepily and then closed her eyes.

"She just ate," Nora said. "She should be good for an hour or two."

Flynn arrived a short time later. He barely gave Grace a glance and set about his work. Maeve explained

Gavin's injuries and her talk with the captain. Flynn's quickly disguised amusement didn't escape notice.

The next patient to arrive was a gentleman wearing a pressed linen shirt and a jacket. He had a lanky frame and a face with craggy, yet aristocratic features. "Before I was delicate in health, I was a strapping man, would you believe?"

"Aye, I can tell you had all the lassies followin' you about, you did," Maeve teased. It amused Flynn how her brogue grew thicker when she jested or when she was provoked.

"I had eyes only for my Corabeth," the man told her. "She was an Irish beauty, she was. She had hair like yours." His eyes glistened and he took a moment to continue. "Gave me three fine sons, she did."

Maeve didn't want to ask about his sons and cause the man any more grief. Too many people had lost their loved ones, and she suspected this man had experienced loss.

"She and my Daniel, they died the same week," he told her. "Knowin' they are together was my only comfort."

Maeve nodded her understanding.

"Robbie and John ran off to America, they did. Found themselves wives and jobs. I'm goin' to meet my granddaughter. Don't let me die before I get there."

Maeve's heart went out to the man.

Flynn had led him to the table and listened to his heart. "You're not going to die on my watch, sir. I think you picked up a bit of a cold in that drizzle yesterday. Stay warm and drink a lot of fluids, and you'll be feeling fine in no time."

"How does his throat look?" Maeve asked.

Flynn asked their patient to open his mouth. "Somewhat red."

"I suspected as much from the sound of his voice. A wool sock filled with salt and heated on the bricks beside your fire will make that feel better." She went to a crock and scooped a portion of salt into a small bag. "This should be enough."

"That's just what my Corabeth used to do for our boys," he said and accepted the salt with a smile. "Is that your baby there?"

Maeve glanced down and patted Grace's bottom through the sling. The baby still slept soundly. "The little one was found abandoned aboard ship. My sisters and I are caring for her temporarily. We call her Grace."

"Might I just touch her fair head?" he asked.

"Yes, of course." Maeve lifted the baby and adjusted her so the old man could better see her.

He touched her hair and rested a long finger against her cheek. At the sight of his spotted and wrinkled hands alongside Grace's pure fair skin, Maeve got tears in her eyes.

"I remember when my babies were this tiny," he said. "It's one of the many times I've seen God's hand as plain as day. So innocent and unblemished is a new baby. Sent straight from heaven to a mother's arms."

"Are you a poet, sir?"

He chuckled. "Hardly. A cobbler. You take care of that little one now."

Their patient left and Maeve closed the door behind him.

"You are good with people," Flynn told her.

She glanced at him.

"Exceptionally good."

"Thank you."

He raised an eyebrow. "Do you believe a sock filled with salt will cure him?"

She shrugged. "I don't know, but the treatment feels good, and it's familiar and comforting. I have found that sometimes comfort and confidence are the keys to healing."

"I thought as much."

"Did I do something wrong?"

"Not at all." He let his gaze fall to the sling she settled back into place. "Is the baby doing well?"

Maeve nodded. "Grace is a contented little dear."

"I didn't know you'd named her."

"Yes, that's what Nora calls her."

"Are you concerned your sister might get too attached?"

"I'm concerned we'll all get too attached. What do you think will happen when we arrive if no family is found and we never learn where she came from?"

"I have no idea."

"Do we have a hope of keeping her?"

"Do you want to keep her?"

"I don't think any of us want her to go to a foundling home. We do know something about little girls in this family."

"I'll put in a good word for you," he assured her. "But keep in mind that someone might eventually claim her."

"If they showed no care for her until then, that someone wouldn't deserve her."

He wanted to reach out and touch her hair…rest a hand upon her arm or her shoulder to reassure her. She never hid her feelings. She wasn't ashamed to show how much she cared about people. It was a quality that drew him in, made him want to be one of the people she loved and cared for so honestly and openly.

The thought caught him off guard. Everything about her unnerved him. She still studied the baby, so her long lashes were in sharp relief against her porcelain cheek. When she looked up, she pierced him with that guileless look he'd come to find so very attractive.

Every other woman looked at him with a predatory gleam or a glimmer of appeal. This one always met his eyes with honest concern or open friendliness, with nothing motivating her desire to speak with him, except her wish to ask an opinion—or express a concern. And in addition to her honesty and beauty, she was as bright as any student he'd ever known, with a natural instinct for making people feel safe and cared for.

The thought of her being hurt if the baby's parents claimed her disturbed him. "Remember, she has family somewhere," he warned.

"I remember," was all she said.

The following day was the Sabbath. The Murphy sisters dressed in their best dresses, which were still drab and plain in comparison to many of the other women's, and joined the others in the hold for prayers and singing.

There were two services for worshippers among the passengers—one for those who spoke only Gaelic and one for those who spoke English. While the sisters understood their native language, they had decided to join the English-speaking service in preparation for their new lives.

The men stood and the ladies seated themselves upon rows of trunks and small kegs. As Flynn entered the hold with Kathleen Boyd and her mother, Maeve followed her sisters and took a seat on the center aisle.

Quite naturally, the people separated themselves into another division as they gathered: the well-dressed, well-to-do passengers on one side and the working class on the other.

Maeve didn't miss the interaction as Kathleen spoke to Flynn and gave him a smile before seating herself on a keg as though it was a plush armchair in a grand parlor. With a self-satisfied expression, she arranged her voluminous skirts before scanning the nearby passengers as though they were her competition.

She didn't bother looking across the aisle at the poor faction.

A waving hand caught Maeve's attention, and she glanced over a row to see Sean McCorkle sitting with his brothers. Pleased to see him doing well, she gave him a warm smile.

Captain Conley strode to the front and opened the Bible, from which he read a chapter from the book of James. "'Every good gift and every perfect gift is from above and cometh down from the Father of lights, with Whom is no variableness, neither shadow of turning.'"

Maeve glanced at Nora. Baby Grace had grasped on to her index finger, and Nora looked upon her as though the act was unique. Nora met Maeve's gaze and smiled sheepishly. She turned her attention to the reading.

Maeve was having a little trouble concentrating, too, but it wasn't the baby distracting her. Her thoughts kept going back to Flynn arriving with Miss Boyd. Perhaps they'd met in the corridor, and their arrival together had been mere coincidence. It was no business of hers, but she had her finger on the pulse of these husband-hunting maidens aboard the *Annie McGee*.

Determinedly, she shook off her unkind thoughts. Hadn't she and her sisters discussed their need to find husbands only a few weeks before? Their situation wasn't that much different. Yes, all the female attention was laughable because of the young ladies' obvious flirtations, but she stood in no place to judge. However, a more straightforward approach might better serve them. Flynn deserved better than a woman who viewed him as a prize to be won.

The captain took a seat beside his missus. The gathering of worshippers observed several minutes of silent prayers.

In the silence, Grace sucked her fingers energetically, and Maeve smiled to herself.

A commotion interrupted the peace. Maeve looked over her shoulder to locate the source. Mrs. Fitzwilliam, dressed in a royal-blue sateen dress and a feathered hat, stood and pulled her skirts aside. "There's an animal!" she shrieked. "I felt it against my skirts."

Chapter Ten

One of the sailor apprentices darted about the edge of the gathering, searching. Maeve imagined a rat and shuddered. She'd heard rodents got onboard ships and lived off the provisions, but as of yet she hadn't seen one of the critters.

A few of the women actually climbed atop the trunks and kegs in fright and another dashed from the room, hysterical.

A movement startled Maeve, and she had to overcome her hesitancy to look more closely. At the corner of a trunk, a black cat, with a white underbelly and white paws, peered from its hiding place.

Maeve stood and hurried the few rows back, passing Mrs. Fitzwilliam, who now stood in the aisle, fanning herself with a silk fan, and knelt to scoop up the frightened feline. "I think this may have been what you felt against your skirts."

"Surely there are rules prohibiting animals running wild aboard this vessel," the woman said in a scornful tone.

"Cats keep down the rodent population, ma'am," Captain Conley replied. "Thank you, Miss Murphy. Seems

you're always rescuin' wee ones." He motioned to someone toward the front of the hold. "Roddy, take the cat
above."

"Yessir." The young fellow hurried to do the captain's
bidding. Maeve handed over the animal, and resumed
her seat.

Men assisted the ladies in their awkward skirts back
down to the floor.

Nora and Bridget were trying not to laugh when
Maeve joined them. After that it was more difficult than
ever to concentrate in the quiet, and the captain called
the service to an end with a song.

Being the Sabbath, nearly everyone gathered around
their fireplaces, and even the sailors were scarce that
day, many taking coffee in the forecastle. The sisters
donned their hats to protect their eyes and skin from the
sun. There wasn't much of a breeze, so they made little
progress sailing upon the bosom of the broad Atlantic.

Aideen and Mrs. Kennedy joined them at their fire,
and Nora showed them how to bake a two-inch flat cake
between two cast-iron skillets above the flames. Maeve
had seen plenty of burnt cakes she suspected were raw
in the middle, and listened to Nora's explanation for pre-
venting a similarly poor outcome.

She plucked Baby Grace from the crate that had
become her bed and held her in the crook of her arm,
without the sling. The infant's eyes were open, but she
squinted against the sunlight. Maeve adjusted herself
so Grace was shadowed by her upper body. Grace still
frowned, but she studied Maeve with her delicate mouth
in an O.

"Did I see you with a bag of sewing?" Mrs. Kennedy
asked Nora.

"Yes, I'm working on a few pieces for the baby."

"We would love to help you sew for the wee one," Mrs. Kennedy said. "It's the very least we can do to repay you for your kindness in sparing us from eating our own cooking."

The women laughed together. "You're learning," Nora told her.

"I *am* a sempstress," Aideen reminded her. "In fact, I have a trunk aboard with fabric and ribbon and lace. Most of it is special pieces I couldn't bear to leave behind. Do let me make Grace something lovely and feminine."

Until now the baby had worn pieces of Dr. Gallagher's shirt fashioned into makeshift clothing and a couple of hand-me-down gowns a generous passenger had offered.

"She could wear it the day we dock," Bridget said excitedly.

Nora's expression grew somber, and Maeve suspected it was because of her concern about Grace's fate once they were in Boston.

"We have time to make each of you a dress for that day," Aideen suggested.

"We could never accept such an extravagant offer," Nora said with a shake of her head.

Bridget's face fell. It was obvious she would have loved a new dress, something pretty and feminine, but she wouldn't argue with her older sister in front of the other women and embarrass all of them.

"My material and skill at sewing are the same as your preserved eggs and ability to cook," Aideen said softly. "It's all I have to offer."

Nora's face grew pink under the brim of her straw hat. The way Aideen had presented her case made it seem that Nora would be rebuffing her gift if she didn't accept. Nora glanced at Bridget, and the two exchanged a look.

"I didn't mean to imply your gift wasn't special," Nora told her. "I was embarrassed that we don't have anything of equal value to offer."

"How did you ladies understand that verse in James this morning?" Maeve asked. "'Every good gift and every perfect gift is from above and cometh down from the Father of lights, with Whom is no variableness, neither shadow of turning.' I think James was saying that God doesn't change or choose favorites. His gifts are for everyone."

Nora gave her a perplexed look. "Did you just change the subject?"

"No. That verse was about gifts, was it not? All good gifts come from God. When we give out of love or kindness or compassion, those are good gifts."

Bridget had come up with a plan to erect a tent over the crate where Grace slept, so she'd be protected from the sun. She had cut a cast-off skirt and was hemming the edges. "No gift is more valuable than another as long as it's given in love. That's what I was thinking."

"Like the widow who gave her last mite," Aideen agreed. "And Jesus said she'd given more than the rich people who put many coins in the offering. The widow was poor, yet she gave all she had."

"So an egg and a dress are really of the same value," Mrs. Kennedy added.

Nora threw up her hands. "All right. You've all convinced me. It would be prideful to say no."

Bridget clapped her hands and gave Aideen a hug. "Oh, my! A new dress. I can hardly conceive of it, can you, Maeve?"

Maeve shook her head and placed Grace in the shaded bed. "'Tis a blessing indeed."

She couldn't remember ever having a dress that wasn't

made over from one of her older sisters' or fashioned from coarsely woven wool. "I'm so thankful it's not raining like yesterday. We'd have had to spend another day below."

"They say it rains more in America," Aideen shared. "We might be surprised by the climate."

A group of children ran past, Emmett McCorkle dragging a rope with a stick attached to the end. The others tried to step on the stick. Sean brought up the rear with a barely discernable limp. The boys drew up short when they nearly ran into a family out for a stroll.

"Hello, Miss Murphy," a dark-haired man said with a bright smile.

Beside him, his wife, dressed in a lavender dress with lace inserts and cuffs, spoke to the three daughters accompanying them. "Greet Miss Murphy, girls."

"Hello, Miss Murphy," they chorused.

The youngest separated from the others and ran to stand before Bridget. She wore a dress made in a royal shade of purple, with contrasting white lace at the neck and wrists and a sash at her waist. "We saw fishes jumping in the water!"

"You did?" Bridget sounded interested. She turned to encompass those around the fireplace. "Mr. and Mrs. Atwater, these are my sisters, Nora and Maeve." She introduced Aideen and Mrs. Kennedy, as well. "Ladies, this is Mr. and Mrs. Atwater, Laurel, Hilary and Pamela."

Pamela was the one looking up at Bridget with a bright smile. The other two hung back and only spoke to appease their mother and at her urging. All three girls wore stiff-brimmed bonnets with satin ties, and their mother wore a broad-brimmed hat festooned with silk flowers and bright artificial cherries.

"Your mother hasn't joined you for your stroll?" Bridget asked Mr. Atwater.

"She's having tea on the foredeck. Enjoy your afternoon, ladies." Mr. Atwater tipped his bowler in a formal gesture and led his family on past.

"His mother is traveling with them," Bridget explained once they were out of earshot. "Her name is Audra, and frankly, she is more friendly than those two. Mr. Atwater's name is Beverly and she's Miriam. They're nice, don't get me wrong. It's just very plain that I'm the hired help."

"The young ladies are all pretty, with their father's dark hair," Aideen said.

"I do admire their hair," Bridget agreed. "Each day when I help them dress it, I long for tresses that stay within their bounds and don't defy pins or ribbons."

"You and your sister do have riotous curls," Aideen agreed. "But both of you have hair that is lovely. Yours is dark and lustrous, and Maeve's is bright and catches the sun."

"Thank you," Bridget told her with a grateful smile.

"Will you accompany us to our stateroom later?" Mrs. Kennedy asked. "We will look through trunks and select material for your dresses."

The sisters agreed.

"Tea sounded good when it was mentioned," Maeve said. "I believe I will put on a pan of water."

A squabble broke out a few cook fires away; three passengers argued over their ration of oatmeal. In these close quarters, it wasn't unusual to overhear the occasional quarrel.

"I'm so glad we have you for neighbors," Mrs. Kennedy said.

On their other side, a gentleman and his nephew kept

to themselves. The Murphys spoke to them occasionally, but they weren't overly friendly. Another passenger had stopped to sit with them, and it was apparent they knew each other.

Mrs. Fitzwilliam and her manservant, Stillman, strolled past, with Stillman holding her parasol over her head. He gave Maeve an almost imperceptible nod, but Mrs. Fitzwilliam kept her gaze straight ahead.

The children ran up behind them and carefully maneuvered around the two adults.

"What's this game you're playing?" Mrs. Fitzwilliam called.

The boys halted and doffed their hats.

"It's tag, but with a stick of wood," Sean explained. "Me brother Emmett is the fastest boy on the ship, so he keeps the stick away from the rest of us. 'Specially me. I ain't as fast as I used to be."

"You're the young man who was injured on the dock, are you not?"

"Yes'm. I'm all better now. The doc and Miss Murphy took real good care o' me."

"Have you proper food and lodging?" the woman asked.

"Real good food," Sean replied. "What's lodging?"

"Your sleeping quarters," Stillman clarified.

"Oh, yes! We got real comfortable bunks. Ain't never had blankets and pillows afore. We like it here."

Mrs. Fitzwilliam's harsh expression softened. "See that you don't mow down adults strolling the deck now."

"No, ma'am." Sean stuck his hat back in place and the children clamored away. Mrs. Fitzwilliam and her manservant walked on past.

Seeing Sean playing with the other children blessed Maeve. She offered a silent prayer of thanks.

The ladies drank their tea, and Nora fed Grace. Bridget read a book while the others worked on Grace's underslip and dress, made from the embroidered front of one of the doctor's shirts.

"Dr. Gallagher's shirts are cut from fine linen and obviously well made," Aideen commented.

"One of the other ladies told me he's from an extremely well-to-do family," Mrs. Kennedy replied. "They own a home in England, as well as an estate in Galway. It's a mystery what he's doing here."

Aideen's attention shifted away, and her fingers grew still on her sewing. Maeve followed her gaze. A man in a wide-brimmed felt hat stood at the rail, a cheroot between his teeth, gazing out over the ocean. From the crow's-feet at the corners of his eyes, it was plain the cowboy squinted into the sun as a habit. Maeve had read of the men who herded cattle and horses across the American West, but she'd never seen one.

This man wore the hems of his trouser pants tucked into tall boots, and leather galluses crisscrossed his back. His mustache and sideburns would be the envy of all the young men in Castleville.

At a commotion farther down the deck, he turned his head to observe his surroundings. Spotting the women seated around their fire, he touched the brim of his hat.

Aideen blushed and fixed her attention on her needlework.

Maeve and Bridget exchanged a look, and the man took his time walking away.

"You're the doctor's assistant, aren't you?" the visitor beside them called to Maeve.

"I am," she replied, twisting her upper body to face their neighbors. "Maeve Murphy." She introduced the others.

"Michael Gibbon," he said. He didn't share their Irish brogue. "I've been visiting family in County Kirk and am on my way home."

"You're not Irish, then?" Maeve asked.

"English by birth," he replied. "But I've been in America for the past nearly twenty years."

Bridget finished the tent over the cradle and settled on a stool to join the conversation. "We've only met a few Americans so far," she told him. "We're headed for Faith Glen. Do you know it?"

"I know it well. My wife and I lived there until her death, and then I moved to Boston."

"I'm sorry for your loss," Maeve and Nora said at the same time.

"Thank you, ladies."

"Please tell us about Faith Glen," Bridget begged.

"It's a lovely little community," Mr. Gibbon replied. "The people are friendly. It's over an hour's ride from Boston, and I never tire of cresting that last hill and gazing down upon the village. There's a town square with spirea and lilac bushes that bloom in the spring. You first notice the white clapboard church facing the square. The General Store and Rosie's Boardinghouse sit on either side of it. If someone had painted the scene, he couldn't have done a better job of creating a welcoming atmosphere."

Maeve released a sigh of longing. "I cannot wait to see it," she breathed.

Nora spoke up. "Since you lived there, perhaps you know a man by the name of Laird O'Malley."

"I knew him, yes," Michael said.

The sisters all sat forward. "Tell us!" Bridget coaxed.

Michael searched each of their faces. "Was he someone important to you?"

Maeve's heart sank.

"Was?" Nora asked.

"I'm afraid he's been dead for several years," the man replied.

Maeve met Bridget's crestfallen expression. "Apparently, he deeded a house to our mother," she told the man. "We have the deed in our possession."

The man's face changed with recognition. "Your mother, you say?" He rubbed his knee as he continued. "There was always talk in the village about a woman Laird had loved and lost. He kept to himself and never got close to anyone that I know of. Lived in that cottage by the ocean and tended his garden. Roses, herbs, all manner of flowers and trellised vines. His garden drew a lot of attention."

He looked at the sisters one by one. "So, your mother was the woman he loved? She must have been a beauty."

"She was beautiful," Bridget agreed.

"Is the cottage still there?" Nora asked.

"Is it occupied?" Maeve asked.

"I couldn't say," Michael answered. "It's been several years since I was in Faith Glen, and I haven't kept in touch. You have the deed, you say?"

Nora nodded. "We've set our hopes on a place to live."

"Well, I hope for your sake it's still there. From what I remember, it was a charming little place."

"So Laird never married?" Bridget asked.

"No, no. He died alone."

Michael's news put a damper on their mood that evening.

"This was the risk we took," Nora told them later. "We had no way of confirming who Laird O'Malley was or if he still lived."

"We won't be able to ask him how he knew Mother," Bridget said.

"But we still have the deed," Maeve insisted. "Whether he's alive or dead, we have a legal document and a letter."

None of them mentioned the cottage might not remain.

"'Which of you by taking thought can add one cubit unto his stature?'" Aideen quoted. "You're here now."

"Aideen is right," Maeve said. "Worrying about it won't gain us anything except wrinkles. Between the sun and worry, we'll turn into old crones if we're not careful."

The other ladies laughed.

"Let's finish here and go select fabric."

Aideen and Mrs. Kennedy took the Murphy sisters to their stateroom and opened trunks filled with the most exquisite bolts of material any of the sisters had ever laid eyes upon.

With Aideen's help, Nora chose a vivid blue linen.

"Nothing fancy," Nora said.

"We're going to play up your tiny waist," Mrs. Kennedy told her. "The current fashion is perfect for you, with a fitted bodice."

"And a high neck," Nora insisted.

"Yes, of course. A high neck is daywear. And I think a paisley shawl with fringe will complement the dress. We can add a matching sash to a hat."

Maeve had difficulty even picturing her eldest sister in something so exquisite. She couldn't wait to see her in a dress worthy of her stately beauty.

"And now you," Aideen said to Bridget.

"With that dark auburn hair and those hazel-green

eyes, she should wear green or gold," Mrs. Kennedy advised.

"I have the perfect thing!" Aideen announced and searched through stacks of rolled fabric. "Here!"

The fabric she chose was a striking green sateen. "We can add gold ruching and she can carry off ruffles and a crinoline," Mrs. Kennedy decided. "Perhaps even ribbon streamers at the elbows."

"It's beautiful." Bridget's eyes sparkled with delight. Maeve hadn't seen her so happy for a long time. She and Nora looked at each other with tears in their eyes.

"I can't believe I'm going to have such a beautiful dress." Bridget touched the material in awe.

"And now *you*," Mrs. Kennedy said to Maeve, pulling her forward. "You're too tiny for ruffles or pleats. We don't want to dress you like a Dresden doll. And your hair requires specific shades that don't clash."

"May I suggest something?" Aideen asked her aunt. She went to yet another trunk and opened it. The roll of fabric she removed took Maeve's breath away.

"It's French silk plaid," Aideen told her. "You're small enough to carry it off, where on a larger person we could only use it for trim or the interior of pleats. It's taffeta."

Maeve touched the orange, yellow, green and blue plaid reverently. "It's so beautiful, I don't know what to say."

"Simply say whether or not you like it."

"I like it very much."

"What would you say to trimming it with braid?" Mrs. Kennedy asked Aideen. The two women were completely caught up in their plans and held a discussion about the placement of the braid.

"And perhaps you could add one of your fancy-work collars," Aideen replied. "We'll need something for her hair that matches. Not a hat, because it would dwarf her, but a small headpiece. Lace and ribbon, I think."

"The maturity of the style will complement your petite stature," Mrs. Kennedy assured Maeve.

Maeve had often been mistaken for a girl, so wearing a dress that showed her off as a mature young woman would be a joy. The idea of fashionable new dresses was still so foreign, she had to get used to it.

She wondered what Flynn would think of her in a pretty dress, but captured that errant thought. He would certainly never look twice at her when he had the lovely and elegant Kathleen interested and available—and many other women besides. Women with money and social standing. Maeve was the hired help.

Why she even thought about him puzzled her. She hadn't come on this journey to snag a rich husband. Even had she wanted to, she didn't stand a chance.

They visited in the stateroom for another hour and eventually bade their friends good-night to go above deck and observe the luminous water in the dark. When the moon was bright, the ship seemed to glide through liquid fire. Maeve could watch it endlessly, but her sisters tired and went to their beds.

She strolled the deck, occasionally greeting one of the other passengers. Two women approached, walking the opposite direction, and in the gaslight below the chart house their forms and faces came into view. Mrs. Fitzwilliam and Kathleen's conversation halted when they spotted her.

"Good evening, ladies," Maeve said.

Kathleen leaned toward the other woman but didn't bother to lower her voice. "I can't normally say this, but the darkness improves that dress."

Mrs. Fitzwilliam said nothing, and they walked past as though Maeve hadn't spoken.

The women's rudeness and Kathleen's insult stung. Maeve swallowed the hurt, dismissed their insults and continued on. Finally, she stopped at the rail near their cooking area to enjoy the play of light on the water. Her thoughts traveled to Aideen's reaction to the cowboy and Michael Gibbon's description of their new home.

"Good evening, Maeve."

At the sultry deep voice she turned to discover her employer. The moon glimmered on his black hair.

"Good evening, Flynn."

Chapter Eleven

"Did you enjoy your Sabbath day?" Flynn asked.

"Indeed. Did you see many patients?"

"Only two who complained of fevers and stomach pain."

"What did you do for them?"

"I checked the water in their cabins and found it rancid, so I had fresh brought to them. I'm thankful the water supply is sufficient for the trip. And we'll be making a stop for fresh very soon. Some don't realize the harm contamination causes."

Maeve studied the moon. "We met a man from Faith Glen."

"Did you now. Did he tell you about your new home?"

"He told us Laird O'Malley has been dead for quite some time. He had no current information about the house, though when last he saw it, he said it was charming."

"Now you're concerned it might not be there or that your deed isn't binding."

She nodded.

"My offer stands, Maeve. I won't have you or your sisters left without a proper home. I'll see that you're taken care of."

"Taking advantage of your charitable nature would be my last choice, but I do thank you and will remember in case we have no other option."

They stood in companionable silence for several minutes.

"How did you keep from laughing when that woman sprang from her seat in fear of the cat this morning?" he asked. "You went to her aid as though her indignant tirade was the most natural thing in the world."

She shrugged, but a grin inched up one side of her lips. "I don't know. I'm always the first to jump into a situation without thinking. It's a character flaw."

"I disagree. I think it's a charming quality and one I admire very much. Some of us sit on our hands deliberating until it's too late."

"You don't. You handle emergencies quite efficiently."

"Medical emergencies, yes. Others require more thought."

"There wasn't much to think about," she said. "It was just a cat."

"But no one else got up, in case it was indeed a rat."

"I saw the furry creature and knew it wasn't."

"You're far too modest."

"I'm just a simple girl, Flynn. I don't worry about ruining fancy clothes or getting my hands dirty. I just do whatever is needed at the time."

"Some people don't need fancy clothing to improve their beauty."

Flynn didn't know why he'd said that. He wasn't the sort to heap compliments upon young women or to use insincere flattery. But nothing he ever said to Maeve was insincere. She might wear plain clothing and have a few calluses on her hands, but she was far from a simple girl. She was an intriguing young woman whose beliefs and feelings ran deep.

He didn't know anyone he'd rather have working at his side…or anyone with whom he'd rather stand at the rail and watch the moon play upon the water.

"What I meant to say was you're not a simple girl, Maeve. Besides being kind and beautiful, you're bright and intelligent and quick-witted."

She didn't react for a moment, and he wondered if she would, but finally she raised her face to the heavens. "No one other than my mother and da ever told me I was beautiful."

"Your sisters take your appearance in stride, because they're both lovely, as well, and the rest of the world is jealous or threatened. If no young man has ever complimented you, then there's something wrong with the male population of Castleville."

She turned and looked up at him. Her wide eyes reflected the fiery dance of light on the ocean. He shouldn't have such tender feelings toward her, and he shouldn't let words like that trip from his tongue, but he did…and he had. His words were all perfectly true.

He did feel something for Maeve, however, and it was becoming more and more difficult to ignore that.

He leaned forward and pressed a kiss upon her soft lips, thinking only of her sweet countenance and how good her presence made him feel. His impulsiveness was completely out of character, but kissing her seemed like the right thing to do.

She didn't draw away, which pleased him and lent him a measure of confidence. He'd thought about kissing her for days now. It was a quandary why the idea toyed with him and wouldn't leave him alone. He had no intention of letting himself have feelings for anyone. But he was drawn to test his imagination and confirm that reality never measured up.

Perhaps he just needed to do this and then he would be able to forget about it.

She gently rested her fingertips against the front of his shirt, catching him woefully off guard. Perhaps she'd simply needed to check her balance, so he gently grasped her upper arm and held her steady.

Now he doubted his foolish thinking: he wouldn't be able to forget about this. The memory of her kiss and her scent would be with him forever.

A breeze caught a strand of her hair and blew it across his cheek. The soft tress tickled his ear. He eased away, straightening, and stood upright, still holding her arm.

She reached for the rail, but didn't take her attention from his face. Raising her other hand, she placed her fingertips against her lips. "No one's ever done that before."

"Kissed you?"

She nodded.

He'd given Maeve her first kiss. Something inside his chest thrummed with tension. Was that his heart? Had he made a foolish mistake? Reaching for her hand, he took it in his grasp and caressed the back with his thumb. He didn't want this to adversely affect their working relationship. She stirred emotions he couldn't risk feeling. She was refreshingly open and honest. Without guile. And perhaps she was too naïve for her own good, he admitted to himself. But he didn't want to lose whatever this new feeling was that warmed his heart and added a buoyancy to his spirit that he hadn't known for a long, long time.

"I apologize if it was unseemly—or if you found it unpleasant," he said.

He suspected she blushed, but the darkness hid it if she did. She didn't pull her hand from his, instead she turned her face to the ocean. "It was not unpleasant."

The ocean air smelled better than he remembered, the breeze cool on his skin. His pulse had an unnatural rhythm that he now noticed. The warmth of her hand seeped into his being and gave him a hope he hadn't expected to know. He hadn't felt this way for a long time… maybe not ever….

Other feelings crowded these out, however. Guilt. Fear. Most especially fear. He had no business letting himself form any sort of attachment. It was wrong to start something he had no intention of following through with.

It wasn't fair to Maeve.

He released her hand and faced the rail, looking out across the display of light on the water for several silent minutes. Finally, he turned to her. "I apologize. That was inappropriate. I'm your employer, and it's wrong to place you in an uncomfortable position."

"It's all right, Flynn."

He'd told her to address him as such when there were no patients present. Why did his name on her lips suddenly sound too intimate? "No. No, it's not. Forgive me. I think I should see you safely to your cabin."

She raised her chin in a stubborn refusal. "I'm quite capable of seeing myself to my cabin when I'm ready."

"Very well. Good night, then." He headed for the ladder that led below deck.

Thoroughly confused, Maeve watched him go. After sharing such a tender moment, his abrupt change caught her off guard, even more so than the kiss.

The kiss.

She skimmed her fingertips across her lips in amazement. Nothing had prepared her for such sweet depth of emotion as she'd experienced when he'd kissed her. No wonder couples fell in love and courted and married. No wonder God had ordained a man and a woman to leave their parents and cleave only unto each other.

No wonder he'd come to his senses and hurried away.

The beautiful Kathleen was surely a more appropriate recipient for his romantic intentions.

She didn't regret having been kissed. She wouldn't. The experience was something of value she could tuck away. A couple of verses came to mind, and she said them aloud. "'Lay not up for yourselves treasures upon earth, where moth and rust doth corrupt, and where thieves break through and steal, but lay up for yourselves treasures in heaven, where neither moth nor rust doth corrupt, and where thieves do not break through nor steal.'"

She didn't own anything of value, and that was okay, because the Bible taught that material things were only temporary. Heavenly things were eternal, the things with value. Love, joy, peace—those were the real treasures.

The memory of Flynn's kiss would bring her joy, so she tucked it away. No one could take it from her.

The scent of fragrant tobacco reached her, and she glanced aside. Several feet away stood the cowboy, again at the rail with his cheroot. She'd heard about the wide-open spaces of America, the vast plains and unexplored wilderness. She supposed being cooped up on a ship was more difficult for some individuals than for others.

His presence brought her out of her reverie. She turned and quickly headed below deck.

Most of the women were already in their bunks. Maeve was thankful for the blessedly cool evening. The cabin often grew stuffy with so many people living and sleeping in it. Thankfully, everyone had agreed that all surfaces should be scrubbed twice a week, and their bedding laundered weekly.

Bridget had been holding Grace, but the baby fussed, so she quickly handed her to Nora, who loosened the infant's clothing and tried to make her more comfortable. A crying baby would not ingratiate them with their cabin mates. So far the others had been kind and understanding, but the sisters couldn't afford to push their tolerance.

Bridget left Nora on her lower bunk and climbed above to her own.

"'Rest tired eyes a while. Sweet is thy baby's smile. Angels are guarding and they watch o'er thee.'"

Nora's sweet voice as she sang the familiar lullaby with its lilting melody and trills on the syllables gave Maeve gooseflesh along her arms. Listening, she changed into her nightclothes.

"'Sleep, sleep, *grah mo chee,* here on your mama's knee. Angels are guarding, and they watch o'er thee.'"

The cabin grew still and silent; not even a rustle of bedclothes stirred as Nora continued her song. Maeve climbed up and stretched out upon her narrow bed. She had to consciously relax her muscles.

Maeve's mother had sung the tune to the three of them in their childhood years, and she suspected the tune was as sentimentally touching to the other women.

"'The birdeens sing a fluting song. They sing to thee the whole day long. Wee fairies dance o'er hill and dale for the very love of thee.'"

Maeve's throat tightened with bittersweet homesickness and the poignant reminder that they'd left behind everything familiar to risk this journey to a new land. Tears welled in her eyes.

"'Dream, Dream, *grah mo chee,* here on your mama's

knee. Angels are guarding and they watch o'er thee, as you sleep may angels watch over and may they guard o'er thee.'"

After Nora sang another verse, she fell silent. The baby obviously slept now, for she was silent. The only sounds in the cabin were a few soft sniffles and a stifled sob. Maeve recognized Bridget's tiny hiccupping cry. She climbed out of her bunk and up to join Bridget on the narrow mattress. She'd shared a bed with her sisters their entire lives, and lying with Bridget now lent them both comfort. Maeve smoothed Bridget's hair down, so it wasn't in her face, and Bridget snuggled back against her.

Maeve tucked her arm around her sister and closed her eyes.

She could use a few of those angels watching over her, as well. And maybe a few more to help her guard her heart.

Chapter Twelve

The next day, the doctor acted as though nothing had happened the night before. In a way, Maeve was relieved. Things wouldn't be awkward between them if the incident was forgotten.

Odd how she thought of it as "the incident" now. As though she'd spilled tea on her skirt or had some other trivial mishap. But it was best left that way, so she focused on her work.

A sailor arrived around noon, a gash in the flesh of his palm, received while cutting open a fish. Flynn thoroughly cleaned it, much to the dismay of the cringing sailor, neatly placed six stitches in it and sent the man on his way.

"You should come above deck and watch the dolphins play," the bandaged sailor told Maeve on his way out the door. "Don't know when ye will see a sight like this again."

Flynn washed his hands. "Let's go. I'll carry up water and boil it, so we'll have a fresh supply."

Passengers stood gathered at the rail. Unable to see over their heads, Maeve found an opening to weave her way forward. Dolphins rolled in the water, and porpoises danced around the prow. The flying fish's aerial darts drew attention, as well.

Off to the west an island could be spotted, and a nearby Englishman mentioned they'd be stopping for water and to leave off a stowaway who'd been discovered.

Maeve heard sailors above and gazed up, finding Gavin on a mast. Her heart raced. Apparently, he looked down at the same time. "Top o' the mornin' to ye, Miss Murphy!" he called, and even from this distance, his broad smile was evident.

The other sailor in his company asked something of Gavin, and it appeared Gavin explained who she was. The sailor tipped his hat.

Maeve blushed and gave a friendly wave.

She took a stroll around the deck and spotted the captain's wife reeling in a net. She greeted the leathery-skinned woman.

"Good day to you." Martha Conley spilled the contents of the net into a wooden tub, picked out a baby shark and threw it overboard.

"Gavin McCorkle mentioned you provided him and the other sailors with fish."

"Cure mackerel several days a week, I do," she replied. "Help yourself to as many fresh as you'd like for your meals today."

"I couldn't take your food," Maeve said with a shake of her head.

"Nonsense. The ocean is filled with fish. Catching them gives an old woman something to do."

"That's very generous of you. Thank you."

Martha grabbed a scrap of canvas lying on the deck and rolled half a dozen mackerel into it. "Used to treat ills aboard ship, I did. Before we had a ship's doctor every voyage."

"You did? What medical experience do you have?"

"None to mention, save what I did here. Lost too many to sickness and fevers, we did. Those aren't days I'd want to live over again."

"I completely understand. I used to treat the people of my village, and all I had were herbs I collected and what little knowledge I'd learned from my mother and the midwives."

"Fine thing it was, Dr. Flynn workin' so hard to get the laws changed so there's a doctor aboard every ship now. He's a good man."

"He got laws changed?"

"Not single-handedly, but he used his influence and his money to get a better passenger act passed. This one requires enough sleeping space for each person, plenty of clean water and clean cabins and galleys. People don't die all the time as they used to. Not on our ship so much, but others, where the owners only cared about profit, not people."

Maeve could plainly see the doctor's involvement. Flynn was a man with deep moral principles and a commitment to healing.

"That man deserves a good turn," she added. "After losin' his wife and sweet baby, the way he did."

Maeve's heart skittered. *Wife? Baby?* She must have looked puzzled.

"Cholera, I think it was. Dreadful sickness. Heard tell that after they died, he quit practicin' and devoted himself to research. It was too late for his family, but I suppose in his mind, findin' ways to save others relieved the pain."

Maeve knew exactly what it was like to be unable to

save the people she loved. For a man who had devoted his entire life to healing, she could only imagine his helplessness and self-blame.

"Thanks again for the fish, Mrs. Conley."

"Any time, dear. Say, will you and your sisters join us for supper tomorrow evenin'? The cap'n and I like to have guests join us."

"I would love to, and I will ask my sisters."

Maeve made her way to the galley where she passed along Mrs. Conley's invitation and asked Nora to store their fish until suppertime.

That night Bridget dined with the Atwater daughters, so Nora and Maeve fried the fish in a hot skillet and asked Aideen and Mrs. Kennedy to join them.

Nora had been given a small bag of potatoes, and they baked them at the edge of the fire.

"The sea air makes a person hungry, I've discovered," Aideen said. "I surely don't want to let out all my seams before we reach port, but it might be necessary."

The ladies laughed and enjoyed their meal.

Sean and Emmett McCorkle skidded to a stop in front of them.

"Hello," Maeve greeted them. "Have you eaten supper?"

"Yes'm," Sean replied. "We eat in the galley. Sometimes I see your sister there."

"This is Nora."

Sean glanced at the pile of bones on a tin plate. "I can throw those away for ye."

"Why, thank you, Sean." She handed him the plate.

Emmett ran right along beside him and returned like a shadow.

"Tell us what keeps you busy during these days aboard ship," Nora said to Emmett.

He lowered his gaze to the deck and attempted to slip behind Sean.

His older brother sidled away and pulled him forward. "He's been gettin' lessons with one of the families. Numbers and letters and the like."

"Why, that's wonderful," Nora told him.

"Sometimes I sit in, too, iffin' I ain't got no errands to do for the cap'n."

"Good for you. You need to know those things."

"Cap'n Conley says we'll be pullin' into a port tomorrow. Me an' me brothers are gonna go see a jungle!"

"A jungle, you say?"

"Don't worry. The cap'n is sendin' someone to look out for us."

"It's very good to know you won't be eaten by a wild animal."

Emmett's eyes widened.

"It ain't that kinda jungle," Sean said. "Just birds and monkeys an' the like. I hope they got coconuts. The doc told me coconuts was good to eat."

"I hope they do, too."

"Do you have any more jobs for us? We gotta get goin'."

"Can't think of anything right now."

"Okay. Well, 'bye."

The boys shot off, narrowly missing a collision with a couple out for a stroll.

Maeve exchanged a look with Nora, and they both grinned. Maeve prayed aloud that the McCorkles would find a good home once the ship landed. The other ladies agreed with resounding *amens*.

The following morning the *Annie McGee* sailed into a small harbor on a lush island. If they wanted to go on land, the passengers were instructed to venture ashore with a knowledgeable companion and were strongly advised to stay within sight of the ship at all times. They were warned that the ship would only be anchored for three hours, while casks of water were filled and loaded.

"Let's ask the doctor to be our companion," Bridget suggested while they prepared for the day, with the other women bustling around them in the crowded cabin.

Bridget took a faded pink bonnet from the large bandbox they'd carried aboard, the one that held all of their hats. "No one wears these coal scuttles any more," she said, brushing lint from the stiffened claret silk. At one time, it had been lovely headwear for a banker's wife. The woman had given it and a few others to their mother as payment for cleaning her house.

"It's a fine bonnet," Nora assured her. "Look how nicely that organza is pleated on the inside of the brim. It's a perfect frame for your pretty face."

"It was nice once," Bridget said. She traded it for a sized and wired straw bonnet with the same shape. "This one will be cooler. The crown is lined with cotton."

Nora took a similar one from the box and Maeve fished until she found the bonnet she preferred. She had replaced the frayed trim with green ribbon only last year. "No one will care which hats we wear."

She and Nora concurred that they should ask Flynn to accompany them, and Bridget went to find him.

He joined them wearing another of his white embroidered shirts and a handsome straw hat. He remarked about the wisdom they'd used in choosing hats to protect their heads and faces from the sun.

There was no dock, so those wishing to disembark waited in line for small rowboats to take them to the island.

What they found was a tiny fishing village, its brown-skinned inhabitants friendly and in the business of trade. Carts and wagons lined the dirt path from the shore to the rustic little community.

Each of the sisters had brought along a few coins from their wages. They purchased nuts, fruit and dates. Bridget bought a necklace made of carved ivory beads and wore it with her plain homespun skirt and blouse.

There were also prepared foods, native to the people of the island, but Flynn advised them not to eat the unfamiliar dishes, because the questionably prepared foods wouldn't sit well on their stomachs.

Flynn took time to delve into the undergrowth and pull from the earth a pouch full of roots he claimed had excellent medicinal qualities.

While her sisters looked at carvings, Maeve waited for Flynn at the edge of the junglelike area. He returned and showed her the tubers. She took one, brushed off black dirt, and sniffed it. She wrinkled her nose. "It has an unpleasant scent."

"I know." He grinned.

It was the first time she'd seen him smile, the first time they'd shared a private moment, since…the incident. Attractive dimples appeared on either side of his smile.

She recalled Mrs. Conley's account of the deaths of his wife and child. The information explained a lot. She should let the revelation go; his personal life was none of her business. But curiosity and compassion overcame wisdom.

"Martha Conley told me about your losses."

Her words took Flynn by surprise. He looked down into her eyes and read sympathy…compassion he couldn't handle. He knew exactly what she was referring to, and he didn't want to talk about it. "We should go wait for a boat to take us back."

"I know what it's like to lose people you've tried so desperately to save."

"Let's go find your sisters." He moved to walk away.

"Flynn."

She stopped him with a gentle hand on his shirtsleeve. He could have easily moved on, but her touch held him. Her fingers were warm.

"I hadn't realized you'd been married."

He stood in place, but looked away, over her shoulder. Her eyes were too much right now.

"What was her name?"

His mouth was dry. "Johanna."

"And your child—a son or a daughter?"

"A son." The word pained him. His child's name was difficult to form on his tongue. His stomach dropped. "Jonathon."

He hadn't said it in years. Speaking his little boy's name made his blood pound in his ears.

"How old was he?"

She was relentless. "Barely three."

"I'm so sorry," she said softly, with as much emotion as one who truly understood would display. "You want to run from everyone who speaks of it."

He nodded.

"When someone tells you your wife and son are in a better place, you rage inside and think, 'No, *this* is where they belong. With me. They were robbed of their lives. *I* was robbed. This isn't better. It's not what God intended. It's *wrong.*'"

It was like she'd been in his head and heard all his unspoken sufferings. Slowly he let himself look at her. For such a tiny person, she packed a big wallop. His belly felt as though he'd been kicked by a horse.

"When someone tells you Johanna and Jonathon are at peace, you want to scream at them, because though it's true, it happened too soon. Eternal peace should come at the end of a lifetime, not when it did. Not too early."

The knot forming in Flynn's throat wouldn't go up or down. He swallowed in a futile effort. Anger surfaced, and it was directed at her for voicing those private thoughts—for knowing them, for speaking the names of his wife and son. Who did she think she was, this snip of a girl, to invade his private grief and insinuate her frighteningly accurate assessment of his feelings into his conscious mind?

"Just let it go," he said, his tone more forceful and his voice thicker with emotion than he'd intended.

She acquiesced with a single nod. "All right."

That was it? She'd flayed him open like one of Mrs. Conley's flopping mackerel and then decided evisceration was sufficient? If she knew that much about him, did she know he lived with the guilt of being unable to save them? Did she know what that felt like?

He couldn't ask.

She removed her fingers from his arm. "Just know you have a friend who understands. And cares."

He didn't want understanding, and he definitely didn't want caring. He was doing just fine being left alone. He didn't need anyone to dredge up feelings too painful to endure.

She moved ahead of him, back toward the island village. He forced his feet to move, but he walked as stiffly as a tin soldier.

Chapter Thirteen

They didn't speak much as they tended to patients that afternoon. Brief questions were met with brief answers. And it seemed as though there truly was no escaping the woman, because she was at the captain's overcrowded dinner table that evening.

The captain and his wife sat on either end, with Flynn between Kathleen and her mother, and all three Murphy sisters on the opposite side of the scarred plank table.

Captain Conley and Martha were down-to-earth, simple people. She enjoyed company and cooking for a variety of passengers. They didn't distinguish between social classes or they would never have asked Kathleen and Estelle to sit at the same table with the Murphys.

Flynn had never known a meal in this cabin to go severely wrong, so he hoped that would be the case this evening.

However, he could tell already that Kathleen wasn't happy with the guest list. She aligned her fork and spoon on the tabletop and gave Nora the once-over. "Where is that child you're always carrying?"

"Our friends are watching her this evening. Grace is an exceptionally good baby." She turned to Flynn. "A generous passenger stopped me in passing today. 'I have a spare glass nursing bottle with a gum nipple,' she said. 'Would you be in want of it?' As you can imagine, I was delighted. 'I surely would,' said I. Grace has enjoyed two bottles of goat's milk since then."

"Well, that is thrilling news," Kathleen said.

"It's going to make my life so much easier," Nora continued with a smile, obviously not picking up on the sarcasm.

"Did you ladies go ashore?" Martha asked, including all the females in her query.

"We did." Bridget touched her necklace. "I bought this. Someone carved all these beads from ivory."

Mrs. Conley had probably seen a hundred ivory necklaces, but God bless her, she admired Bridget's. Flynn had always liked that down-to-earth woman. She got up and dished steaming stew from a black kettle into individual bowls.

"What have you made us this night?" the captain asked.

"Ballymaloe," his wife replied. A traditional Irish stew. "I bought lamb on the island." The fare smelled delicious.

She set a bowl in front of her husband and then before each guest. The captain didn't wait until everyone was served, just picked up his spoon and dug in.

Martha set a crusty loaf of bread directly on the table and tore off a hunk for herself before sitting.

The *ballymaloe* was filled with tender bits of lamb, onions, barley, parsnips and carrots and smelled exceptionally good.

The Murphy sisters picked up their spoons and tasted the stew appreciatively. "This is delicious, Mrs. Conley,"

Nora told their hostess. "What a treat to have vegetables, too."

"I bring enough to last the voyage, if used sparingly."

Kathleen and Estelle watched the others for a moment before dipping their spoons into the mixture. Kathleen tasted it. Her reaction amused Flynn. Accustomed to extravagant slices of braised meats and fancily prepared side dishes, this food was not the Boyds' usual fare. But there could be no objections to Martha's cooking, as they should have learned the last time.

In the past, Kathleen had been a good companion. They shared a history. Now, he questioned their friendship. He often enjoyed the opportunity to speak of familiar people and places in her company, but when others were around she showed a different side—this unbecoming superior side.

"Very tasty," Estelle said.

"Did you make any purchases?" Martha asked the others.

"I bought fruit," Maeve answered.

"I got Grace a gourd rattle," Nora said.

"We stayed onboard and sent a sailor to purchase shellfish." Kathleen took a sip of water. "There's nothing else of value to be found. Only cheap trinkets made by the natives."

The conversation fell away for a moment.

Bridget's spoon paused over her bowl, but she didn't look up.

"I gathered roots," Flynn mentioned. "A particular sort that are easy to find in the rich, dark soil on the islands and rarely found elsewhere."

Maeve placed her hands in her lap to address him. "I was wondering. Has anyone ever tried to take a few of those tubers and plant them in America? Transplant them."

Deep in thought, Flynn set down his fork. "I don't know. One of the researchers I studied under in England has a greenhouse where he grows hard-to-find species of herbs. Growing these roots may have been done, but if it has, I don't know of it."

Kathleen's sharp gaze moved from his face to Maeve's, where her eyes narrowed.

"Set aside two," Maeve told him. "And I'll try planting them in the garden we're expecting to have when we get to Faith Glen."

"Splendid idea." He reached for bread and tore off a piece.

Maeve resumed eating her meal.

"My dear," Kathleen said to her. "I'm so impressed with your frugality. The cut of your dress shows that it must be a least a decade old, yet you've so cleverly remade it into a serviceable piece. And in such a practical color, too. Who could possibly spot a dusty hem on a skirt of such an earthy brown? Definitely the mark of a sensible nature."

Flynn glanced from Kathleen to Maeve, inwardly cringing.

"Besides, with that hair of yours, you've color aplenty in your appearance. You've no need for more eye-catching attire."

Bridget was the one who appeared incensed at Kathleen's backhanded compliments. Adding Maeve's naïve nature to the fact that she gave people the benefit of the doubt, Flynn suspected she didn't even realize she'd been insulted. He'd been angry with her all afternoon, but that emotion quickly faded as protective anger on her behalf changed his attitude.

Maeve almost lifted a self-conscious hand to her hair, but instead kept it restrained in her lap.

"There's a lot to be said for a sensible nature," the captain's wife said. "Some people set a lot more store by their hair or the cut of their dress than they do kind-heartedness. Never read in the Bible that fancy clothing is a fruit of the Spirit, now, have you, cap'n?"

Captain Conley plainly intended to keep out of the conversation. He mumbled something unintelligible and stuffed a piece of bread in his mouth.

"I didn't wear my best dress, either," Kathleen said, though she was dressed in an elegant gown of deep blue. "Why risk ruining nice things on this voyage? Tears and stains are inevitable."

Flynn wondered how Martha had planned this particular group of dinner guests and supposed she had invited the Murphy sisters after he and Kathleen had been invited. She may have forgotten who she'd already asked, but he suspected she rather enjoyed combining incongruent personalities and watching the outcomes.

"And you, dear," Kathleen said to Bridget. "I've noticed you on deck, and tonight you've done something different with your hair."

Bridget's face brightened. "Yes. One of our new friends helped me."

"Well, I admire your courage for trying."

Bridget's cheeks turned pink. Maeve turned and looked at Kathleen, as though a light had dawned and she'd recognized the intentional barbs delivered with each of the "compliments." She cast a frown on the dark-haired woman across the table.

"Faith Glen, you mentioned," Estelle Boyd asked, changing the subject. "Do you have family there?"

"No," Nora replied and didn't go further.

"We've inherited a cottage," Bridget supplied. "A lovely place near the ocean, with a garden."

According to Maeve, the sisters weren't sure about that, but Bridget wisely made a point of letting Kathleen believe they had a home once they arrived. He could only imagine her remarks if she knew the Murphys were uncertain of their future.

"Well, isn't that nice?" Estelle said.

Everyone finished their meal and Nora jumped up to help Martha remove the bowls and forks.

Maeve refilled the water glasses.

Accustomed to servants, Kathleen and Estelle remained seated.

Flynn recognized the heavy bowl of baked custard that Martha set on the table. Nora placed small dishes at each setting.

Maeve remained standing long enough to scoop out a serving for each person. Kathleen held up her palm to stop her from placing a bowl in front of her. "None for me, thank you."

Maeve set down the dish in the middle of the table and took her seat on the bench once again, near Martha at the end.

"You and your sisters are hardworking, mannerly young women," Martha told her. "Any young man who takes one of you for his wife will be fortunate."

The sisters looked only at their dessert dishes, and Maeve deliberately refused to lift her gaze. She dug into her custard.

Kathleen looked pointedly at the other women. "I wish I was as brave as the three of you. I go without desserts to fit into my dresses, and it's clear you don't give your figures a second thought."

Each of the Murphy sisters paused in enjoying their custard.

"Why, the bench doesn't even know a one of them is there," Martha said with a snort. "They're light as duck down. If anything, they could use some meat on their bones. Now your mother there, she likes a good custard, she does."

Having just finished her last bite, Estelle had been eyeing Kathleen's bowl. She dabbed her mouth with her handkerchief—the captain's wife didn't set the table with napkins—and gave Kathleen an apologetic glance.

"Thank you for another delicious meal, Mrs. Conley," Flynn told their hostess. "I've never eaten from your table when I didn't thoroughly enjoy the fare."

"Cookin' keeps me busy," she said.

"You told me fishing keeps you busy," Maeve said to her.

"Aye, fishin' and cookin'."

"I've offered her a house anywhere she pleases, but she's got the ocean in her blood as much as I." The captain fumbled on a nearby table and found his meerschaum, which he packed with tobacco and lit.

The fragrant scent curled around them.

"And I've told 'im a thousand times I'll live in a house when he does. We could raise a few sheep, keep a cow and have a little garden, mind you. But the old goat won't hear of it. I may as well be whistling jigs to a milestone."

It was obviously a conversation the couple revisited often.

"And you, Mrs. Boyd," Martha said to Estelle. "Where is it you have a mind to settle?"

"In Boston," the woman replied. "Our barrister has rented something for us, temporarily. Only until we're sure what the future holds for us, of course." She gave

Flynn a pointed look. "Why don't the two of you have a walk on deck? It should be a lovely evening."

Times like this he got the distinct impression Kathleen's mother would have liked to see the two of them become more than friends. He'd come out and told her on more than one occasion that their relationship wasn't like that, but she didn't seem convinced. She probably made Kathleen crazy, too.

Maeve's blue-eyed glance followed him as he stood and pulled back Kathleen's chair. Her perusal disturbed him, as did most things about her, and he wasn't sure why. He gave her a hesitant smile, but she looked away.

He thanked their hostess once again and ushered Kathleen from the cabin.

Maeve and Bridget took a walk around the deck later, and she was thankful they didn't run into Flynn or Kathleen. They did discover an interesting sight when they reached Mrs. Fitzwilliam's fire, however. The woman and her hired man were not alone. Two children sat with them, apparently enjoying some sort of dessert from blue-and-white china bowls.

As the sisters drew closer, Maeve made out Sean and Emmett McCorkle keeping the woman company. Sean was chattering on about a school of porpoises he'd seen that day.

Mrs. Fitzwilliam didn't look their way or notice the Murphy sisters, so they walked on past.

"Mama used to talk about looking for the good in people," Maeve said. "Apparently, Mrs. Fitzwilliam has a side we haven't seen."

"Well, I don't believe Kathleen Boyd has a single redeeming quality, no matter what Mama said," her sister replied.

Maeve lay awake on her bunk that night, her mind in turmoil. Bridget had simmered over Kathleen's thinly veiled insults for the better part of an hour, but Maeve had simply tamped down her hurt. It was disturbing that another human being could be so unkind…and frightening that Flynn, a decent, honorable man didn't seem to recognize her glaring flaws.

Maeve wasn't worldly or experienced, but she recognized a wolf in sheep's clothing when she saw one. She liked to give people the benefit of the doubt but, as Bridget had predicted, she couldn't come up with any redeeming qualities to tag on the woman.

It had been apparent that Mrs. Boyd was pushing for Flynn to marry her daughter. At one time Maeve had believed the match was a wise one—they were from the same social class, moved in the same circles. But now… now she tried to picture the doctor cleaving to a woman so proud and haughty, and the imaginings made her feel sick.

She thought of what Flynn had been through, losing his family. He deserved someone kind.

"Lord," she prayed. "Give Flynn wisdom to make decisions. Send Your Spirit, the Comforter to heal his grieving heart. Your Word says You heal the brokenhearted and bind up their wounds, so Lord, I ask You to bind up Flynn's wounds of grief and guilt. Lord Jesus, be a healing balm to his heart and his mind. Show him You're holding him close and loving him. Take away the pain that's eating at him like a sickness. In the mighty name of Jesus, amen."

She rolled to her side and another thought came to her. She couldn't cast it aside. "And, Lord, I forgive Kathleen for being rude and haughty. She must be an awfully unhappy person to treat others so unkindly. Help Bridget be merciful. Help me be generous and kindhearted, Lord. Show Kathleen the truth of Your way, which is to love others. And if she's the wife You have planned for Flynn, please, please, *please* change her heart."

The cabin was stuffy that night. She threw off her sheet and tried to get comfortable.

"Are you all right, Maeve?" came the soft voice from the bed at the head of hers.

"Yes," she whispered. "Are you?"

"Yes," Bridget replied. "You're beautiful, you know. Inside and out, just like mother used to tell us."

"As are you," Maeve returned.

"Ssshh," came Nora's censure from below.

Maeve smiled and closed her eyes.

Chapter Fourteen

The following day they treated several patients for stomach complaints. "As many times as I tell people not to buy food from the islanders, they eat it anyway."

Flynn mixed peppermint oil with water and dosed it out most of the morning.

During a lull in the stream of patients, he said to Maeve, "I'd like to apologize for Kathleen's comments last night."

"It's not your place," she said.

"All the same, you and your sisters are gracious. Kathleen's barbs are uncalled for."

"She does have a tongue that would clip a hedge," Maeve replied. She should keep her questions and thoughts to herself. "Are you planning to marry again?" He seemed surprised by her straightforward question. Would she never learn? After a moment he replied, "Why is everyone focused on getting me married?"

"Don't you want to marry?"

It was obvious that he struggled to reply. "It's the natural way of things, to marry, to make a home and a family," he said finally.

She paused in rolling a strip of bandage torn from a

worn sheet. "You didn't really answer my question. You merely stated a fact, like the sky is blue or cows give milk."

"Are you always this direct?"

"I guess so. My life hasn't been given over to small talk, and skirting around issues doesn't solve anything."

"And you're convinced I have problems to solve."

"You're avoiding your feelings. I'm praying for you," she answered. "I know God has a plan for you. The Bible says it's a plan for good and not for evil. He wants you to experience the fullness of life He offers. He's given us so much.

"It's hard to understand why things happen, why we lose our loved ones. There are a lot of things I can't explain. But I do know God wants only the best for us. He loves us."

He opened a palm in question. "How is it so easy for you to trust Him after all you've lived through?"

"Because He's the One who saw me through those things and brought me out on the other side. He's still bringing me through, with this move to a new land."

At that moment Gavin McCorkle showed up bleeding from a cut above his eye. He'd been hit by a padlock a fisherman had used as a weight on his fishing net.

"You can't barely see three feet before you," he told Maeve as Flynn cleaned the gash. "The fog is downright eerie, 'tis. But the fish are crowding each other out to get into our nets."

She hadn't been on deck yet. "Is Mrs. Conley up there with her net?"

"Aye. Has the biggest haul of all, she does. The cap'n's even helpin' her haul 'em in. We're near another island, but Cap'n Conley doesn't want to risk the reefs with such poor visibility."

"We took on plenty of fresh water already," Flynn agreed.

Flynn put in one suture to hold the cut closed.

A tremendous peal of thunder startled the three of them, and Maeve dropped the scissors she'd been holding. Her heart beat at an excessive rate.

Gavin jumped down from the table. "Orders are to double-reef the topsail if a storm comes upon us!"

He shot out the door.

Another roll of thunder encompassed them.

"I'm going topside to have a look," Flynn said.

Maeve set the supplies aside and followed him.

The fog Gavin had spoken of had lifted, but the sky had grown black as night. The day was as eerie as Gavin had declared. A violent gale arose as they stood near the ladder. Maeve held down her skirt hem, which threatened to fly upward.

Those who'd been at their cook fires extinguished them, gathered all their belongings and headed below deck for shelter. Sailors busied themselves securing sails and lines. Forked lightning zigzagged down from the heavens.

An angry storm at sea was a terrifying and majestic thing to see. Maeve would remember this sight all her days.

Rain descended in torrents, and they turned and climbed down the ladder as fast as they could. Flynn paused to maneuver a heavy door, one Maeve had never noticed before, over the opening.

"Be careful as you make your way to your berth," he told her. "Tell the others to tie themselves to their bunks for safety's sake. And stay calm."

One end of the ship rose as though on an angry billow, and Flynn caught her before she struck the wall. The next moment, the same end of the vessel plunged downward. "Here. I'll see you to your cabin."

He took her securely by the upper arm and led her through the passageways until they reached her destination.

Cries of the terrified women greeted her upon entering. Untethered bandboxes and clothing lay strewn about the floor. Nora and Bridget had been waiting for her. Nora comforted the fussing baby. Bridget flung herself at Maeve. Her body trembled so forcefully, her teeth chattered.

"Dr. Gallagher said we must lash ourselves to our beds!" she said loud enough for the others to hear. "Do so quickly now and stay calm."

The females used sheets and blankets to tie themselves by their waists to the frames of their beds.

Successive peals of thunder drew shrieks, and the constant plunging of the ship had more than one woman losing the contents of her stomach.

Maeve's belly felt queasy, but she had a strong constitution and prayed her way through the fear.

The cabin grew stuffy, and the smell of vomit reeked throughout. Grace let out a tremulous wail and cried pitifully.

"Sing, why don't you, Nora?" Maeve called down.

"Now?"

"Yes. Everyone enjoyed your lullaby."

Nora cleared her throat. The first few notes were shaky. "'The primrose in the sheltered nook. The crystal stream the babbling brook. All these things God's hands have made for very love of thee.'"

The ship still rocked upon the ocean, but those who'd been crying quieted to listen.

"'Twilight and shadows fall. Peace to His children

all. Angels are guarding and they watch o'er thee as you sleep. May angels watch over and may they guard o'er thee.'"

Grace had quieted, too. Perhaps Nora's voice had comforted her when she'd begun to sing. At any rate, her song had brought a measure of comfort to the baby and their fellow passengers.

Soon after, the rocking of the brig lessened as the wind and waves abated. The sound of thunder moved off into the distance.

Still they waited to be sure the worst of the storm had passed. Half an hour later, Maeve loosened her bindings and hopped down. "Are all of you all right? Is anyone hurt?"

"I bumped my head on the bunk," an older woman said and rubbed the area.

"Let me have a look." Others were making their way out of their beds now and a few rolled up their soiled linens. Maeve probed the woman's skull. "You might have a headache, but you're fine."

She turned to the others. "No one will object to an additional wash day, so you may wash out your bedding, ladies. I'll ask a mate to string the lines as soon as the sky is clear." She turned to her sisters. "I'd better go straightaway to the dispensary in case anyone was hurt."

"I want to make sure the Atwater girls fared well," Bridget told her. She worked her hair into a braid and hurried off.

On deck, the leaden clouds had parted, and as though in defiance of the contending elements, the late-afternoon sun made an appearance.

The dark sodden deck shone in the light. Overhead, canvas sails snapped in the breeze as they were unfurled. Maeve should have gone below, but something held her in place. She felt as though she was waiting for something, though she wasn't sure what. She listened and waited.

Searching the sky, she was treated to a view of the changing color and departing darkness. As the last remaining clouds scuttled out of view, the reason she'd lingered manifested itself, stretching wide across the sky.

The most magnificent rainbow she'd ever witnessed confirmed God's promise to the ages and His people. *Lo, I am with you always, even unto the end of the age,* she heard as plain as day.

A tear trailed down her cheek. Swiping it away, she smiled through blurred vision. God was good. His promises endured. He was going to see them to America safely. He would provide them with a home and security, and meet their needs. Anything less than solid trust and devotion was foolishness.

The affirmation of His enduring love buoyed her spirits. She caught herself wishing Flynn was here to see it, and then in a split second, she shot down the ladder and dashed along the corridor.

He'd arrived at the dispensary and was picking up the few supplies they'd abandoned when the storm hit.

"Come now!" she shouted.

He dropped something he held and ran after her. Up the ladder they scrambled, and came out on deck. "What's wrong?" he asked. "Who's injured?"

"No one. Look!"

A line creased his brow, but he shifted his attention to where she pointed. His expression softened.

Maeve said nothing. He'd as much as accused her of talking too much, of asking too many personal questions, and admittedly she was guilty of those things. So for once she held her tongue. She let God do the talking this time.

Again Maeve appreciated the majesty of the rainbow, but her interest was in Flynn's reaction. Emotions played across his finely chiseled face. His brows were as black as his hair, his nose straight and well-formed. He had a solid jaw and an expressive mouth. His eyes, fringed by black lashes, were dark and fathomless. When his face relaxed and lines of concern smoothed away, she realized what a handsome man he was.

Gradually, life resumed its natural rhythm around them. A few hardy souls came out and cleaned their cooking areas of debris. Riggers called to one another from above.

Huge birds flew overhead, as large as geese, pure white with jet black-tipped wings. Maeve supposed they were residents of the nearby island, which was now visible, but behind them.

Finally, Flynn turned to her and spoke: "Thank you."

She wasn't sure exactly what had taken place during that interlude, but she was glad she'd been prompted to go get him. She simply nodded.

"Let's get back to work," he said.

That evening they were treated to a splendid sunset, the colorful likes to which none other during their trip could compare. Bridget didn't join them for their evening meal, as she was dining with the Atwaters in the captain's cabin.

"I wish I had your fearlessness," Maeve said to Aideen, in a mocking singsong tone. "To stuff yourself on that mackerel and not care a whit."

Aideen, who had been told all about Kathleen's barbed compliments, chuckled and popped another bite in her mouth. She chewed with her eyes closed as though the smoked fish was smooth ambrosia.

"Maeve," Nora warned in her matronly, older-sister tone.

"Oh, I forgave her," Maeve told her. "I'm just going to laugh about it now. You know you want to laugh, too."

A tall man in a black suit approached them, and Maeve recognized him as the man who worked for Mrs. Fitzwilliam.

"My mistress asked that you accompany me to her stateroom," he said.

"Is she sick?"

"She is requesting your presence, miss. That's all I know."

Maeve set down her plate and brushed her hands together. "Well, let's go, then."

He led the way down the ladder and to a door on the opposite side of the lower level from where Maeve and her sisters slept. After rapping on the door, he opened it.

A set of mother-of-pearl inlaid folding screens shielded the room from view. She supposed it was a good solution to spare the woman's privacy when her servant was a man. It did set up a dramatic effect.

"Have you brought her, Stillman?" came a woman's voice from beyond.

"Yes, ma'am. Miss Murphy has arrived."

"Send her in."

"Mrs. Fitzwilliam will see you now." He gestured for her to proceed around the screen.

She had certainly met the most interesting people on this voyage. Maeve skirted the screens.

Lying atop a bed dressed with elegant satin draping and huge tasseled pillows was the woman who'd dressed her down the first day on the *Annie McGee.* She wore a silk dressing gown in a luscious shade of mauve and a pair of matching slippers with rhinestone embellishment.

"Are you feeling poorly, Mrs. Fitzwilliam?"

"I think I shall not make it through the night."

"Was it the storm? Perhaps some peppermint oil will settle your stomach. You had a rough go, I'd wager."

"It was not the storm, although that was an experience I do not wish to endure on any future occasion."

"What is it, then?"

"I fear it's my heart."

Chapter Fifteen

"I'd better send for Dr. Gallagher, then. I'm not a physician, you know."

"I don't want that man here."

"Why not? He's a fine surgeon."

"Because he looks like my dear departed Walter in his youth, and I couldn't bear for him to turn those eyes on me today of all days."

"But he's better equipped than I to treat a heart condition."

"I fear my heart is broken, and I doubt there's anything he can do about that."

The woman could add more drama to a conversation than even Bridget.

Maeve tugged an easy chair closer to the woman's bed. The contents of the bedside table were on the floor, apparently tossed there during the storm, so she knelt and set them back in place. Among jars and a leather-bound journal was a daguerrotype of a dashing, dark-haired man in a finely cut suit. A watch chain draped from inside his vest to a pocket, and he seemed to study the camera with a look of annoyance. Maeve placed it upright on the table.

Mrs. Fitzwilliam covered her face with a flowered handkerchief. "I dream of him nearly every night. Mr. Fitzwilliam was industrious and always full of ideas. He could make even the drabbest day come to life. I never lived a dull moment in all our married years. We were going to travel abroad once he found an assistant he trusted with his business affairs. That just never seemed to happen, so our voyages were always business related."

Maeve settled on the chair and spoke softly. "You must miss him very much. When a person so full of life, like your husband, is gone, it sometimes feels as though a candle has been extinguished and the whole world is dreary without them."

Mrs. Fitzwilliam slowly tugged the handkerchief away from her eyes. She looked at Maeve. "That's it exactly. How do you know this?"

"That's how I felt when my mother went to glory. Even though we were poor and she and my father worked hard every day, she always found ways to make the most simple meal entertaining. She sang so beautifully, her voice could lift anyone's mood. Even in a work dress and apron she carried herself like a queen.

"My father adored her, and my sisters and I learned so much about life from her. For the longest time after she died it felt as though the spark had gone out of our family. But then, little by little, I would see things about my sister Bridget that reminded me of Mother. Or I'd hear Nora say something my mother said. Only today, as the boat was pitching and the thunder was crashing, Nora sang a lullaby in the same lilting voice as Mother.

"She left us a legacy of her beautiful spirit, her wisdom and her kindness. She's no longer of this earth, but she lives in our hearts."

Mrs. Fitzwilliam's eyes shimmered with tears that

spilled over. She blotted her nose with the handkerchief. "He does live on in my heart. And in my dreams. Sometimes they're so real, I wake up thinking he's still here and I will see his head on the pillow beside me.

"Sadly, we never had any children of our own. I was Walter's second wife, you see, and he had a daughter. He indulged her, much to my dismay. She grew into a selfish young woman without a lick of sense. Her offspring is a foolish spoiled snip of a girl, whom I was attempting to raise on my own after her mother left her in my care to chase after a French artist."

"So you do have some family?"

"I treated my husband's granddaughter as my own. I gave her everything a young girl could ask for—singing lessons, clothing, a parlor all her own in which to entertain her friends."

"Where is she now?"

Mrs. Fitzwilliam flattened a fleshy hand against her breast as though she was in pain. "The foolish child ran off six months ago. She met a ruffian of poor character, and when I refused to allow her to see him, she packed a bag and sailed off to Boston with him."

"So, you're going after her?"

"Of course I am. I can't let Mary fall to ruin when she has a perfectly good home and someone to care for her."

"Of course not. How old is Mary?"

"Eighteen now. Her birthday was only last month." She sniffled into her hankie. "I fear I'm losing my mind, Miss Murphy."

"Why do you say that?"

Mrs. Fitzwilliam finally roused herself upward to sit on the edge of the bed. "Have you ever glimpsed someone who looks so much like the person you lost that your heart catches? When you look more closely, it's not them at all."

"Aye," Maeve replied. "I could have sworn I saw my da on the dock when we were boarding, but it was just a silver-haired fellow in a homespun shirt. When he looked my way, he looked nothing like Da."

Mrs. Fitzwilliam nodded. "I used to think I spotted my Walter, too. And twice recently, I thought I saw Mary. Both times I glimpsed a girl with the same black hair, but when I looked again there was no one there. Do you think that means Mary is dead, like Walter?"

"No, of course not. You know better than that. She's on your mind is all."

"Does it mean I'll be placed in a sanitarium soon?"

"Certainly not. You've had a lot of concerns on your mind, is all. Sometimes our mind plays tricks on us. A woman in my village lost her baby at birth. Every night for months she awoke to the sound of a baby crying, until she was on the verge of hysteria."

"The poor woman."

"I'll be glad to help you find Mary when we get to Boston. I'll help in any way I can."

The older woman met her gaze directly. Her dark auburn hair had come loose from its fancy bun, and those blue eyes didn't appear quite as cold as they once had. "That's kind of you, Miss Murphy. Thank you."

"Call me Maeve."

"You may call me Elizabeth."

"Shall I help you dress your hair now?"

She pointed to a case on the floor. "My brush and comb are in there."

Maeve gathered the items and returned.

"How is the young boy faring? The one whose leg you saved?"

"Sean is quite well. He's running errands for the captain now. There are three McCorkle brothers. Seems they came up with a plan to escape a workhouse and board the ship. Things went awry when young Sean got hurt.

"Gavin is a rigger. I saw him overhead today. Little Emmett is caring for the sailors' chickens and goat. Mrs. Conley won't let them eat in the galley with the crew. She feeds those boys like kings, she does."

"Should they need anything—a place to stay, clothing…you come to me. Do you hear?"

"Yes, ma'am. I can't do this as intricately as you, but I can give you a serviceable bun. My sister Bridget could fashion it more stylishly."

"It will suffice, Maeve. Thank you." She gave her a sheepish look. "I just needed someone to talk to who could understand my distress. You seem like a kind and understanding person."

"We all need that. It's perfectly normal."

"I don't really have anyone, except Stillman. He was my husband's valet. Since Walter's been gone, he's been with me, as I didn't have the heart to let him go, but he is a man, after all."

"How are you feeling now?"

"Foolish."

Maeve ignored that. "I mean your chest. Any pain?"

"Nothing time won't heal."

"Very well." Maeve paused. She didn't want to leave without one last offer. Finally, she decided if it was rebuffed, she wouldn't care. "Would you care to join me and my sisters at our fire tomorrow evening and share a meal?"

The invitation seemed to toss the woman into a wave. She floundered for a moment, but then caught herself.

"I would love to join you. Thank you for the invitation. I'm sure Stillman will appreciate a night off."

"All right. We'll see you then."

Her opinion of the woman had changed a hundred percent. Immediately she recalled her prayer, asking for God's help in being generous and kindhearted. She'd directed that request toward her feelings about Kathleen, but quite obviously God thought she needed to treat everyone the same way.

She still didn't see herself inviting Kathleen to their fire any time soon, but stranger things had happened. She wasn't going to count anything out just yet.

Wait until her sisters learned who would be joining them the next evening.

Mrs. Fitzwilliam was an entertaining dinner companion. In her younger days, she'd traveled with her husband on business. She shared stories of India, Japan and even Africa.

"I am most likely the only person here who has ever ridden an elephant," she said at one point.

"I've ridden a donkey," Bridget said, and they shared a laugh that drew attention from their neighbors.

"*Everyone* has ridden a donkey," Maeve admonished her.

"I haven't," Mrs. Fitzwilliam proclaimed. And again they laughed heartily.

The Murphys had included Aideen and Mrs. Kennedy in their dinner plans and combined resources.

"The fish is exceptional," their guest said.

Everyone was growing weary of mackerel, but no one spoke of it. Plenty of fish was not a hardship in any way, shape or form. Their countrymen back home would love to haul in a catch like this and put it on the table for their families.

In a way Maeve felt bad for leaving so many people behind to fend for themselves, but on the other hand, she felt fortunate to have escaped the poverty and oppression.

Nora had outdone herself with a kettle of rice pudding.

Mrs. Kennedy was holding Baby Grace, so she asked Nora to save her a serving.

"I do so admire your courage for eating that pudding," Bridget said to Maeve. "You're so brave to blow yourself up like a puffer fish and not care a whit that your drab, ill-fitting dresses no longer fit."

"Bridget," Nora cautioned, but her voice had no true censure behind it. In fact, she quickly hid a grin.

Mrs. Fitzwilliam looked taken aback by Bridget's teasing, so Nora shared how a particularly rude passenger had behaved at the captain's table.

"Oh, dear," Maeve said to her oldest sister. "You haven't dressed for dinner. I'll make your excuses while you run along and change. Don't worry yourself if it's a rag. No one on this vessel has any fashion sense. They'll never know."

Nora did laugh at that.

"I am amazed at what some people consider a suitable dinner dress," Aideen told them, sipping her tea with her pinkie in the air. She turned to her aunt. "Why look at your hair! How generous of you to employ a blind maid."

They laughed over that, and even Mrs. Fitzwilliam got into the spirit, once she was convinced they weren't making sport of *her.* "I hope I never sounded like that," she said, turning a repentant gaze on Maeve. "I do apologize for anything unkind I said to you in the past."

"All is forgiven," Maeve assured her.

"But truly," Mrs. Fitzwilliam said to Maeve. "That's an interesting lace collar you're wearing. Did the mice get to it?"

Nora choked on her tea, and Bridget patted her on the back until she stopped coughing.

They were enjoying themselves so thoroughly, no one noticed the couple strolling nearby until they were practically on top of them.

"You ladies are certainly enjoying your evening," Flynn noted. "What is all this merriment about?"

Beside him stood Kathleen, her shiny dark hair in place, a paisley silk shawl wrapped around her shoulders.

"Nora did something incredible with this rice pudding," Maeve replied. "It seems we have enough to feed the crew. Would you care for some?"

Flynn glanced at Kathleen, and it was plain he wanted to accept. "That sounds nice," he said and led Kathleen forward.

The ladies scooted closer together to make room for two more. It wasn't a problem, since they had Aideen and her aunt's space to use. Maeve got a stool for Kathleen and sat on a mat.

Kathleen sat with her skirts tucked aside as though she didn't want to soil them by allowing them to touch one of the other women.

Nora placed a serving of rice pudding in a clean dish and handed it to Kathleen.

Everyone grew silent, waiting for her refusal.

The sound of the waves against the side of the ship was loud in the ensuing silence.

As though she sensed every eye upon her, the young woman glanced from person to person. Apparently refusing the offering in front of so many was too rude even for her, because she accepted the bowl and a spoon. "Thank you."

Flynn took his with a smile and tasted it. "Mmm. Indeed, this is the best rice pudding I've ever eaten in my life. And I'm partial to rice pudding."

"Evenin', Dr. Gallagher," their neighbors called over.

Flynn greeted them.

Kathleen took a bite.

"So what were you sharing such a hearty laugh over?" Flynn asked.

"Well…" Maeve studied the starlit sky.

"I'm afraid their amusement was at my expense," Mrs. Fitzwilliam said, surprising Maeve by coming to her rescue. "I was bragging about having ridden an elephant in India. They could not picture it. I wasn't quite as full-figured as I am now."

The baby fussed, and Nora got up.

"Let me," Bridget said. "I'll go." She grabbed a tin cup and headed across the deck in the moonlight.

Maeve took the baby from Mrs. Kennedy and changed her nappy.

"Where did she go for milk?" Kathleen asked.

"To milk the goat," Nora replied. "The sailors generously let us milk her whenever we need to, day or night."

"Why don't you just gather a whole bucket at once and save yourself the additional trouble?" she asked.

"Because it would be contaminated in the hours it was left exposed." Flynn's tone revealed his aggravation at the question.

Maeve stood and carried Grace over to their guests and extended her toward Kathleen. "You're welcome to hold her."

Kathleen just looked at Maeve with a blank expression, so Maeve placed Grace in her arms and stepped back.

The young woman looked as though someone had dropped a mud pie in her lap. She grimaced and held Grace as far from her as possible, without letting go. The baby fussed at the awkward position.

"Oh, here, like this." To Maeve's utter amazement, Flynn took the infant and nestled her into the crook of his arm. Grace immediately settled in and opened her eyes wide in the darkness.

"She's such a sweet little thing," Nora said.

"Still no idea how she came to be abandoned?" Mrs. Fitzwilliam asked.

Nora shook her head. "'Tis a mystery, it is."

"Quite obviously someone didn't want to get up and milk a goat three or four times a night," Kathleen remarked.

"Her own mother wouldn't have had to milk a goat," Maeve pointed out. "Nature takes care of that detail rather ingeniously."

"Oh." Kathleen pulled her shawl around her.

Bridget returned and Nora filled the glass nursing bottle.

"Do you wash it between feedings?" Flynn asked.

"Yes, doctor," Nora replied with a grin. "The nipple, too. Do you want to feed her?"

Flynn didn't reply for a moment, but then he nodded and took the bottle. Grace knew better than he what was required and latched on hungrily.

Seven women watched the only male in their midst, a tall broad-shouldered man, as he held and fed the tiny infant, a babe not even as long as his forearm. It was one of those moments that doesn't require comment, because it's so pure and beautiful on its own.

Maeve couldn't help wondering what he thought as he held Grace, truly acknowledging her for the first time, and not distancing himself. He must be thinking of his Jonathon, of the wife he loved and lost. He must be thinking how fleeting and fragile life is—and, in the face of a newborn baby, how beautiful.

Chapter Sixteen

When Grace was finished, Nora took the bottle. "Put her on your shoulder to work up a bubble now."

He did as instructed, propping Grace on his shoulder and patting her gently. She emitted a very unladylike sound and he chuckled. "Right on cue."

"I should take her to bed." Nora reached for the baby.

"Bridget and I will do the dishes," Maeve assured her.

Aideen got up. "I'll help."

"We should be going." Kathleen stood. "Thank you for your hospitality."

"You're quite welcome. It was our pleasure," Maeve said.

"Yes, do come back," Bridget added, as though they'd just had someone into their parlor for a tea party.

Flynn thanked them, as well, and the couple strolled away.

"That was interesting," Aideen remarked.

"I don't know what I'd have done if she'd refused the dessert," Maeve said.

They busied themselves with the dishes.

This week on the Sabbath, the boundaries in the hold were nearly obliterated. Aideen and Mrs. Kennedy, along with Elizabeth Fitzwilliam, sat with the Murphy sisters for Captain Conley's Bible reading and during silent prayer.

The McCorkle brothers sat directly behind them, and were the most boisterous singers in the room. When the service ended, Mrs. Fitzwilliam turned around and spoke to each lad.

After lunch, serious work began on the dresses. The Murphy sisters gathered in the other ladies' stateroom, where all the supplies were handy, and applied their efforts to cutting the fabric.

"I'm terrified of making a mistake," Nora said, the scissors trembling in her hand.

Mrs. Kennedy took the shears from her and all of them watched in fascination as a loud *snip snip snip* sounded and the fabric parted in perfect precision. Aideen wielded her own impressive pair of scissors to cut facing and bias strips.

"What about underclothing?" She glanced up. "Do you ladies have proper underslips and pantaloons? What about chemises?"

Nora's complexion turned pink. "No one will see our underclothing."

"It has nothing to do with who will see them and everything to do with how beautiful and self-confident you feel."

"And pantaloons will make me feel self-confident?" Maeve's eldest sister challenged.

"Yes," Aideen replied emphatically. "We shall fashion several sets, and you will not set foot on that gangplank without a proper ensemble beneath your dress."

Bridget smiled from ear to ear.

Nora acquiesced with a pretty shrug. "If you feel that strongly about it."

Maeve sat with Baby Grace in her lap and watched her sisters with their new friends. "When we're living in Faith Glen, we shall travel to Boston to visit you. And you're welcome at our cottage any time."

"Oh, I would love that," Aideen told her. "I don't think I've ever had such pleasurable company."

They went on deck for a quick afternoon meal, and Maeve boiled water. "We were running low, so I purchased some lovely tea from one of the ladies I met."

"Thank you, Maeve," Nora said. "Afternoon tea sounds delightful."

Bridget agreed and added, "I do wish we had biscuits."

"Or those sweet little lemon cookies we once enjoyed at a wedding," Maeve added.

"You're making my mouth water." Mrs. Kennedy closed her eyes. "Let's pretend."

A scuffle broke out several fires away. The occasional argument was common, but this was beyond a verbal disagreement. The women sat in stunned silence as two men shouted and took punches at each other.

"Oh, my." Bridget rested a hand on her cheek.

One man chased the other across the deck, his boots making a loud racket on the planks. The man being chased carried a lumpy bag, and when he got to the side of the ship he paused, heaved it upward and threw it overboard.

Quite obviously incensed, the man in pursuit lunged forward with a loud growl. The sisters had seen the Donnelly brothers fistfight on rare occasion, but this didn't seem like a spat between rowdy brothers. Tight-fisted hits were met with grunts. They grappled to the deck, stood and circled each other with bent knees.

A flash of steel glimmered in the sunlight.

Both men stilled.

The first lunged.

The second slid to the planks, a crimson stain spreading across his shirt front.

The other, the one who'd thrown the bag overboard, wiped his bloodied dagger on the leg of the injured man, sheathed it and ran.

"After him!" someone shouted.

Already on her feet, Maeve shouted for someone to go for Dr. Gallagher, and darted to the bleeding passenger on the deck. She fell to her knees beside him.

The bearded man's eyes were already glassy. Blood trickled from the corner of his mouth. Still conscious, he rolled his eyes toward her. Attempting speech, he choked instead.

She tore open his shirt to find a deep wound that had obviously pierced vital organs. She tore off her shawl, rolled it and pressed the wad against the wound. She knew of nothing to do for him. He was rapidly bleeding to death. "If you need to make peace with God, I am believing this is your last chance."

He turned his head aside, spat and gasped, "Pray."

"You want me to pray with you?"

He nodded, grimacing so wide his bared teeth shone in the sunlight.

Heart racing now, Maeve leaned close to the dying man and asked God to forgive him of any trespasses and take him to glory.

He nodded as though agreeing with her prayer, but his eyelids fluttered.

"Henry!" A woman collapsed to her knees near his head. As though she didn't know what to do with her hands, she shook them before cradling his head in her lap. Sobs tore from her throat. "Why didn't you just let him go? You foolish, foolish man! Why couldn't you have stayed with me, Henry? Why? Why?" She shot her panicked gaze to Maeve's. "Why aren't you doing something for him?"

"I'm trying to stop the flow of blood, ma'am. I don't know what else to do. I'm not a doctor."

Henry's eyes fluttered shut and back open. He couldn't seem to focus on the woman.

"Don't you die on me, Henry! We're startin' a new life in Illinois. Don't you dare die. We've got five children to raise!"

Maeve's stomach clenched.

Henry's eyes closed and he emitted a deep ragged breath, then didn't draw another.

"*Henry!* Don't you die, Henry!"

Behind her, Maeve heard Bridget's sob and then Nora urging her away.

Finally, Flynn arrived and knelt beside Maeve. "What's happened?"

Relieved to see him, Maeve lifted her blood-soaked shawl to show him the stab wound in Henry's belly.

"Do something!" the woman shrieked. "Don't let him die!"

"Ma'am," Flynn said softly. "He didn't have a chance. This wound perforated too many of his organs. Even if I'd been here and immediately attempted surgery, I couldn't have saved him. He lost blood too fast."

She threw herself upon the dead man's chest and sobbed.

Maeve wanted to comfort her, but her hands were soaked with blood. She released the shawl, sat back on her knees and looked at the other faces in the gathered crowd, just now seeing how many people had watched that scenario unfold.

From behind her, Nora stepped around Flynn and knelt beside the woman. She draped an arm over her shoulder and spoke softly. "Come away now, *ma milis.* I'll make you a cup of tea and you can lie down. Where are your children?"

The woman raised her head. Her expression registered shock, confusion. "Oh, dear God. The children." She looked at Nora then. "They're back near our fire."

Nora checked the crowd. "Does anyone know who this woman's children are?"

A woman stepped forward. "I do. Their fire is beside ours."

"Will you look after them, please? I'm going to take her to lie down."

"Take her to our rooms," Mrs. Kennedy offered. "It's quiet there. Private."

Once Nora had led away the grieving widow, Flynn ordered the nearby men to help him carry Henry's body to the prow, where a coffin would be made.

Maeve got up and stared at her hands, then her skirt, which was hopelessly stained. She was angry. Angry that something like this could happen in the middle of a day filled with sunshine and salt spray. On the Sabbath, no less. A hideous crime leaving a woman with five fatherless children to raise.

The crowd had dispersed. A couple of the apprentices carried buckets to the scene and poured water on the deck. The water diluted the thickening blood, which ran into the cracks between the planks.

"Blood is depressin' tough to remove from the deck," one of them said.

Maeve's skirt was ruined. Angrily, she reached for the button and ties in the back and stepped out of it. Not caring who saw, she wiped her hands on the wool, then used it to pick up her shawl before she stomped to the rail in her pantaloons. There, she flung the bloody clothing into the ocean.

Without a backward glance or a sideways look, she marched to the ladder and ran to her cabin to wash and change.

Most of their mates had gone to the cabin, too. A few of them spoke to her, telling her she'd done all she could, most lamenting the fact that a man with a family had been struck down in the prime of life.

"They said that other fella stole their sack of provisions, he did, and Henry was simply goin' after what rightly belonged to 'im."

"'Tis a pity, it is."

"Poor woman. Five hungry mouths to feed and her man dead and gone. Can't help but wonder what will become of them now."

Maeve couldn't bear the talk. She picked up her Bible and made her way to the dispensary, where she could be alone. She poured more water into a basin and used Flynn's soap and brush to scrub her hands again, taking extra care to get under her nails.

The look in Henry's eyes as he lay dying was yet another picture of despair and hopelessness she would never erase from her memory. Her hands were clean, but she continued to scrub until her skin was red and irritated.

She poured more water and washed her arms and her face, as well. Finally, she dried her skin, and her motions slowed. The horror of what had happened caught up to her. The enormity of this voyage and their uncertain fates overwhelmed her.

She backed up to the wall for support. Her chest was tight and her lungs near to bursting. She tried to hold in the emotion, but her face crumpled and scalding tears ran down her cheeks. Sliding to the floor, she sat in a huddle with her knees drawn up, her face buried in her clean skirt, and cried great heaving sobs.

She'd never cried this hard or this much. She'd been strong for her sisters and Da when Mother had died. She'd been strong yet again when Da had passed on. She'd been so resilient that sometimes she felt as though she must not have a tear in her.

But here they were, buckets of them, enough to soak her sleeve and the fabric over her knees. Blindly, she reached up to a drawer for a bandage rag on which to blow her nose and let herself simply breathe for several minutes.

Slow, even breaths.

If she felt this badly, how did Henry's poor widow feel? And his children? How young were they?

The door opened.

Please not a patient, Lord, she prayed. She'd thoughtlessly left the portal unlocked.

A clean, pressed white shirt in her peripheral vision assured her differently, however.

Flynn.

"Maeve?" he said, spotting her huddled on the floor and walking toward her. "What are you doing down there? Are you all right?" He drew up short at the sight of her. "Ah, Maeve."

"I'm fine," she said, but her stuffy voice and nose belied that proclamation. She could only imagine what her face and eyes looked like. And her nose.

He went to the basin of water she'd used, wetted a cloth and wrung out the excess water. "Place this over your face for a few minutes."

She obeyed and breathed through the damp cotton.

The cool cloth felt good on her skin, especially over her burning eyes.

He took one of her hands and splayed it open to examine it. "What have you done to yourself?"

After releasing her, he was gone for a moment and returned. With strong, warm fingers he rubbed glycerin into her raw skin. The massage felt better than she'd thought anything could. Her entire arm relaxed under his attention.

He let her shift that hand to hold the rag to her face and ministered to her other in the same way, applying the cool glycerin, massaging it into her flesh. Her other arm relaxed and tension gradually left her body.

Slowly peeling away the cloth, he dabbed glycerin with the pad of one finger under each eye.

He had another plan, because he went for more supplies and returned with peppermint oil. After he massaged a dab onto each of her temples, the oil spread coolness to her aching head, and the scent roused her flagging spirits.

Or perhaps it had been his tender care that had lifted her from despondency. She didn't feel as hopeless as she had only a short while ago.

He urged her to her feet and guided her to one of the chairs, then pulled another near and sat before her. "There was nothing you could have done differently. What I told his wife was the truth. His wound was fatal. You comforted him in his dying moments."

"I prayed for him. He asked me to."

"You did more than most people would have."

She nodded. "Perhaps. But knowing that doesn't change what happened or take away the futility I feel over one human being taking another's life. It's senseless."

"We're only people," he said. "We do everything we can, but we're not miracle workers."

She agreed.

"What would your da say if he was here?"

Puzzled, she looked at him. "My da?"

He nodded. "Was he a wise man?"

She didn't have to think too hard. The corner of her mouth quirked up. "He'd say, 'Maeve, me fine daughter, aimin' to cure the ails of this world is like hopin' to mind mice at a crossroads.'"

Flynn chuckled. "You must take after him, because it sounds just like something you would say. So he *was* a wise man."

"That he was."

She ran her fingers through hair that had fallen loose and tugged it away from her face. "It all rose up strong today, all the pain I've been pushing back and keeping inside and thinking I was over it."

"Maybe that's good."

"Maybe it is."

"You're the bravest woman I know."

She looked into his dark eyes. "No, I'm not."

"Yes. You jump right in and take a situation in hand. In fact, I'm a little bit concerned for you, since that seems to be your habit. I don't know what you'll get yourself mixed up in next."

"Well, I'm thinkin' about those fatherless children and Henry's widow. The Bible tells us to take care of widows and orphans."

He shook his head. "Here you are, not concerned about your own future, because you trust God has that in hand, but instead thinking how you can do something to improve their future?"

"Well…" She thought a minute. "Yes."

He laughed, and those dimples winked at her.

Without thought for consequences or propriety, she placed her palm against his warm cheek. The texture of his beard was pleasantly rough. "Thank you, Flynn."

"My pleasure." Quite spontaneously, he leaned forward and touched his lips to hers, a kiss that seemed as natural and pure as rain on a spring day.

Chapter Seventeen

It was a kiss of comfort, a bond of mutual understanding. This kiss showed care and compassion. Nothing more.

But if that was true, why did she feel as though she'd been swept overboard and caught up in a turbulent current? He threaded his fingers into her hair, and she longed to stand and have him wrap his arms around her.

Now she kissed him in return. Earnestly, without thought for anything as simple as comfort. She wanted to drown in his kiss.

The thrill of it was as amazing as last time…yet terrifying on the other hand. She feared she might burst into tears again, and that would never do. The beauty of it buoyed her and kept her on the chair when she might otherwise have toppled to the floor. Only one thing kept her from losing herself in his embrace.

Last time he'd apologized.

She inched away, and he released her.

"Will you be telling me you're sorry again?" She searched his dark mahogany-colored eyes. "I don't enjoy being someone's regret."

"I can't regret kissing you, Maeve."

"Are you not promised to your Miss Boyd?"

Something moved behind his eyes. Was that regret or surprise? "No, I'm not. Kathleen and I are friends."

"She and her mother speak differently. You and she seem so comfortable in each other's company. She doesn't see herself as your friend."

He frowned in confusion. "I've never let her think I'm interested in more. We have mutual friends, memories of our home. We talk and that's all."

"You feel nothing for her." It wasn't a question.

"Friendship, Maeve. Only friendship."

"You have never kissed her?"

"Not once," he assured her.

"Then these kisses of ours…perhaps they do mean something?"

The look in his eyes was definitely confusion. "I—I don't know what to say."

She stood on trembling legs and picked up her Bible from a counter. "You can't avoid your heart forever. Maybe if you faced your feelings you'd recognize what is it you want."

"Just because you run directly at a problem without forethought doesn't necessarily mean it's the only way."

This time she did think before she spoke. And she held what she really wanted to say in check. "I came seeking privacy. I'll be leaving now."

"You might want to stay away awhile longer. The council is deciding the fate of the man who stabbed Henry to death."

"The council?"

"Yes. Remember the group of men who were selected by their fellow passengers to mete out justice during the journey?"

"What about the captain?"

"He is like a judge. The council is comparable to a jury."

"What do you suppose they'll decide?"

"Murder is met with swift punishment in any country as well as on the sea."

She headed for the door.

He didn't try to stop her, but he followed.

On deck, passengers were gathered around the prow, much as they had the day Bridget Collins had been buried at sea. A man in a gray suit stood to pronounce the council's decision.

"We didn't deliberate long," he said. "And we've come to a unanimous decision. This man who refuses to give his name will be thrown overboard immediately."

A murmur went through the crowd. Maeve felt sick to her stomach. She'd lived in a peaceful little farming community her entire life. The most momentous events had been births and deaths by natural causes. She'd never before witnessed a murder or an execution. "Can't we take the man to Boston and give him a trial?" she called out.

"Massachusetts law wouldn't recognize a crime committed aboard ship," the speaker replied. "We're the judge and jury here."

"What of imprisonment?" she asked.

There were more murmurs from the gathering.

"Again there's the issue of who's responsible for his imprisonment."

Another member of the council spoke up. "And meanwhile would you have us feed the vile man from our own provisions? Why, he tried to steal Henry Begg's food right from his children's mouths. And when Henry called 'im out, he killed him. He showed Henry Begg no mercy, and he deserves none."

The man was hauled out into the open. Had an evil look about him he did, and a contemptuous glare. Sweat soaked his hair and ruddy face. His hands had been restrained behind his back, a rope tied about his shoulders and another at his feet.

"You have one last chance to state your name for the ship's record and to notify any family you may have," Captain Conley said.

The prisoner spat at him, but the captain was far enough away to avoid being hit.

Captain Conley opened his Bible and read a passage. The words didn't register with Maeve. He finished, closed his Bible and nodded at the mates who held the prisoner in place.

They hauled him up to the stern and balanced him there for a moment as wind whipped their hair.

Maeve's heart beat hard and painfully. She didn't want to watch, but she couldn't tear away her gaze. *Lord, take his soul.*

A sailor lashed out with a mighty shove, and the nameless man plunged headfirst into the waters below.

Her surroundings wavered in her vision. Maeve closed her eyes. Flynn grasped her by the shoulders and held her in place from behind. She hadn't realized she'd been swaying where she stood. At the sound of soft weeping, she opened her eyes and spotted Henry's wife surrounded by children of various heights and ages. The youngest was a chubby baby on her hip; the head of the eldest came to her shoulder. One small boy clung to her skirts, looking confused.

A moment later, the sound of bagpipes floated on the salt-laden air, adding another dimension to the event and stirring memories of home.

A plain pine box drilled with large holes was carried through the crowd and placed reverently upon the deck.

Now a funeral.

"'So when this corruptible shall have put on incorruption, and this mortal shall have put on immortality, then shall be brought to pass the saying that is written,'" Captain Conley read. "'Death is swallowed up in victory. O death, where is thy sting? O grave, where is thy victory? The sting of death is sin, and the strength of sin is the law.'" He turned. "Come now, Mrs. Begg, and say your last goodbyes to your husband."

She walked forward, still holding the toddler, and reached toward the pine box with a trembling hand, but then drew it back. The youngsters who were old enough to understand what was happening, cried openly. She ushered them away from the coffin and stood trembling.

Sailors in their best clothing worked two lengths of rope around the box and hoisted it up and out over the water. The bagpipes played a haunting melody, a familiar hymn, with which those standing in watch sang along.

Maeve couldn't sing. Her throat had constricted. She'd cried out every last tear earlier, so though her eyes still burned and her nose stung, she had nothing left.

Once the sailors lowered the ropes, the pine box pitched into the ocean.

Maeve couldn't allow herself to think of Henry's body, just as she'd been unable to think of her father's. At least Da's remains were on a lush hillside in his beloved homeland and not buried under tons of water and— She caught herself.

Henry Begg wasn't there in that fleshly vessel, she reminded herself. He'd gone onto heaven to await his family. Neither could she dwell on the poor Begg woman's shock and grief.

She went for a cup from their cooking area and placed a few coins inside, then made the rounds of the cook fires, asking her fellow passengers to share with the unfortunate widow. The cup was brimming when she delivered it to Mrs. Begg. "I know it's not much. And it won't go far, but I shall pray for it to be multiplied."

The woman thanked her, and Maeve joined her sisters in Aideen and Mrs. Kennedy's stateroom.

Their previously lighthearted mood had vanished, and the ladies worked together with somber determination.

"It's easier on my eyes to do this in the sunlight," Aideen commented. She had picked up a basted bodice and begun stitching darts.

"Put it away for now," her aunt told her. "We can sew in the morning."

There was a rap at the door.

"Is Miss Murphy here?"

"There are *three* Miss Murphys here." Aideen grinned at Sean McCorkle.

"Miss Maeve," he specified.

Maeve walked to the door.

"The doc asked for you. There be a passenger havin' a baby, and he asked you to attend. I'll be showin' ye the way."

"Excuse me, ladies."

The others waved her on.

The passenger was one Maeve had only seen in passing, but had never spoken with. On seeing her, she'd wondered when this baby was due to arrive. Maeve introduced herself.

"Margret Madigan," the woman managed. It was obvious she'd waited until birth was close at hand to send for help. She had prepared sheets and blankets.

"Have you had other babies?" Maeve asked.

"Aye. Three previously. One didn't survive his first month. I had a poor supply of milk, I did."

"We'll not let that happen again," Maeve assured her. "We have plenty of provisions and I'll see that you have a portion of goat's milk for yourself."

The woman grimaced and gripped the sheet on her bunk with white-knuckled fists. She or someone else had laid out folded flannel and provided two buckets of water.

"I'm going to wash in this one," Maeve told her. "And I want anyone who has any contact with you or the baby to do the same." She washed her already sore hands. "Are you feeling as though you have to push yet?"

"Aye," Margret replied.

"Is it all right if I have a look before you do that?"

"Let the whole crew have a gander if it moves this along any faster," Margret replied.

An older woman had remained in the cabin, and she and Maeve exchanged a look. The mature woman's eyes sparkled with amusement.

"Yours isn't a familiar accent," Maeve said as a distraction.

"Scottish," was Margret's brusque reply.

"Have you names selected, be this a lass or a laddie?"

"I hoped not to jinx the babe's fate," the woman replied.

Maeve wouldn't have another funeral this day if she could help it.

As the evening lengthened, Margret's efforts became more and more focused. The other woman bathed her perspiring face with cool cloths and spoke softly in a language Maeve couldn't understand. Her tone was soothing and encouraging.

Margret emitted a sharp cry and bore down.

"One or two more like that, and we'll see this baby's pretty face," Maeve told her. "There 'tis. And a curly head of hair, this wee babe has. Rest easy now for the next big push. This next one will do it."

Margret's next push expelled a good-size boy child into the world. Maeve quickly wiped his face and used her finger to clear his mouth. When he didn't cry, she turned his head down and swatted his bottom. "There you go, laddie. That's a fine healthy cry."

She handed the babe to the older woman, who cleaned him with the fresh water while Maeve attended to the new mother.

"He's a big one, he is," Maeve told her.

Margret didn't take her eyes from the baby, waiting until he was wrapped in flannel and placed in her arms.

She looked at his fingers and opened the wrap to examine his feet. She pressed her lips to his head and inhaled. Her eyes closed and a tear slid from under her lashes.

"Shall I go fetch your husband?" Maeve asked.

"My husband is waiting for us in Boston," she answered. "I thought I'd make it until we arrived, but this little fellow wasn't waiting."

"It's fitting somehow that after a fine man went to heaven today, another has just come into the world, don't you think?"

"I was down here all day, but I heard about the Begg fellow's untimely death," she answered. "I'd be devastated if I lost my husband."

"He's a handsome boy, Mrs. Madigan. Does he have a name now?"

"I have a son named after me father and a daughter named after me husband's mother. My father-in-law's name isn't fit for a child, so I'll not be givin' it to this boy."

"What is it?"

"His name was Urquhart."

Maeve had to agree the name might be a burden.

"What is your father's name?"

Maeve dried her hands. "His name was Jack. He was a fine, tall handsome man, with a heart as big as the sky."

"Jack is a very good name. Jack Madigan has a pleasant ring to it, does it not?"

"Aye."

"My husband will like it, as well. Actually he'd like anything that wasn't Urquhart."

Maeve laughed. "Let's get you into some dry clothing. You must be hungry now. I'm going to get you a meal and a cup of milk. Drink plenty of water, too. We took on a fresh supply."

"I wish I could repay you," Margret said, allowing Maeve to hand the infant to the other woman in order to help her change.

"Your smile and that healthy little fellow are sufficient reward. Dr. Gallagher pays me to assist him, you know. He will come listen to Jack's heart and look him over."

"Thank you."

Maeve tucked her into her bunk and handed the baby back to her. "Rest now."

"God bless ye, Miss Murphy."

Flynn got the message Sean delivered from Maeve, and immediately went to examine the newborn. Mrs. Madigan's strapping baby boy was as big as Baby Grace, yet two weeks younger. Flynn took the baby from her, laid him on a top bunk and listened to his rapidly beating heart. After looking him over from head to foot, he pronounced him healthy and gave him back to his mother.

The woman had already eaten and had something to drink, as evidenced by the dishes on the nearby floor. "Maeve took good care of you, I see."

"An excellent midwife, she is," Mrs. Madigan agreed. "And a fine young woman."

He could well imagine. As efficient and full of compassion as Maeve had proven herself, she was surely a blessing in assisting babies into the world.

"I named him Jack. That was Miss Murphy's da's name."

"I like it."

Leaving baby and mother behind, Flynn went on deck and stood at the rail, looking out across the obsidian ocean. The moon was obliterated by clouds tonight, so the water was black and fathomless.

It had been an exhausting and depressing day. Images danced in his mind. One of the most haunting had been the look on Maeve's face and her condition when he'd found her alone in the dispensary. The most thought-provoking had been her questions.

Her optimism and cheerful attitude had previously never waned in any situation, therefore her obvious devastation had been difficult to observe. She was feisty and painfully straightforward. So much so that she made him look inside himself and see things he didn't want to expose or admit.

He was looking now, and he didn't like what he saw.

He had much to consider as far as his feelings were concerned. Grief, regret and guilt weren't easy to face. Nor was his attraction to Maeve.

But consider he must.

Chapter Eighteen

Maeve had been right to confront him. He had no business kissing her without making his intentions clear. He wasn't a man who toyed with others' feelings.

He'd told himself he was an honorable man, a widower still working his way past grief and unwilling to bring any more complicated feelings into the equation. But perhaps he should have given more thought to the feelings and expectations others had for *him*.

According to Maeve, Kathleen had led her to believe there was more between them than there was.

Thinking over the barbed words that had spilled from her lips as she had insulted the Murphy sisters, he guessed she wasn't too proper or genteel to deliberately slur her fellow passengers, no matter how she disguised her claws—or to spread rumors about a romantic relationship that did not exist outside of her own mind.

And this was the woman he called a friend? Try as he might, he couldn't think of one thing other than their long-time acquaintance that made her a friend. Her background explained a lot about her general sense of entitlement, but it couldn't forgive her for being unkind.

Now Maeve…there was a woman who'd be a good

friend. But he didn't think of her in that way. He thought of her differently. Reverently. Kindly. Warmly. He thought of kissing her.

And if he was perfectly honest with himself, he wanted to think of being able to open up and love someone again. He just didn't know how.

It had been a long time since he'd let himself love anyone—even God. He was rusty at praying.

But Maeve's example inspired him. Perhaps opening his heart to the Lord could be the first step in opening his life to a chance at happiness again.

"Lord, I'm thankful You haven't forgotten me, even though I've neglected You. I have to admit I spent a lot of time wondering where You were and why You didn't care."

He swallowed hard. "But You do care. It's evidenced all around me. If You sent Maeve to shake me up and open my eyes to my self-pity, then help me not resent that. Or her.

"If You sent her to point out my glaring flaws, then I thank You. I could use wisdom to make decisions and to let myself heal. I'd appreciate Your showing me the changes I need to make and where to go from here.

"Sometimes I feel as though my future is as black and bottomless as this body of water. I can see into it no better than I can see the ocean's floor."

A cloud parted just enough to let a glimmer of moonlight reflect off the water's surface. He studied the heavens. How many times had he crossed the Atlantic now? Six times? Maybe eight? And he'd never taken time to simply stand here and behold a night sky laden with stars. Tonight they were hidden, and he wondered about the irony.

He remembered the captain's reading over Henry that

day, and the scripture returned to him. "O death, where is thy sting? O grave, where is thy victory?"

Because of God's mercy and redeeming grace, death was only cessation of life upon this earth. His Johanna... his Jonathon were inhabitants of an eternal kingdom. He'd always believed that. He knew the truth in his heart, but he had never had the courage to release them. He'd suffered their deaths every moment of each day since they'd been gone. "Come unto me, ye who labor and are heavy laden, and I will give you rest."

That rest had to mean peace. Had to mean laying aside those things he'd carried like sacks of boulders until the burden crippled him.

Quite plainly now he saw that he must release those he loved in order to have any kind of peace in his heart. He wanted that rest.

His heart thumped. He'd avoided thoughts of them for so long that allowing himself to remember them was frightening. He'd hidden that part of his past—that part of *him* away—and he didn't know if he could change.

Johanna first.

He let himself remember her sweet face, surrounded by silky, fair hair. She'd been tall and slim and carried herself with grace and dignity. She'd been raised in a wealthy family and trained to run a household and servants, but she'd been generous and accepting. She had been devoted to him and their child.

She would want him to be content. To move on.

And his boy.

Jonathon had possessed fair hair like his mother, but his eyes had been hazel—brown one moment, green the next. He'd been a fun-loving, active little fellow who'd run to his da at the end of the day. Flynn's arms ached with overwhelming emptiness. This was why he hadn't let himself think of them…why he guarded his thoughts so jealously.

"Into Your care I give them, Lord Jesus." He almost choked on the words, but he spoke them anyway. "Thank You for providing a way for them to dwell with You until we're together again."

He sagged against the side and held himself upright with his fingers gripping the rail. "Lord, please give me good memories to sustain me, and erase the images that bring such unbearable pain."

Waves lapped against the side of the ship.

He'd been running from this for so long.

Words resonated in his heart—clear and unmistakable. *Be still and know that I am God.*

In other words, stop running from the memories. He needed to let them overtake him. Anything less was a disservice to what he and Johanna had shared, and a betrayal to his son.

He searched for a good memory, and it came to him. A day at a fair. Jonathon had loved the pony rides and begged to ride again and again. Flynn had patiently walked beside him in a field with a figure-eight path worn into it.

The sun had warmed Johanna's hair to rich gold that day. He'd purchased her a comb with ribbon streamers, and she'd worn it in her gilded tresses. They had shared laughter…and created memories.

Memories to last a lifetime, he realized now. *His* lifetime.

Nothing could take those away from him, but he'd thrown them away. He took them back now, tucked them safely into his heart. "Thank You, Lord. Thank You for the time we had together and the memories we created."

A stiff breeze ruffled his hair and buffeted clouds away from the moon. A handful of stars winked at him.

There was something he needed to do. It was too late tonight, but tomorrow he had to speak with Kathleen.

Things were quiet at the dispensary when Flynn told Maeve he would be gone for a while and went in search of the Boyds.

Estelle was in their stateroom, but she told him Kathleen had gone above for fresh air. "You've never come in search of my daughter before," she said with a curious tone. "Is everything all right?"

"I want a word with her," was his only reply.

Long, purposeful strides carried him along the starboard deck until he spotted her in a lavender dress and a hat with a matching ribbon trailing down her back.

What surprised him was the man standing beside her. A wide-brimmed hat shaded his eyes from the sun, and he wore a plain shirt and trousers, which were tucked into tooled leather boots with inch-and-a-half heels. Flynn had met Western men on his travels, and had on more than one occasion listened to stories of Indian wars and cattle drives. Some of these men were ranchers, who owned huge parcels of land and raised horses for the army.

At his approach, Kathleen spotted him and stepped slightly away from the cowboy. "Flynn! What a pleasant surprise to see you on deck this morning."

"I do seem to indulge my passion for work most of the time." He extended a hand toward her companion. "Flynn Gallagher."

The man had strong work-roughened hands. "Judd Norton. Pleasure to make your acquaintance. The ship's doctor, if I'm rememberin' correctly."

"Yes, sir."

"Mr. Norton purchased horses from somewhere near County Galway," she told Flynn. "Waterford, wasn't it? Now he's on his way home."

"Heard of a gentleman who was sellin' his stable of Irish draft horses," he told Flynn. "They're excellent cross-country animals and economical to keep. It didn't take me long to figure out I wanted 'em, so I boarded a ship. I'm gonna breed 'em with my Spanish mares. I have high hopes for excellent riding horses."

"Where are you from?"

"I have a spread in the Nebraska Territory."

Flynn thought a moment. "Quite a distance to travel before you ever got to the ocean."

The man agreed. "I'd never been that far east b'fore. I admit I'm hankerin' for wide-open spaces that don't include waves or sharks."

"Were you looking for me?" Kathleen asked, turning the conversation.

"I don't want to interrupt your visit."

"Not at all," the American said. "I spend a lot of time right here and appreciate anyone who takes pity on my boredom. Miss Boyd made my mornin' pass more quickly." He touched the brim of his hat, but didn't remove it. "Miss. Nice to meet you, doc."

He sauntered away.

"What brings you out here?" Kathleen asked.

"Would you like to sit or are you comfortable standing?"

"I'm quite comfortable, thank you."

He took a place beside her, but not too close. He'd had a lot of time overnight to think about how he would say this. There'd be no wrapping what he had to say in sugar. "I've been self-evaluating. This trip has given me a lot to think about and stirred up some things that have lain buried."

"What makes this trip different?" she asked.

"I'm not certain," he answered, but he was pretty sure Maeve was the difference. She hadn't allowed him to hide.

"And what have you been thinking of that makes you look so serious?"

"How long have we known each other?"

A surprised look came over her face. "Fifteen, sixteen years, perhaps."

"You're aware, I'm sure, that our parents formed an alliance at some point. They were hoping to take my mind off Johanna and Jonathon and spoke to me of marrying you."

Her dark eyes widened. The subject of his marriage and the family he'd lost had always been off-limits. "You've never before spoken their names in my presence."

"I deliberately put them from my thoughts. It hurt too much to think of them. I've devoted myself to research."

"And legal dealings to do with immigrant ships," she agreed. "No one could blame you for that."

"The more I buried those feelings, the less sensitive I became to everything around me. I'm only beginning to see what I've done." He glanced at the water and back at her. "I've determined I shall change that behavior now."

"I do hope that's good news, Flynn. Are you ready for a change in your life? What did you promise your parents when they inquired?"

"I told them you and I were only friends and nothing more. I told them there could never be more between us. Kathleen, I apologize for being insensitive and not realizing you might have thought there was hope for marriage."

She seemed to absorb his words. "I believed you only needed time. I suspect you're about to tell me something entirely different."

Her tone held a surprising edge.

He nodded. "I'm sorry if this pains you, but there will never be more between us."

This would be the time to tell her she was special and desirable and another man would be lucky to earn her favor, but the words wouldn't come. Eventually she would make some man's life a living nightmare. Flynn was fortunate it wouldn't be him.

"Mother and I left everything behind," she told him. "She sold our property and a home that had been in our family for three generations to follow you to America."

"I had nothing to do with that. I've actually spent a very small portion of time in America and most of my time in Edinburgh. I never encouraged you to sell your property."

"You never encouraged me on any count."

"Thank you for seeing that." She knew. She wasn't a fool. "Your mother wanted to leave Ireland ever since your father died, did she not? I still don't know where I'm going to settle."

"But you have a home in Boston."

"It's a convenient place to stay between trips. You're still welcome to use it until you find somewhere to live."

"How generous of you."

"It was never my intention to lead you on." She was probably expecting him to say they would remain friends, but he didn't see that happening. He didn't want to be friends with someone who could treat others so unkindly.

"This is for the best," she told him. "I can see that."

He nodded, though he didn't understand.

She gathered her voluminous skirt that dragged on the deck without whatever feminine frippery she couldn't wear aboard ship and headed away from him, her posture stiff.

"The fortunate thing about this," she said pausing in her exit, "is how utterly forgettable you will be."

Chapter Nineteen

That morning, for the first time during a voyage he regretted leaving the sunshine behind to go below. Flynn felt as though a weight had been lifted from his shoulders. The reason for his ease was more than setting the record straight with Kathleen. Last night he'd faced his pain and allowed God to begin a healing process. Like any healing, it might take time, but he'd sought the Great Physician, and His power and love were unfailing.

He wanted to tell Maeve all that had taken place, but their last conversation had left things between them uncomfortable, and all morning she'd been cool.

At noon he took a stroll along the port side and discovered Martha Conley casting a net over the side of the ship.

"Would you miss the sea if the captain were to agree to settle down on land?" he asked her.

"Not for a minute. I do this to keep my sanity and feel productive. Rather be tendin' a garden, I would. I've eaten enough fish to last all me live long days. Green things, that's what I long for."

"But you've come along with him all these years."

"The sea's his mistress," she told him. "He loves her and I love him, so here I be."

The next person he spotted was a man sitting at an easel. The fellow wore a paint-spattered smock and a wide-brimmed straw hat. Fully expecting to find a sea-scape, Flynn approached the painting.

Instead, the man was painting a portrait of a woman. Glancing about, Flynn had spotted no one posing who looked like this person. "Who is she?" he asked.

"Her name is Sharon."

"An Irish lass?"

"Romanian. A traveler."

Flynn had heard of the clans that roamed the countrysides of Europe. The artist's voice held regret.

"But you're headed for America."

"I'm not her kind. Travelers don't marry outside their own people."

"And you paint her from memory."

He shrugged. "It's a knack I possess. But she is an indelible image on my heart."

"It's a wonderful painting. She's a beautiful young woman. I thought I would see a painting of the sea on your easel."

"My stateroom is full of them. B-19. Please come select one."

"I'll buy one from you."

"I need only paint and canvas to exist, so they're not expensive."

"Later this evening, perhaps."

Back in the dispensary, Emmett McCorkle was standing not far from the door.

"Young Emmett waited for you," Maeve told him. "I offered to help, but he wouldn't even tell me what brought him."

"Well, why don't we go into the other room back here, and you can tell me what brings you down here on such a fine day."

He ushered the boy into the room and closed the door. A few minutes later, he returned for water, rags and a scalpel.

"May I be of assistance?" she asked.

"It's a personal matter," he replied. "Go on upside for air. We won't be long."

A moment later Emmett cried out. Maeve left the dispensary. She found Aideen and Mrs. Kennedy at their fire and joined them for a cup of tea.

"A woman inquired about you only a few minutes ago," Aideen told her. "She mentioned the number of her stateroom and asked you to call on her."

"Was it an emergency? Why didn't she come to the dispensary?"

"I have no idea. She didn't say."

"Thank you for the tea. I needed the refreshment."

She made her way to the stateroom Aideen had mentioned and rapped on the door. A woman opened it and invited her in with a smile.

"What can I do for you?"

"We're fine, Miss Murphy. I have noticed you from time to time. My daughter and I beg you to take a few things off our hands."

"I'm not sure I understand."

"Come this way." The room was sectioned off with freestanding folding screens, and behind them were trunks and hatboxes and chests of every size and shape. "I'm sorry," the woman said. "I haven't even introduced myself. I'm Beth Mooney, and this is my daughter, Clara."

Clara was probably about twelve or thirteen, with sleek dark hair and an olive complexion.

Beth urged Maeve forward. "Clara has undergone a growth period recently, and though we've packed all these dresses and underthings, it's obvious she will no longer be able to wear them once we arrive. It seems she will need practically a whole new wardrobe."

Maeve still hadn't figured out what Clara's exceeding height had to do with her. "I'm afraid I don't understand what it is you want from me."

"We were hoping you would try on a sampling and see if you might get wear out of them. They're well made and still quite fashionable."

Now Maeve understood. The Mooney woman wanted to pass along clothing from her daughter and thought Maeve would be a suitable size to inherit. "Oh. I see."

"Here's what we'll do," Beth told her. "The screens adjust like so, and you just step behind there and try on something. This one is nice." She stuffed a voluminous green dress into Maeve's arms. "Go ahead. I'll unfasten your buttons for you. Don't be shy."

Maeve reluctantly tried on the emerald dress. It was fashioned with pleats in the skirt and lace at the neck and each wrist. Never had she worn fabric so elegant or fine.

Beth urged her to come stand before their full-length mirror and fastened the back closed. She plucked the large pins from Maeve's hair and the ringlets sprang free and draped her shoulders. Though the style was definitely suitable for a younger girl, the vivid garment enhanced her hair and skin.

"I had no idea this color would be suited to you, but it's striking."

Maeve couldn't disagree. "I could never accept such a

generous offer," she said with a shake of her head. "The things are too nice to give away."

"Give them away I will. I'll offer them to charity once we land if you don't want them."

"I'm afraid I don't have room to store them. We share our cabin with several women."

"Take a few now and leave the rest here until we land. There's a pretty dressing gown and a nightdress Clara just discovered have grown too short, as well. Surely you can use those."

"It's generous of you. Thank you."

The woman made a stack and offered to carry more for her, but Maeve assured her a few items were plenty for now.

"Well, you come get them if you want something else before we dock."

Maeve carried the clothing to her cabin. Mrs. Mooney had noticed her. Noticed her shoddy clothing? Noticed her small stature? While she was thankful and the woman had been generous and thoughtful, it stung to know others perceived her as needy.

She hung the dresses on the hooks near their bunks and folded the nightclothes into the trunk she shared with her sisters. She could hear Bridget now, exclaiming over the clothing.

She met Emmett in the companionway, walking rather stiffly for one so young and agile. The lad had filled out and the sun had kissed his skin and encouraged freckles. He looked far healthier than he had the first time she'd laid eyes on him. He ducked around a corner and was gone before she could speak.

The doctor was sterilizing a scalpel when she entered.

"Beautiful day, isn't it?" he said.

"Lovely."

"The laddie had a boil thrice the size of a Norse silver penny on his backside," he explained. "I doubt the boy has been able to sit for a week. Finally told his brother, and Gavin made him come to me."

"That explains why he wouldn't let me 'ave a look."

"No lad wants to show a pretty lady his bum," he agreed with a grin.

She wiped down the counters.

"It's a good day when no one is sick aboard a ship this size," he said.

"I was thinking about visiting a few people," she told him. "If I have your permission, that is. I am wondering how Goldie is getting along and if she needs any additional ointments for those burns."

"Why don't I do that while you call on Henry's wife and Mrs. Madigan and her baby? That way we'll both be attending patients and will finish up twice as quickly. It would be nice to enjoy the weather on deck this afternoon. And I'd like to talk with you."

"Very well. I'll be on my way."

"Meet me under the forecastle when you've finished."

Henry Begg's widow and her five children shared a cabin with one other woman who had several children and her mother traveling with her.

"Is your daily allotment sufficient for your growing children?" Maeve asked.

The woman nodded. "Our countrymen have shared with us, as well."

It was common, just as when Maeve's father had died, for neighbors to share their own provisions.

"And you?" she asked the widow. "Are you eating? Sleeping?"

"Don't have much of an appetite, but I want to sleep all the time."

Maeve stayed and talked with her awhile longer. "Take the little ones for walks on deck," she told Mrs. Begg. "They need the exercise and the fresh air will help you."

The visit with Margret Madigan was far easier. Maeve found the mother and her little ones seated at their fire. She and the baby were flourishing, and her two other children, though small, were good company for her and adored their new brother, Jack.

Flynn waited for her where he'd indicated. "The day was too nice to spend the entire time below deck."

His new attitude surprised her. "You're different today."

"You're absolutely right. I am." He guided her on a leisurely stroll. "I left a note on the door of the dispensary. In case there's an emergency, everyone will know we can be found up here."

Maeve had stopped for a bonnet before stepping up into the sun again. It shaded her face, but she couldn't bring herself to tie it under her chin, so she let the ribbons dangle. A gathering at the rail caught her attention and she joined them to see what was of interest.

The top fins of two enormous whales could be seen cutting through the surface of the water. "I've seen whales from a distance, while standing on the cliffs above the village, but never this close or from this vantage point. They are magnificent."

"I've never been to Castleville," he told her. "What's it like?"

Together they moved away from the others and walked a little farther. "The shoreline below the cliffs is trimmed with golden sands and rocky outcroppings. When we were children, we used to walk an hour or more to make our way to the bottom. We felt safe because the Donnelly brothers, Scully and Vaughan, came with us. Adventurous and strong boys, they were. There are caves to the north, but Da warned us of the dangers, and we never dared explore them."

"Your childhood sounds happy."

"We didn't have much, but we didn't realize it. Things were good before the famine. Before the sicknesses came."

"They get snow in America," he told her. "Have you ever seen snow?"

"No, never. Da saw snow in the mountains as a lad."

"There are extremes of weather, because the ocean isn't absorbing heat. So winter is cold and summer is hot. Once it snowed when I was in the city. It's pretty, but it's also an inconvenience. Shopowners must remove it from in front of their doors, and it makes the streets more difficult to travel. You and your sisters will need coats and winter boots."

"I don't know that I'll like that."

He chuckled. "We Irishmen are indeed spoiled by ideal weather."

"What was it like to grow up rich?"

No one had ever asked him that before. He had to think about it. "Like you, I knew nothing different. Not until I was older and understood the struggles of those going hungry after the blight and farmers losing their homes. For us the blight was inconvenient, but not a major problem. We simply ate more fowl and lamb. For others it was life and death."

"And on top of the hunger came disease," Maeve said.

"Money didn't draw a line there," he told her. "My father is a surgeon. I went to the finest school in England to become a physician. We had no tools or medicine to fight cholera or relapsing fever. No one was spared."

She agreed and nodded her understanding.

He rested a hand on her shoulder and led her to the side of the ship, where he dropped his hand and studied her. "You spoke to me as no one ever has, when you suggested I should face my feelings."

"I shouldn't have—"

"Yes, you should have." He was nervous to tell her what he'd done. He took a deep breath.

Chapter Twenty

"Last night God showed me some things. Plain as day. I can't deny His guidance."

Maeve glanced across the water and then back at his face, waiting patiently for him to continue. He'd never started a conversation like this before—not one that included God. Her curiosity was piqued.

"You are perceptive, and you were right. I'd been hiding from my feelings. I had buried every emotion that remotely reminded me of my former life—all the memories, the bad and the good, as well."

"You were simply protecting yourself. It's understandable. It's human nature to shield a wound."

"But I was missing so much by denying even the pain. I couldn't bear to live with it, so I never let myself think about it. I still have to deal with feeling as though I failed my wife and son…but I'm no longer ignoring the guilt, so now I can finally learn how to deal with it."

She understood the regret. There was always the question of whether or not she could have done something differently that would have changed the outcome for others. She lived with the burden of having let them down, even though she knew she'd done all she knew to do. How much worse must it be for him—a man who studied and had the finest medicine and equipment at hand—to helplessly stand by and lose the two people he loved most in all the world?

"I do understand," she assured him. "Truly I do. But there's no known cause and no cure for cholera, Flynn. You are not responsible for letting them die."

"The cause is so *close* to being discovered," he said. "I know with certainty the spread has something to do with drinking water or waste or other contamination. I have funded all my own research. I searched for a partner to join me, but was unsuccessful. My efforts are too late for Johanna and Jonathon, of course, but not for future victims."

"Perhaps you'll have more of an impact in America and your colleagues will listen. Is there as much cholera in America?"

"New York experienced outbreaks in the early thirties and late forties. Most say the '32 epidemic spread from London. New York was and is squeezed into over-crowded wards by an influx of immigrants."

"What about Ontario and Quebec City? I've heard many people left County Galway bound for northern areas."

"The worst of the coffin ships landed there," he told her. "They developed quarantine stations on an island, anchored ships and kept passengers secluded until health officers allowed them into the country. Hundreds and hundreds died right on the ships."

"Those are the ship's conditions you devoted yourself to improving."

"Something needed to be done. The only businesses flourishing along the coast were coffin makers and un-dertakers. Now if shipowners don't comply and still overcrowd or don't supply adequate clean water, they are fined so heavily they can't continue to operate."

"And you know that the death of your wife and child are no more your fault than those of all the other people, while your measures meant that untold lives have been *saved.*"

"I know. But I have trouble accepting that I'm a physician and I was helpless to save them."

"I understand, Flynn. I felt helpless, too, when my neighbors grew sick and died. When my own father caught influenza and didn't recover. Nothing I did made any difference. I thought if I'd had more knowledge, if I'd had better medicines, they wouldn't have suffered the way they did. They would still be alive and life wouldn't have had to change. I have longed for those days before the blight, before death came knocking at every door in our village."

He nodded his understanding. "We have so much in common, Maeve. But you didn't shut yourself off as I did. God showed me plain as day what I'd been doing by not letting myself remember my wife and child. Last night I welcomed the memories."

"I'm happy for you."

"There's more."

She studied him curiously. What more could there be? His realization and vow to change was monumental. She waited.

"When I left the dispensary this morning, I sought out Miss Boyd."

"Kathleen?"

"Yes."

"To share all this with her? I suppose that was fitting."

"I only touched on these things. She wouldn't have understood."

Before she could digest his words, a sweeping breeze caught her bonnet, and sailed it up into the air and dropped it in the ocean. Maeve reached up to her tousled hair and belted out a surprised laugh.

She and Flynn watched her bonnet drift on the current, growing farther and farther away.

She laughed again as it finally sank into oblivion. "A fitting demise for the old girl," she sputtered and pealed out yet another burst of laughter.

Flynn wore an expression of complete confusion. "What's so funny? You're not upset?"

She took the pins from her hair and let it fall about her shoulders and catch in the wind. "No, I'm not upset. It was at least ten years out of date and secondhand to boot."

His dark gaze took in her wild hair. "I don't think another woman exists who would laugh if her bonnet was carried off and dropped into the Atlantic."

"Life's too short to mope about headwear."

He'd been wearing half a smile, but it disappeared with his next words. "I spoke with Kathleen about her mistaken beliefs."

Chapter Twenty-One

"I told Kathleen I'd never had feelings for her."

Maeve stared at him. "You told her that?"

"Not in those precise words, but yes."

She pushed her hair away from her face and looked out at the ocean. Why had he told her this? In a short time they'd developed a relationship that completely puzzled her. Theirs was a relationship unlike any that she'd ever had with a family member or even a friend. She was comfortable talking to him about experiences and even many of her feelings—things she'd never told anyone before. She found herself wanting to know more about him. He'd confided a careful measure with her, but there was much more below the surface.

Talking about Kathleen seemed different somehow. Maeve had assumed he was fond of the woman—that he intended to marry her. Apparently, that wasn't the case.

Maeve collected her thoughts. What exactly had she prayed? She'd asked for Flynn's grief and guilt to be lifted and for Kathleen to see the truth. She'd meant the truth about God's love for her and how He wanted her to treat others, but maybe Flynn seeing the truth about

Kathleen was an answered prayer, too. *You're an amazing God.*

"How do you feel today?"

"Relieved. Unburdened."

"Well, then, I'm pleased for you."

"I'm more than pleased, Maeve. I'm relieved and thankful—and actually anticipating any more changes God wants me to make. I'm able to remember my wife and our life together. I can think about my son now, and, even though it's painful, it's no longer more than I can bear."

His revelations were a lot to take in. She went over everything he'd told her, absorbing these changes in his attitude.

After a minute he asked, "I didn't even ask you how Mrs. Begg and Mrs. Madigan are."

Maeve explained how her visits had gone. "And your call on Goldie?"

"I found her at her fire. She's done a fine job keeping her dressings and bandages clean. She probably has several more weeks of healing, but as long as she's as diligent as she has been, she'll heal well. I warned her she may have discoloration, even once the skin renews itself."

"I doubt she'll care about that, as fortunate as she is to have not been more seriously burned."

"Now that I've had occasion to speak with her when she's not suffering, I've seen what a positive and spirited woman she is. Her husband is attentive, and I don't think that's just because of this accident."

"I saw that, too. Remember how he didn't want to leave her side for an instant?"

"I suppose we should return and see if anyone's left

messages. I want to make a fresh cotton paste for Goldie and leave it with her."

Maeve accompanied him to the dispensary, and they resumed their tasks.

That evening, Aideen and Mrs. Kennedy had dinner with the captain, so the sisters cooked their supper and ate together with only the three of them gathered at the fire.

"This is a change," Bridget remarked.

"I enjoy having the other ladies with us, but sometimes being alone is nice, too." Nora uncovered the skillet cake she'd made. "I'll let this cool."

Maeve told them about the woman who'd given her her daughter's clothing that day.

"I wish the dresses would fit me," Bridget said. "I would dearly love so many new pieces of clothing. I'm perfectly green with envy."

"You're not envious," Nora cautioned, like a mother.

"All right, I'm not envious. But I do wish someone my size would grow out of her clothing."

"Why, you've always received my outgrown clothing," Nora told her, feigning a serious expression.

"You know that's not what I mean, and your dresses weren't new when they fit *you,*" she lamented.

"You never had anyone to impress anyway," Maeve teased her. "Vaughan Donnelly always thought you were beautiful, even barefoot and dressed in Nora's hand-me-downs."

"Vaughan Donnelly was a toad," Bridget returned.

Maeve laughed.

"He helped Da mend our roof last year," Nora reminded her. "And he and Scully dug Da's grave, if you'll remember."

Bridget ate the last of the stirabout. "Maeve speaks of

him as though he was a romantic interest. Nothing could be more ridiculous. He married someone else, if you'll recall."

"I merely pointed out that you've always been beautiful, even without expensive dresses."

Bridget gave her a sidelong look that revealed her skepticism. "I might just wear those new dresses of yours anyway, even if the hems come to me knees and the cuffs bark me elbows."

"I'm not that much shorter than you! You're exaggerating."

"I'll be a leader in fashion when the ship docks. Soon all the American women will want skirts to their knees, so their knickers show."

"Bridget Murphy," Nora admonished. "Don't be vulgar."

Maeve and Bridget exchanged a mischievous look.

"Did I mention the dresses look like something a twelve-year-old would wear? They might suit your maturity level, after all."

Bridget couldn't hold back her amusement at that remark, and the two of them giggled like schoolgirls.

"Honestly, sister," Maeve told her. "You may find some underpinnings that will suit you, but I dare say most will be too small. You're welcome to whatever you want, however. You can even use the fabric if it strikes your fancy."

"Some day I shall have a closet full of beautiful clothing," Bridget told them. "Why, I won't wear the same dress twice in a month."

"I need a new bonnet," Maeve told them and shared her tale.

"I believe we should toss all of them overboard before we get to Boston," Bridget said.

Maeve sliced the flat cake that Nora had rested on the bricks to cool and prepared her next words. "Dr. Gallagher is not interested in marrying Kathleen Boyd."

Now she had her sisters' attention. "How do you know?" Nora asked.

"He told me so today. Last night I told him she had indicated their relationship was more serious, and this morning he told her there was no future for the two of them."

"I had assumed they had an understanding," Nora said. "I guess none of us realized it was one-sided."

"How did she take it? Did he say?"

"He didn't give details, no."

Bridget got a gleam in her eye. She picked up a slice of cake and leaned forward. "Maeve, I dare say he's sweet on you. It makes perfect sense now."

"That's impossible."

"Of course it isn't. It's plain he admires you. He seeks your opinion and relies on you."

"That's merely part of our doctor-assistant relationship."

"Tell me he hasn't shared with you more than talk of poultices and warts."

Maeve's cheeks grew warm. "There have been no warts that I know of."

"You two discuss more than rashes and coughs, now. Admit it's true."

She shrugged. "It's true."

"Aha!" Bridget took a bite of her cake. "This is a tasty sweet, Nora. Thank you." She enjoyed her slice and brushed her fingers clean before returning her attention to Maeve. "Once the man saw you beside Miss Boyd, Maeve, his decision wasn't difficult to make."

"It wasn't like that at all."

"No, how was it, then?"

Maeve picked up their dishes. "God revealed some things to him."

"Of course He did. And one of those things was that you'd be a far more suitable wife than Miss Boyd."

"That's quite an assumption," Nora piped up. "But I have seen the way the man looks at you, Maeve. There may still be some things God hasn't revealed to him."

"Do you really think he likes me in that way?"

"I've only seen him with you when Miss Boyd was there, as well, so I can't really say. But I did observe that he didn't look at her the same way he looked at you."

"He's from a family of physicians," Maeve said. "They own homes in three different countries. He's been to university and studied in England. He's met fascinating people. I'm only a simple farm girl who grew up barefoot and dirt-poor. What could a man like him possibly ever see in me?"

"The same things we see," Nora told her. "A generous, compassionate, gifted and beautiful woman who has a lot of love to give."

Maeve explained then how Flynn had lost his family and blamed himself for so long.

"And it took a simple farm girl who grew up barefoot and dirt-poor to show him he needn't blame himself." Nora stored away their cooking utensils.

Maeve smiled. "Perhaps."

Bridget released a sigh. "It's ever so exciting. A shipboard romance."

"Don't be putting the cart before the donkey," Maeve warned her.

"If you're to be marrying into the Gallagher family, you'd best be removing donkeys from your vocabulary."

Maeve picked up the bonnet Bridget had discarded.

She waved it above her head. "Stop with your match-making or I will pitch this over the side of the ship."

"No, you won't. You're far too practical."

"Watch me."

"If you think I care, you're mistaken."

Maeve stood and marched away.

From behind she heard her sister leap to her feet, so she ran. Upon reaching the railing, she threw the bonnet as high as she could.

A minute later it was a blot on the surface of the glistening water.

Standing with both hands on the rail, Bridget leaned forward. "I wish it had been daylight, so I could have appreciated the sight of it swooping out over the waves. Perhaps a dolphin has it now."

"And is taking it home to his dolphin wife."

They laughed together.

"We can do Nora's tomorrow." Maeve's tone was impish.

"We cannot."

"Well, we can't afford to lose any more of ours or we'll burn in the sun."

"You're so right. Nora's 'tis."

Maeve barely slept for thinking of Flynn and her sisters' disclosures about the way he looked at her. Considering him in a romantic way had been forbidden these past weeks. He was her employer. She'd believed he was courting another woman.

He would remain her employer for only another ten days or so. And now she was aware he had never been courting another woman. Kathleen Boyd was not his sweetheart.

Maeve had been a fine one to point out to him how

he'd buried his own thoughts and feelings. She had pretended no interest in him whatsoever, while a deeply buried longing wished he would look at her twice.

He was a marvel. Handsome, mannerly, educated. He'd traveled the world and learned more than twenty Castleville villagers put together would ever know. He challenged her thinking. His nearness took her breath away, and sometimes, at the mere thought of him, butterflies fluttered in her belly.

She hadn't dreamed she had a chance with a man as fine and smart as Flynn Gallagher. What could he possibly ever see in her? Nora had suggested he found her compassion, gifts and beauty appealing. She didn't see herself like that, but he himself had said she was beautiful.

Maybe there was hope. *Show me the way, Lord. Make it plain enough for a simple girl like me to see.*

As the night drew out, she considered the married couples she'd known and tried to think of ways the pairs were different and yet compatible. Her parents' relationship had always seemed ideal, but now that was in question, due to the curious letter from Laird O'Malley.

The gentleman who'd come to the dispensary with a cold and who had been on his way to visit sons in America had spoken reverently of his wife. Maeve remembered her name because of the way he'd said it. *Corabeth.*

Would a man ever say her name like that? Would Flynn?

She thought of the big McHugh man's devotion to Goldie. She'd guess they shared a similar background, however. His dedication to his wife had been endearing.

Mrs. Fitzwilliam had been married to a man of her own station, too. A person could go mad from this kind of back-and-forth thinking. Maeve deliberately closed her eyes and forced herself to focus on something else. She thought of Grace and wondered how things would turn out when they landed. She thought of Mrs. Conley and her desire to settle on land and grow a garden. There was another devoted couple…

It was a long night.

Chapter Twenty-Two

Maeve was up before any of the others in their cabin. She washed in tepid water and wet her hair to control it. After gathering it in the most severe braid she could muster, she fastened it on the back of her head. A look in Bridget's hand mirror showed her that it looked nothing like Kathleen's sleek dark style.

After examining each of the dresses she'd hung the previous day, she selected one she thought would fit the best. The underskirt was a whole new experience, and she had to wear one of the hand-me-down chemises because of the dress's square neckline.

"Bridget," she whispered. "Wake up and fasten the back of this dress for me, please."

Her sister blinked at her. "What day is it?"

"Thursday. Now please come help."

Bridget wiped her eyes and climbed down from her bunk. She blinked at her sister. "Oh, my. It's not so bad."

Maeve presented her back.

The dress fit pretty well, with the exception of the bodice. There hadn't been as much of Clara Mooney to stuff into this portion. Maeve wasn't twelve, quite obviously.

But she exhaled and waited for Bridget to fasten the hooks.

"I expect you'll not be takin' a deep breath today," her sister whispered from behind.

"But it looks pretty, does it not?"

"Aye. It looks lovely, it does."

Nora roused and left Grace asleep on her bunk to stretch and dress.

Others were waking now, too.

"I'll go start our fire for breakfast," Maeve offered. "Shall I put on a pot of oatmeal?"

"Aye, that would be nice, *ma milis.*" Several lamps had been lit, and Nora got a better look. "Look at you, Maeve Eileen Murphy. You're a heartbreaker to be sure."

Maeve escaped the cabin and made her way on deck.

First thing that morning, Flynn was summoned to the Boyds' stateroom.

"She refused to let me send for you." Estelle Boyd rinsed a cloth in a basin of cool water and placed it on Kathleen's forehead. "She's been feverish all night. Today, when she started vomiting, I told her I was sending for you and that was that."

Flynn might have thought her illness was feigned, as it had been the last time—if she'd come seeking him. But the fact that she hadn't wanted him calling on her today convinced him she was truly ill.

"Fever and vomiting," he said. "Other symptoms?"

"I ache all over," she told him. He'd never seen her without her hair fashioned in a stylish knot. Her face was pale. She wore a dressing gown and was lying on her bed with a sheet over her. Her mother had placed a bucket on the floor beside her. "I can't bear to roll over. My back and hips hurt severely."

"Have you done anything to injure your back?"

"Nothing. It's not that kind of pain."

He tested her pulse and listened to her heart. There hadn't been any cases of influenza aboard, but her symptoms pointed to it as a definite possibility. "Are you eating and drinking?"

"Mother brings me small meals, and I eat a few bites, but since yesterday nothing stays down."

"I'll go make you a tincture for the vomiting, and I'll check on you every few hours."

"It's not necessary to check on me."

"Actually it is. I'm the ship's doctor, and you're quite ill."

Kathleen waved him away.

Since he'd been called away from the dispensary so early, he hadn't yet seen Maeve. Entering his work area, he drew up short at the sight of the diminutive woman wearing a plain apron over a fancy pleated dress with puffed sleeves. She'd fastened her hair so tightly upon her head, the only curls visible were the little corkscrews that framed her face.

"Maeve?"

"I saw your note," she said, turning. "There has only been one patient, and it was a sailor with a scrape I cleaned and bandaged. Reeked of smoked fish, he did. I wouldn't be surprised if you could still smell it in here."

"You've never worn such a lovely gown before. Is there a special occasion?"

Pleased that he'd noticed, her face grew warm with embarrassment. "Nothing at all. I simply wanted to wear something different."

She was pretty no matter what she wore, but this color enhanced her skin and the blue of her eyes. He missed her usual tumble of corkscrews, however. Her unruly hair was part of her charm. "You look beautiful."

Forcing his thoughts back to his patient, he explained about Kathleen's condition and set about making a tincture to help her stomach ailment.

He returned to see the young woman several times. Her symptoms only worsened as the day progressed. Her condition concerned him, because he didn't have a diagnosis that satisfied him.

"Will you accompany me to Kathleen's stateroom?" he asked Maeve that afternoon. "You've seen a lot of influenza. I wouldn't mind a second opinion."

She gave him a wide-eyed stare. "*My* opinion?"

"Don't depreciate your medical knowledge, Maeve. You have an instinctive sense about these things."

She was obviously reluctant to go with him, but she agreed. She removed her apron, and the parts of the dress he hadn't before seen came into view. A large square neckline trimmed with lace drew attention to her lovely face. Another woman would have worn a jeweled necklace in that open area—an emerald most likely—but Maeve was the jewel. She didn't need adornment. He couldn't allow his gaze to linger or move any lower.

She glanced down. "Is there something wrong with my dress?"

"Not a thing."

He grabbed his leather bag and ushered her out of the dispensary.

"Why have you brought *her?*" Kathleen asked immediately.

"Miss Murphy is my assistant. You know that."

"I don't want her touching me. Poor people carry disease."

Maeve, a shining beacon of grace under duress, showed no reaction to Kathleen's caustic remark. She merely set Flynn's bag on the foot of the bed and opened it. Her composure and dignity made her all the more beautiful.

There wasn't a dress in all the world that could lend that much poise to Kathleen's character.

"I shouldn't need to point this out to you." His tone was stern, but matter-of-fact. "You're the one lying there sweating, and Maeve is the one who's perfectly healthy, yet risking her own safety to be here."

Her dark eyes flashed, and it was obvious Kathleen loathed lying there in her unglamorous and ineffectual state. "Ladies don't sweat, and there's no need to be vulgar."

He held his tongue. Why had he ever considered himself friends with this person? "Describe your symptoms this afternoon, please."

"I told you all that this morning."

"Tell me again now."

Exasperated, she tucked the sheet under her arms. "I'm feverish. My stomach is reeling. And now your boorish behavior has given me a headache."

"She didn't have a headache earlier," he said to Maeve. Turning to address Mrs. Boyd, he asked, "Have you been on deck at all or eaten today? One of us will stay here with Kathleen so you may have an hour to yourself."

The older woman's expression showed deep concern, but also appreciation for the opportunity to leave the stateroom. "That's very considerate of you, Flynn. I shall go stretch my limbs and have something to eat."

"I'll stay with her if you need to return to the dispensary," Maeve offered.

Maeve was kinder than necessary, kinder than Kathleen deserved, and her stature grew more and more in his esteem. Kathleen treated her poorly, yet she was willing to sit by her sickbed.

"You're not leaving *her* here with me," Kathleen said, though her voice was weak.

"I am."

"Look at her. She's wearing a day dress a ten-year-old would wear to tea with her mother."

At that point Estelle interrupted her daughter. Her face had turned bright red, and Flynn recognized her high color as stemming from Kathleen's rudeness. "Mind your tongue, Kathleen!" Estelle said to her daughter, and her tone displayed her indignation. "The doctor and Miss Murphy are here to help you. Don't be ungracious. It's unbecoming of a lady."

Too ill for further argument, Kathleen closed her eyes and ignored them. Again Mrs. Boyd thanked them for the respite. She left the stateroom.

"Go ahead, doctor," Maeve told him. "I'll come get you if her symptoms change."

With a nod, he left her with the patient.

As the day passed, Flynn sutured a sailor's head, removed another's splinter and checked a child's eyes and lungs after he'd been dangerously close to smoke erupting from his family's cooking fire.

The first mate had discovered a sailor unconscious in one of the supply compartments, and Flynn had declared him inebriated and in need of several hours' sleep.

When the day grew late, he again joined Maeve in Kathleen's stateroom, and she reported the young woman's condition the same. "She's been quiet, sleeping mostly."

One at a time he raised Kathleen's lids and looked

at her eyes. She roused only momentarily. Through the sheet, he palpated her abdomen.

Kathleen grunted in pain and swatted his hands away, then turned her face aside and slept again.

"I'll come back later this evening," he told Estelle.

"Thank you for your attention, Miss Murphy." Her mouth was pinched as though she wished she didn't owe either of them thanks, but she'd said the words nonetheless.

Maeve handed her a book. He assumed Estelle had lent it to her. "I'll bring you breakfast in the morning, so you won't have to cook for yourself."

Estelle couldn't meet Maeve's eyes. After an awkward moment, she extended the book. "Please keep it. You can finish it at your leisure."

Maeve accepted the gift. "Thank you. I don't have any books of my own, except my Bible, of course, so I shall treasure this one. I can't wait to see how it ends, but I'll be disappointed once the story's over. I can always read it again, though, can't I? A book is a gift that keeps giving."

Flynn thought Estelle was going to cry. He wanted to himself. He thought of the extensive libraries in two of his family's homes. They owned duplicates of many books so there were the same editions wherever they were staying and they didn't have to move them.

A good many of the immigrants he'd encountered couldn't even read, but Maeve and her sisters did have that benefit. He imagined a life where every penny and effort was spent on daily survival. The Murphy sisters were women of character.

Estelle had quite obviously been affected by Maeve's gratitude over such a simple offering, as well. She composed her features and returned to sit at her daughter's side.

Kathleen had slept during the entire exchange, so they left without disturbing her.

"Did you feel anything in her abdomen?" Maeve asked once they were in the companionway.

"Perhaps some swelling in the area of her liver. Her pain is disturbing," he said. "So many things could be causing the fever."

"What are you thinking?"

"I don't want to guess. There are a lot of things it could be."

"Such as?"

"Yellow fever. But she didn't go ashore at the island, and it's unlikely she caught it at sea."

"But not impossible."

"I don't think so."

She didn't know much about yellow fever, but she knew it was most often fatal. "What else?"

"Puerperal fever is contagious between women who have given birth, doctors and midwives. Since no one else has the same symptoms, it can't be that."

That one was unfamiliar to her.

"And there's jaundice, but I don't know how she'd have picked it up."

"And again there haven't been any other cases, and she didn't go ashore at the island."

"It's puzzling to be sure. We will know for certain if the whites of her eyes turn yellow."

"Or her skin," she added. "But either way, there's little we can do but wait. In the meantime, why don't you come join me and my sisters for our supper?" she asked.

"Thank you. I'd like that." He followed her up the ladder and across the deck.

Chapter Twenty-Three

Bridget grinned from ear to ear when she saw the doctor accompanying Maeve. "However did we get so fortunate this evening?"

"Maeve generously invited me to join you. I often eat in the galley, but any time I receive an offer to dine with someone at their fire, I accept."

"We're pleased to share our supper with you," Nora told him. "Sit now and join us. Don't wait for Maeve to light in one place. She'll be flittin' about for a while yet."

"Kathleen Boyd has taken ill," Maeve told them. "It's quite serious, so we must include her in our prayers this evening."

"But of course we will. Is there anything we can do?" Nora asked.

"Perhaps one of you could make her some gruel like Maeve made for Sean. She's not keeping down food."

"Aye, that will give her strength," Nora replied. "I'd be happy to do that." She removed the sling that held the baby. "She's just falling asleep. Would you mind?"

Her request caught Flynn off guard. He'd been self-conscious the last time he'd held Grace, with Kathleen eyeing him. He reached for the baby. It was a warm evening, almost balmy, so she was draped in a piece of light-weight flannel.

Her tiny mouth made sucking motions, and she cracked her eyes open and squinted, as though wanting to see who now held her. The hand that wasn't tucked against his chest waved and trembled, so he took it gently in his grasp and stroked her tiny arm with his thumb. Her eyes closed once again.

Through his shirt, her rhythmic breathing was calming. He understood the sisters' concern for one so tiny and helpless. He hadn't allowed himself to dwell on the situation before, because looking at her had stabbed him with such painful memories. Now he thought of his Jonathon. The dark-haired infant had been as loved and coddled as this one. He'd been a happy, chubby little fellow. He'd never had a day of want in his short life. He'd been accepted and loved. Adored.

Every child deserved to be wanted and loved. Every child deserved a chance to not simply survive, but to thrive.

His heart ached with loss.

He had so many wonderful memories. He closed his eyes and saw the first time he'd laid eyes upon his tiny child. He remembered holding him while fearful of breaking him. He thought of Jonathon lying on the bed between him and Johanna as they admired his sleeping profile. His wife had been happy. So proud and content. He'd loved her immeasurably.

"Are you all right, Flynn?"

He looked up into Maeve's questioning blue eyes. "I am now. I was remembering my Jonathon when he was this small. He had dark hair with a touch of curl. I used to smooth it down, but Johanna would coax it back up atop his head. We laughed about that."

The sisters had paused in their chores to listen.

"What month was Jonathon born?" Bridget asked.

"April."

"A spring baby. How special and appropriate. Grace is a June baby, don't we think?"

"Definitely," he answered. "She was brand-new when your sister found her."

Aideen and Mrs. Kennedy joined them then. "Are we interrupting?"

"Of course not," Nora told Aideen. "The doctor has joined us for supper, and I'm making Miss Boyd a gruel. She's taken ill."

"That's unfortunate," Mrs. Kennedy said. "Is there anything we can do?"

"We could take turns checking on her tomorrow," Bridget suggested. "I understand Maeve sat with her most of the day today. Most likely you missed your assistant at your side attending patients, doctor."

"That's generous, but until I'm certain exactly what she has contracted, it's better if we don't expose a lot of people to her."

"Of course," Bridget replied. "That's wise."

Mrs. Kennedy offered their bag of daily provisions. "It's rice tonight. I know how to prepare it now. May I?"

Maeve opened their own sack. "I doubt you'll hear a one of us decline that offer. While Nora is making the gruel, I'll mix together batter for a flat cake."

Bridget offered a small wrapped bundle. "Mr. Atwater's mother gave me raisins today. Can you use them in the flat cake?"

Flynn was impressed with how they pooled their supplies and came up with a meal. No one seemed out of sorts that they didn't have a table and chairs or fancy plates. If they'd have preferred a steaming roast with vegetables, no one spoke of it.

"You are the most contented lot of people with whom I've ever spent time." He looked from one face to the next. "You share what you have. And you're happy to do it. I can't in a hundred years picture my sisters—or my mother—preparing their meal from the ship's allotment and happily doing all this work."

"We never prepared a meal before we came aboard," Aideen admitted. "Neither of us knew the first thing about lighting a fire or cooking. The Murphys have shown us all we know."

"And bright students you are," Nora praised.

"To be honest, Dr. Gallagher," Bridget said. "Our daily provision is more food than we had in two or three days at home. It had been that way for the past couple of years. We are grateful to have this much and more than happy to share."

"I am humbled to be included." His speech was husky with emotion.

Eventually the rice finished cooking. Maeve had added onions and bits of fried mackerel to make a tasty meal.

Nora prayed, including a petition for Kathleen's healing and Flynn's wisdom in knowing how to treat her. She took Grace from Flynn, so he could eat.

"I almost made a big mistake," Flynn told them.

"What was that?" Bridget asked.

"I nearly allowed grief and discouragement to consume me. It was easy to avoid the things that hurt. I focused all my thoughts and energy on external conditions. Everything that meant something to me had been lost."

The ladies gave him their full attention.

He didn't know why he'd chosen to say this now. He

had carried nearly three years of unacknowledged pain bottled up inside. Maybe it needed to come out.

Maybe he recognized their compassion and knew they would understand.

"Everyone deals with grief in their own way," Nora said.

"Continuing as I was would have led to a colossal ruination of my life and peace of mind."

Bridget and Aideen didn't raise their gazes from their tin plates. Nora and Maeve exchanged a look.

Mrs. Kennedy spoke up. "I was married to a wonderful God-fearing man who was taken from this earth before his time, Doctor. I understand the hopelessness that comes with the cessation of all the dreams you shared with that person. The anguish is difficult to live with. You feel alone in the world, as if no one understands or really cares."

He studied her, thoughtfully. He'd never spoken so openly with anyone, except Maeve. It felt good to talk with the others. "You do share my experience, ma'am. If you don't mind my asking, what does that loss feel like now?"

Mrs. Kennedy appeared thoughtful for a moment. "I still think of my husband often, but sometimes it's as though that part of my life didn't really happen."

"I don't want that to happen. What I mean is, I've just recovered the memories. I don't want to lose them."

"You won't lose them, young man. But they will fade. I never had another opportunity to marry. I think I would have felt more productive and fulfilled if I had. Instead, I have remained a widow to this day."

"Perhaps you'll meet someone in Boston," Bridget said.

Mrs. Kennedy only laughed. "And perhaps a gull will come flying overheard wearing your bonnet."

Her jest lightened the mood and they all shared a hearty laugh.

"Maeve threw Bridget's bonnet overboard," Aideen told him.

He chuckled. "I should have liked to have seen that. The demise of Maeve's own bonnet brought her much merriment."

"We've plans to toss one of Nora's. You are invited."

"The two of you can fling your own headwear in the ocean if you like, but leave mine be," their older sister warned. "I will still need protection from the elements when I arrive in Boston."

"Speaking of arrival in Boston," Aideen said. "We are ready for final fittings on your dresses before we add the trim and do the hems."

"I can't wait!" Bridget turned to him. "We're making dresses. Beautiful dresses! Each of us will have a new one the day we dock. Our generous friends have provided everything—the fabric and trim, ribbon and thread. And each dress is unique."

"Suited to each sister appropriately," Aideen added.

"That will be a sight to behold," he told them. "The young men of Boston will be falling over each other to carry your bags and assist you wherever you want to go."

Bridget laughed, but it was plain she was delighted with his teasing prediction and flattery. "Do you really suppose so?"

"Indeed I do. Not that a one of you needs a beautiful dress to win a man's heart. Your natural beauty is more than sufficient."

"I would never have considered you a man to take risks," Nora told him.

"Risks?" he asked.

"Seems, it does, you've risked life and limb a time

or two to dangle from the parapet at Blarney Castle and kiss Mr. McCarthy's stone."

The others had a good laugh over her teasing remark.

"As a matter of fact, never have I kissed the Blarney Stone." He feigned an indignant frown and pressed a hand to his shirt front. "Everythin' I say comes straight from me heart."

The women did share a hearty laugh over his affected brogue. Because his speech was always so proper, it made his teasing all the more humorous.

Maeve sliced the flat cake into equal portions and passed a piece to each. She'd sensed his eyes on her more than once that day. As soon as she'd gotten to the dispensary that morning, she'd felt foolish for wearing this dress. His appreciative gaze had relieved her discomfort—until Kathleen had pointed out the dress was made for a much younger person.

Maeve had no idea how one could tell— except that the bodice fit so tightly—but she supposed someone who knew about fashion would know. Neither Aideen nor Mrs. Kennedy had remarked.

Truth be told, she was having difficulty breathing and couldn't wait to change for the night. It had been worth the discomfort to hear Flynn's praise, however.

She reached for the empty pan, but Bridget brushed away her hand. "I'll do these dishes. I played games and read with the Atwater girls all day while you worked, so you go for a walk and enjoy the night air."

Maeve straightened. She wasn't going to argue with that.

"Will you join me for a walk around the deck?" Flynn asked.

Aideen extended a shawl, and Maeve accepted it. "That sounds nice."

As they passed fires, more than one person greeted the doctor.

"Will you call on Kathleen yet again tonight?" she asked.

"Yes, I want to check on her once more." They walked at a leisurely pace. "I'm missing something, and I can't figure out what it is. I have diligently sought out any others with the same symptoms. There are none. A contagious disease takes three or four days from the time of contact to reveal itself."

"Then it's not contagious."

"We can't be sure."

"Her mother's fine, she is."

He sighed. "I know. Yes, I know. It's completely frustrating."

A streak of lightning zigzagged across the distant sky. A moment later thunder sounded in the distance.

"Not another storm, I pray," she breathed.

"It's miles away." He rested his arm on her shoulder and drew her close. "And the wind isn't blowing it this direction. Are you afraid of storms?"

She liked his nearness. "We never had many to speak of at home, but no. I simply don't like the idea of being stuck in a cabin below with others who are frightened."

"Perfectly understandable." They stopped at the rail and gazed out across the water, and he dropped his arm to her waist. "My Johanna didn't like thunderstorms. And she was deathly afraid of spiders."

"She wouldn't have liked to clean some of the places I've cleaned, then. How did she feel about pigs? We had one neighbor who kept two pigs and left them to wander in and out of her house through the open door."

"Johanna wasn't a farm girl. She would probably have run them out."

"I tried that when I was there for the birth of one of her children. The pigs just laid down in the doorway and wouldn't budge."

"Were they young pigs?"

"At one time, but not by the weekend I was there."

"Johanna had a cat. A white one, with long silky fur. Even after Jonathon's birth, she would let him jump up and lie on her lap, and she'd stroke his head.

"She used to plan dinner parties down to the last detail. Four courses followed by coffee and dessert in the sitting room. She played the pianoforte for the guests. What a picture that was."

Maeve understood that all this was new to him. Remembering his wife, thinking of his child. She'd encouraged him to lift the cloak he'd kept over his past and let himself feel, and he was doing it.

"Once I married her, I never expected to find myself alone again." His voice held a wistfulness and regret she'd never heard before. "I didn't expect to be sailing across the Atlantic again and again. I don't know how I got here."

"Escaping, most likely. Running away."

"What a coward I've been."

She edged away so she could look into his face. "Not a coward, Flynn. You turned your pain into worthwhile endeavors. Look at all the good you've done. Your efforts to improve ship conditions everywhere are saving hundreds of lives every day."

"I didn't do it alone."

"Why don't you stop and give yourself a little credit, instead of considering your work part of your punishment?"

Without replying, he speared her with a censuring look.

"You've allowed yourself very few comforts," she

pointed out. "Compared to the life you're used to, these ships are barren. I dare say you wouldn't be eating what you ate tonight if you were at home."

"I no longer have a home."

"What about your house in County Galway?"

"I signed the deed over to the nuns. It's now a found-ling home."

"That was a generous thing to do. Another worthwhile gift."

"It was also cowardly. I never had to face the rooms where my son spent his few short years of life."

"Part of your punishment," she guessed.

"My son deserved to live."

"Yes, he did."

"I should have spent the rest of my life with Johanna, watching him grow up and become a man."

"Yes," she agreed.

She'd been foolish to imagine Flynn had any true interest in her. He'd had the love of his life and lost her. Maeve was no society wife. She didn't know the first thing about dinner parties. She was a simple foolish girl.

"It's time I took myself off to bed, 'tis."

Chapter Twenty-Four

Maeve hurried away to the cabin. Her sisters had arrived ahead of her and were already changed.

"Please help me out of this dreadful dress," she said to Bridget.

"You looked so pretty. The doctor couldn't take his eyes off you."

"You're reading too much into things," she warned her sister. "He's still very much in love with his wife."

Sleep eluded her yet another night. Maeve gave up trying to sleep, dressed in her familiar plain attire, went for fresh water and made her way to Mrs. Boyd's stateroom.

"I'm glad to see you." Estelle ushered her in. "She hasn't been fully alert since yesterday."

"Have you been making her drink water?"

"Yes. She doesn't wake, but she'll drink for me."

"We'll use the remainder of that bucket to bathe her now and this fresh one is for drinkin', 'tis."

Estelle helped Maeve bathe her daughter, preserving her modesty with a sheet as they cooled one area at a time. Maeve understood Estelle's desperation only too well. As morning neared, she told the woman to lie on the cot they'd had set up to get some rest and promised she'd remain by Kathleen's side.

Picking up a small Bible, she turned the lamp higher and read through the Psalms. She'd always found it interesting how David's life had often been turbulent. He'd made big mistakes and he'd fled from Saul's army to hide from the man's jealous wrath, but he'd always turned to God in every situation. Some of his writings were desperate pleas and others love songs to his God.

She skipped through more familiar verses to one she'd read less times. *O give thanks unto the Lord; for He is good: because His mercy endureth for ever,* the verses said in repetition.

Were those words repeated so many times so that simple people like her would get the point or because they were written as a song? She read them over several times, imagining how David would have sung them.

It is better to trust in the Lord than to put confidence in man. Or in princes, the next verse said.

It was surely better, then, to put her trust in the Lord, rather than her own knowledge or in any other person. She called on the Lord in distress, too. Many times.

She read down farther, then went back to the beginning and softly read the whole verse aloud to Kathleen. "Kathleen," she said once she'd read it all. "The Lord is your strength and your salvation. You shall live and not die. You and I both will declare the works of the Lord and praise Him. He hears us, and He's our salvation. We rejoice in this day and we are glad in it. God is good, and His mercy endures forever."

Mrs. Boyd sniffled from her cot, and Maeve supposed she had overheard her.

It didn't matter how Kathleen had treated her. Maeve

was called to be at her side, to minister to her and pray over her, and so she would.

Sometime later, she must have fallen asleep in the chair, for a soft tap at the door startled her awake.

Flynn entered the unlocked door and joined her. "How is she doing?"

"The same."

"How long have you been here?"

"I couldn't sleep."

Estelle rose from the cot and straightened her hair. "She's been here half the night."

"What baffles me," Flynn said. "Is that no one else aboard the ship has these symptoms. It's as though she's been in contact with someone or something that no one else has. Which is highly improbable."

"The two of you eat the same food," he said to Estelle. "Share meals."

Estelle nodded. "Even when we eat with the captain and Mrs. Conley, everyone has the same fare."

Maeve thought back to the evening she and her sisters had dined at the captain's table along with Kathleen and Estelle. That evening had come to mind more than once, but she'd deliberately worked to set aside the memory of Kathleen's rude behavior.

Bridget had been so proud of her ivory bead necklace.

Mrs. Conley had purchased lamb on the island, and they'd all eaten it with no ill effects.

Maeve had purchased fruit and shared it with her sisters.

They kept going back to the fact that Kathleen hadn't even gone ashore. What was it she'd said? She searched her memory. Something to the effect that she and Estelle had remained onboard as though setting foot on the island was beneath her. *There's nothing else of value to be found,* she'd said. *Only cheap trinkets made by the natives.*

Nothing else?

Her memory screamed Kathleen's words and Maeve grabbed Flynn's sleeve.

He looked to her.

"She said she sent a sailor to purchase shellfish."

He glanced at Estelle, who nodded. "She loves oysters. I don't know where she got that affinity, because I certainly don't share it. She bought fresh oysters as well as smoked, because they last longer."

"When did she last eat them?"

Estelle shrugged. "Several days ago."

"That's it," he said to Maeve and looked at Kathleen's eyes. "The whites are a little yellow today."

"What does that mean?" Estelle asked.

"It means her liver is struggling to handle the contamination."

"What can we do?" Maeve asked.

"Fluid in and fluid out is her best hope."

"She drinks for us," Maeve told him.

"Good. Make her drink as much as you can. A cup every ten minutes. Maybe more of that gruel for her blood."

"I'll make it."

Estelle sat on the chair Maeve had vacated and sobbed into her hands. "I can't lose her. She's all I have in the whole world." She looked up at Flynn. "Please save her."

Maeve's heart dipped, not so much at the plea, but at how she knew Flynn would feel about it. He'd dealt with so much guilt already, and he was a man upon whom responsibilities weighed heavily.

Quickly, before he could react or reply, Maeve picked up Estelle's own Bible and opened it to Psalm 118. She ran her finger down the page and then showed the verses to Estelle. "'It is better to trust in the Lord than to put confidence in man,'" she read. "'It is better to trust in the Lord than to put confidence in princes.' We do what we can do, but we're only human. Place your trust in God now, and look to Him."

Estelle nodded tearfully. "Yes. Yes, I will."

Maeve stopped Flynn with a hand on his arm. "May I speak with you for a moment?"

"Of course."

"You are smarter by far than I am. I certainly would never want to step on your toes or elevate myself."

"Say what you like, Maeve. Do you have an idea?"

"You're now convinced this is jaundice."

He nodded. "It's the only diagnosis that makes sense."

"The mariners along our coast sometimes came in contact with Chinese sailors. My mother learned that the Chinese treated jaundice with licorice or ginger tea."

He thought a moment. "Licorice being a liver detoxifier."

"And the ginger tea helps with the nausea and vomiting."

"I'll send Sean and Emmett to ask all the passengers if anyone's brought licorice aboard. I have ginger root. It's definitely worth a try. Good suggestion."

Maeve headed on deck to prepare the gruel.

She remained with Kathleen and Estelle the rest of the day, following Flynn's directions while he attended to his regular duties and stopped by every chance he got.

Maeve napped briefly on the cot that afternoon. When she awoke, she sent Estelle to sit with her sisters for supper on deck and fed Kathleen strong ginger tea.

She glanced at Kathleen's comb and knew how hopeless the tool would be in trying to tame her hair. She had a wide-toothed comb her father had carved her years ago, and it was the only thing she could work through her curls. She worked her fingers through the mass and bound it in a fat braid. Then she washed her face with the soap Estelle had left out for her.

The lather was emollient and had an exotic smell she didn't recognize. No wonder Estelle's skin was so lovely and unwrinkled.

Flynn showed up a short time later. "You smell like coconut."

"What's coconut?"

"It's a large hard-shelled hairy nut found in the tropics. Inside is milk and white meat. The milk is used for hair and skin products, or for cooking, and the fleshy part for cooking and baking."

"I believe I'd like to try a coconut."

"I should have found you some on the island. The scent suits you."

"It does?"

"Yes. Natural, fresh. A perfume would never do you justice." He leaned over her and inhaled.

His nearness was disturbing, as always.

Without intending to, she leaned into him and rested against his warm strength, her cheek to his chest. She closed her eyes, and the moment seemed so natural and right. He had his own scent, too, one she'd noticed many times—sandalwood and pressed linen.

His arm came around her. "You had a long night, followed by a trying day."

His voice rumbled under her ear.

"I wanted to be here."

"I'll stay with her tonight, so you can go sleep in your own bunk."

Maeve could have remained that way forever. In his

arms she felt safe. It was a feeling she hadn't known for much of her life, a security she hadn't felt since she'd been a wee child.

She felt drained and tired. It would be nice to let someone else carry the load for a while.

That thought roused her back to her senses and she drew away. She'd only just told Estelle to put her confidence in God, not a man. God was carrying her load, and that was that.

At a sound, they both turned.

Kathleen moaned and turned her head on the pillow.

"Kathleen?" All business, Flynn hurried to her side. He touched the backs of his fingers to her forehead.

She blinked up at him. "Flynn?"

Chapter Twenty-Five

Kathleen stared at him. "Flynn, what are you doing in my dream?"

"You've been quite sick," he told her. "We're doing our best to help you get better."

"Oh, Maeve!" she said, noticing her and greeting her as though she was a long lost friend. "I knew you'd come. There's a package on the foyer table for you."

"All right. Well, I'll just get it, then." She met Flynn's gaze with raised eyebrows. "While you're awake, I have some water for you."

"Will you ask Abigail to bring tea?"

"If you'd like tea, I'll make you a pot."

"That would be lovely."

Maeve helped her drink a cup of water. Kathleen settled back on the bed and closed her eyes.

"I'll take a few minutes to go make tea and stretch my legs."

Her sisters already had tea brewed, so she poured a container full for Kathleen.

"Your gracious sisters shared their supper and prayed with me," Estelle told her.

"You'll be happy to know your daughter spoke to me only a few minutes ago."

"She did! What did she say?"

"It wasn't so much what she said as the fact that she roused and recognized Dr. Gallagher and me."

"Well, glory be!" Estelle said. "I'm taking this as a good sign."

"As am I," Maeve agreed.

The breeze on deck was balmy that evening. Maeve turned her face into it and inhaled the salty sea air.

"What is that scent?" Bridget got up and leaned over Maeve to sniff her hair, then her cheek. "Why it's you."

"It's coconut," she replied. "Mrs. Boyd let me use her soap."

"I've never smelled anything like it," Bridget said. "What kind of nut has so much fragrance?"

"It's a very large nut, actually," Estelle explained. "That grows on a palm tree."

Maeve smiled and left them to return to Kathleen.

She slept in her own cabin that night, and while the room was still crowded and stuffy, she at least had her own space and several uninterrupted hours to rest.

Sean McCorkle was waiting for her outside her cabin door when she emerged. His skin had darkened from sun, and his face had filled out. He looked positively healthy. "Sean! Good morning."

"Mornin' to you, Miss Murphy. The captain be wantin' Dr. Gallagher to call on the missus. She be feelin' poorly, she is. I couldn't find the doctor."

"He attended a patient through the night, he did. I'll go tell him right now. Thank you."

Sean darted away.

She took time to start their fire and make oatmeal and tea, which she carried below deck in a shallow crate.

Kathleen was awake when she arrived at the stateroom. Flynn appeared tired, as expected. She relayed the news about Martha Conley, so he gathered his bag and left.

"I've brought breakfast," she said and rested the crate on a trunk. "Enough for you, too, Mrs. Boyd."

After spooning oatmeal into a dish, she carried it to Kathleen. "Are you able to feed yourself today?"

The other young woman accepted the bowl. "I believe I am."

Maeve prepared Estelle a bowl and then sat with her own.

"Mother told me how long you stayed with me," Kathleen said.

"You were alarmingly sick for a few days. Your mother was exhausted from worry and from caring for you."

"I owe you both a debt of gratitude."

"You owe me nothing," Maeve assured her.

"You can be indebted to me," Estelle said to her daughter. "The fright took ten years off my life. I think I developed a wrinkle, as well." She touched a pinkie to the corner of her eye. "Perhaps two."

Her remarks amused Maeve. "Does the doctor believe the danger has passed?"

"Her eyes aren't yellow today," Estelle replied.

Kathleen straightened the covers over her lap. "That must have been highly unbecoming."

After they'd finished their breakfast and their tea, Maeve helped Kathleen wash and dress. Kathleen tried to offer Maeve a pair of silver filigree combs for her hair, but Maeve wouldn't accept them.

"I should like to repay you for your kindness," she said, and her expression was sincere. "Please take them. If you won't wear them, give them to one of your sisters."

Bridget would love to have the lovely combs. That suggestion convinced her. "Thank you."

She slipped them into her apron pocket.

"Flynn said I might take Kathleen on deck for fresh air this afternoon, if she's feeling up to it." Estelle's relief was plain. "I'm remembering what you said and the Psalm about declaring the works of the Lord. I put my confidence in Him, and my daughter is recovered. God deserves the glory for this."

Maeve met Estelle's eyes and smiled for the first time in days. "His mercy endures forever."

Tears formed in Estelle's eyes.

Flynn wasn't in the dispensary and there were no notes, so Maeve headed for the captain's cabin and knocked. Flynn's voice called out to enter and she found Martha Conley on her bed, the captain pacing the cramped space. "Got sick last night, she did."

Maeve joined Flynn beside Martha's bed.

"Hello, dear," Martha told her. "Sorry to be a bother."

"You're not a bother, now. I came to see if I could help. Does she have a fever?"

"A mild one."

"'Er heart is beatin' too fast, 'tis," the captain said from behind them. "I've driven the poor woman to her grave."

Flynn ignored him. "She has a headache and is dizzy."

"Fell down twice, she did," the captain said.

Maeve touched Martha's cheek, then rolled back her sleeve. "Her skin is hot and dry."

"What did you do yesterday, Mrs. Conley?" Flynn asked.

"Hauled in the biggest nets of fish you ever did see. Even had nice big crabs in the catch, I did."

"I'd wager you didn't drink much the entire time, and might not have even worn a hat."

"My hat blew overboard, and I couldn't be bothered to go for another while the fishin' was good."

Flynn stood. "I'm going to leave Maeve to assist you. You got too much sun, and didn't take in enough water. If you aren't cooled off, it could be dangerous." He turned to Maeve. "Get her cool. Remove constrictive clothing, keep her skin wet, simulating perspiration. Fan her. And make her drink water. Lots and lots of water."

"I am so glad you travel with plenty of clean water," she said to the captain.

"'Ave no choice with this doctor aboard. Is she going to be all right?"

"She should be fine. Let's go and let Maeve take care of her now."

"You snap out of it, you 'ear, Martha?" her husband called to her. "I'll not 'ave you passin' on b'fore I've bought you a 'ouse with a garden."

"Is this what it took to get me house?" she asked.

"Fool woman, fishin' all day in the blisterin' sun." He followed Flynn out the door.

"I don't know how you've remained at sea all these years." Maeve helped Martha out of her wrap. "Tell me where to find you some loose underclothes. Here? I've only been onboard these few weeks, and I can't wait to get on solid land. I can't think of a good enough reason to bring me back to the ocean."

"If you had a man who had the sea in his blood, you would follow 'im wherever he took you, you would. 'Tis only my affection for my husband that keeps me here. I fish to keep me sanity—and to be useful."

By evening, Mrs. Conley's temperature had gone down, and she was feeling much better. Maeve cooked for the captain and his missus and left them alone together.

The following day was the Sabbath, and Flynn insisted Maeve attend services with her sisters. The captain read from his Bible, and Martha sat upon a trunk in the first row as usual. Maeve thought he gave her tender looks now and then. She smiled to herself, remembering the crusty remarks that didn't begin to hide his concern.

After the service, Mrs. Fitzwilliam took Maeve's arm and led her aside. "I have truly lost my right mind."

"What's wrong?"

"I imagined I saw her again. I dream of young Mary at night, and then this morning I glimpsed her as I made my way here."

"A lot of young girls have black hair," Maeve told her. "Didn't you say she has black hair?"

"She does."

"And she's on your mind, so it's only natural that you'd associate another girl's appearance with your granddaughter's. I told you I used to think I saw Da in the village. Once I swore I saw him in the field, and when I looked back, there was nothin' there. Our minds play tricks on us. Do you know how to sew?"

Mrs. Fitzwilliam seemed surprised by the question. "I do needlework, yes."

"Join us for our noon meal today. We are putting the finishing touches to dresses my sisters and I will wear when we dock."

"Are you sure it will be all right with your sisters?"

"Goodness, yes."

"I don't want to be a burden. I'm just a lonely old woman, Miss Murphy."

"You're not a burden, and the way to alleviate loneliness is to make friends and volunteer your services."

She joined the sisters, along with Aideen and Mrs. Kennedy, for a meal of crab lobscouse, the crab and vegetables provided by Mrs. Conley.

"This is quite good," Aideen said. "But my mouth is watering for fried chicken."

"A slice of beef," Mrs. Fitzwilliam added.

"A lovely guinea fowl." Nora rolled her eyes comically.

"A real cake," Mrs. Kennedy suggested. "With frosting."

"Strawberries," Bridget contributed.

Maeve tested the biscuits. "'Tis quite a feast you've dreamed up. I'm only glad that I don't have to wash all the pots and pans."

The dishes only took a few minutes to wash and clear away. Nora laid out sheets to create a clean workspace. Now that the dresses had been put together, they took up a lot more space.

Mrs. Kennedy enlisted Mrs. Fitzwilliam's help with the hats, and the two of them struck up a conversation.

Judd Norton, the cowboy from the place called Nebraska Territory, stopped to extend a greeting. Nora invited him to sit, and he thumbed back his hat and joined them.

"Those are interesting boots, Mr. Norton," Bridget observed.

"They're for riding. Pointed toes make it easy to get feet in the stirrups and the underslung heels hold 'em there. 'Course I'm not wearin' my spurs onboard the ship. Riders wear spurs with blunt rowels to prod their horses."

"They're so fancy," Bridget said. "I don't imagine everyone has such a fancy pair of boots."

"No. These are my Sunday boots. I have a pair o' stovepipes I wear on the ranch. Good pair o' boots costs a man half a month's wages."

"I suppose your hat is practical, too," Mrs. Kennedy said. Being a hat maker, she would take notice.

"Yes, ma'am. The brim shades the eyes o' course. Keeps my head cool. Protects my neck from rain and snow. Why, a good hat will protect you from thorns and low-hangin' branches, carry water or grain, fan fires—and last for years.

"You can tell a man by his hat. A plainsman is different from a sou'wester. Mexicans wear a sombrero, sometimes even made of straw."

"Will we see many men wearing this sort of clothing in Boston?" Aideen asked.

"Not likely, miss. City fellas wear fancy coats and boots. Beaver hats."

"Beaver?" she asked, with raised brows.

Judd chuckled. "Trappers sell all sorts of furs for clothing. Beaver is popular because it's sleek and repels water."

"I've only just learned about all the rain and snow," Maeve told him. "Do you see snow in Nebraska Territory?"

"Snow piles so high we tie ropes from the house to the barns and privy so we don't get lost and freeze to death."

"Methinks you joined the good doctor on his trip to kiss the Blarney Stone," Nora told him, with a teasing grin. "That's a tall tale."

"I assure you, miss, it's the truth. In America we call what you're talkin' about spinnin' a yarn, but snow isn't a yarn, I guarantee you. An unexpected blizzard will freeze cattle where they're huddled along a fence line."

"Are all the parts of the country like that?"

"Down in the Southwest, it is dry as a bone, nothin' but cactus and rocks as far as the eye can see."

"And what of Boston, Mr. Norton?" Aideen asked.

"I've only visited in fair weather," he told her. "Where in Ireland did you live?"

She told him where she'd been born and raised.

"Don't reckon you'll find weather as nice or land as green in Massachusetts. But you will find opportunities. Ladies own millin'ry shops and boardin' houses."

"My aunt and I hope to buy a small establishment," she told him. "We've brought supplies to get us started and once we're settled, we'll order more."

"If Boston has too much competition, you might want to consider cities farther west for that sort of shop. Might even be more profitable."

"How does one travel west?"

"Rails are bein' laid to major cities every day. Horses and wagons are leavin' all the time."

"I suppose if we've endured a trip across the Atlantic, a few more miles won't kill us."

The conversation had narrowed down to the two of them: Aideen and the cowboy. Maeve couldn't help noticing the inflection in Aideen's voice or the way Judd cast her an engaging smile. Maeve's own heart fluttered at their sweet exchange.

She met Bridget's gaze. She and her sister shared silent recognition.

"I should be movin' on," Judd said several minutes

later. "Don't want to wear out my welcome. I might want to come back another time. I do enjoy the company."

Aideen's struggle with her expression was clear as day.

Bridget jumped up. "Aideen and I will keep you company on your stroll, if you don't mind."

"I wouldn't mind at all."

Bridget reached for Aideen's hand and pulled her to her feet. They'd only taken a few steps, when she stopped. "I almost forgot. It's my turn to get milk for Grace." She raised a hand and let it drop. "You two go on. I'll catch up with you later."

Judd touched the brim of his hat and extended his elbow for Aideen to take his arm.

Bridget sat back down with a self-satisfied smile and picked up the length of ribbon she'd been assigned to stud with seed pearls for her hat.

"Bridget Murphy." Nora's voice held that cautionary tone Maeve knew only too well. "You had better go milk that goat now. No daughter of Jack Murphy will be found tellin' an outright lie—especially not on the Sabbath!"

None of the others raised their gaze, and Maeve had a difficult time to keep from laughing.

Bridget unwrapped a clean tin cup and marched away.

"We'll have a little milk for our tea," Nora said once she was out of earshot.

The others laughed then.

Some time later, Mrs. Fitzwilliam thanked them and departed. Not long after the cowboy had returned Aideen, they were folding up their sewing because of the impending darkness when Flynn joined them.

"How do the passengers fare this day?" Maeve asked him.

"Quite well. Kathleen is much improved. You saw

Mrs. Conley at service, of course. I treated a few sailors with minor injuries." He glanced at the others, then back. "Why don't we go talk shop somewhere else, so the others won't be bored with our conversation? We can walk."

Maeve excused herself to join him, and they took a leisurely stroll. The passengers' fireplaces they passed provided scenes of merriment, domestic chores and the occasional squabble.

They came upon Mrs. Fitzwilliam and Stillman at her fire. To Maeve's surprise and delight, all three McCorkle brothers sat with them, obviously enjoying biscuits.

"Please join us! It will be a nice change to host the two of you at our fire," Mrs. Fitzwilliam said.

Stillman held out a tin plate of biscuits and they each took one.

"Young Gavin here is the same age as my Mary," the woman told them. "Here he is working and making something of himself. Why, even Sean and Emmett run errands for the captain. They have no family, did you know that?"

"We did," Flynn replied.

"I'll be buying a home when we reach Boston," she said. "I have Stillman here, of course, but young helpers would be a benefit. I would like to offer you young men a place to live. I'm a lonely old woman, and I'd be happy to have your company."

Sean looked at Gavin.

His shaggy-haired older brother appeared thoughtful. "I could work and pay you rent, I could."

"We'll work something out," the woman said.

"We can help take care o' you, like Stillman does," Gavin added.

"I'd be more than glad to pay for your help," she answered.

"We don't want no pay," Gavin insisted. "The Lord says a person should just do good without expectin' nothin'."

"An' you remind us of our granny what used to make us soup and bread when we was little."

Elizabeth Fitzwilliam dabbed the corners of her eyes.

Flynn experienced an unfamiliar glow of hope. He'd taken Sean aboard and given the three of them jobs to prevent them from suffering the fate of stowaways, so he'd felt responsible for their welfare and had been concerned about what would become of them once they landed.

The McCorkles had gone from being orphaned and homeless to having the promise of a good life. There were still a lot of things that could go wrong. The Irish were not welcome in many areas of America. It pained him to think any of these people could be turned away or spoken down to, but he wasn't going to dwell on negative possibilities.

He considered whether or not he should give them a warning, but in the end, he didn't want to discourage them. He'd already mentioned it to Maeve.

"I'll visit whenever I have an opportunity to be in Boston," Maeve told them.

Flynn didn't want to think about what he'd be doing after they landed this time. He'd had plenty of opportunity to think about the things Maeve had said to him. He wanted to deny that he'd been punishing himself by coming on these voyages.

Surviving the elements and risking contagion was like defying the fact that he'd been spared when Johanna and Jonathon had both died.

Doing without and being alone were his punishment for letting his wife and son die.

But since Maeve had forced him to recognize he wasn't to blame, he could say he'd done his time aboard the ships. The laws were in place. He could step back and be confident immigrants were safer than they had ever been. Death counts were considerably lower than ever before.

Was his work done, then?

His self-sacrifice had filled his months and occupied his thinking. What would he do if not this? Go to Edinburgh and become one of the scientists who were so involved with their research that reality blurred in the background?

Emmett showed Maeve a small wooden figure of a whale. He explained how one of the sailors had carved it for him. Maeve admired it appreciatively.

She was good with children of all ages. She fed and changed Baby Grace as though it was the most natural thing in the world. And she interacted with Emmett in a manner that drew out the shy boy and encouraged him to speak. She was efficient and compassionate in everything she did. Maeve would make a fine mother one day. A fine wife. Some man would be fortunate to marry her.

Chapter Twenty-Six

Flynn and Maeve thanked their hostess and resumed their walk. Before they'd gone very far, they came upon Mrs. Conley and the captain, seated on wooden folding chairs, admiring the sky.

"How are you feeling this evening?" Flynn asked Martha.

"My head has finally stopped throbbin'," she answered. "I learned my lesson. I'll not be fishin' the entire day without proper headwear or plenty of water."

"I've learned me lesson, as well," the captain said. "I was mighty fearful of losin' her, I was. 'Tis not a proper home or occupation for a woman, bein' aboard a ship all her livelong days. Loyal to the end, this one is, but I'll not be carryin' her back out to sea, unless o' course she wants her house and garden to be in Ireland."

"You're buying her a house?" Maeve asked, with delight in her voice.

"And settlin' down to till the ground and weed the vegetables in her garden. This shall be my final voyage as cap'n."

Maeve knelt down near Martha's chair. "Where do you want to live?"

"Ireland is no longer the land of my youth. The land-lords have starved our people and burned them out so they can become richer. People like us can't farm a piece of land without the tyrants takin' the crops." She shook her head sadly. "No, we'll be findin' us a place in America."

"They say Faith Glen is a lot like the villages back home," Maeve told her. "Perhaps you'd like to live there."

"Wherever we are, ye can be certain that we will keep in touch, we will, Maeve Murphy."

Maeve stood and self-consciously blinked back tears. "I've become attached to so many during this journey. Parting will be as difficult as leaving home was. I feel as though I've known the two of you a lifetime. I shall miss you."

"You're a sweet girl, you are." Martha reached for Maeve's hand and squeezed it.

"This is likely the last Sabbath before we reach Boston Harbor," Captain Conley told her. "Checked charts this morning, I did. We've had a good tailwind."

"I'll be glad to arrive, but after making so many friends, it will be bittersweet."

By the time they'd made it all the way around the deck a couple of times, the night sky was dark and stars winked at them.

"I thought of something when Mrs. Conley was so ill," Flynn said at last. "Before I realized what was wrong with her."

"Thought of what?"

"I thought about her wish for a home. If she hadn't sought help—or if we hadn't been able to bring down her body temperature and she had died—the captain would have had to live with his regrets. The rest of his days he'd have been sorry he put off buying her a house until it was too late. It's easy to let things go."

"I suppose it is."

"I admire you, Maeve. You sometimes act before thinking, but you always act. You say the things that are on your mind. You tell people what you want them to know before it's too late."

"Sometimes there aren't second chances," she told him. "It's no shame to confess your feelings."

"Not everyone's as brave as you."

"I'm not brave."

"You are."

She looked at him. "Is there anything you might regret not saying or doing if you don't do it before we dock?"

"There is."

Her heart fluttered. "Can you take care of it right now?"

"I'm not sure." He cleared his throat nervously and looked away.

Maeve experienced disappointment. She didn't know what she wanted him to say or do, and she'd resigned herself to the fact that he was still in love with his late wife, but there were things left unsaid between them.

"I would regret never kissing you again."

The knowledge brought her joy—and disappointment at the same time. She, too, would regret parting ways. He would take a piece of her heart with him.

"Well, I've said what I was thinking. But I don't know that I feel any better for it."

"Likely you won't feel better until you've actually done it." She took a bold step forward.

Flynn didn't waste any time. He leaned forward until his warm lips covered hers in a soft, hesitant kiss. She hadn't known kisses could send shivers along her spine or take her breath away, but this one did. The moment felt right, but it was dizzying at the same time. She grasped the front of his shirt and clung to the fabric to keep from falling.

He wouldn't have let her fall, however. He flattened his wide hands across the small of her back and gently held her in place.

She'd given a lot of thought to their previous kisses, surely more thought than was appropriate. When she'd remembered, she'd wondered if their kisses had really been so good or if her memory had blown them out of proportion.

Her memories were not inflated.

Kissing Flynn made her feel feminine…and wanted… and *disappointed.* Disappointed because this was something she could get used to, but she wouldn't have the chance. Disappointed because she'd only just discovered her feelings for him, and their time was drawing to a close.

She released his shirt. He straightened, but kept his palms against her back. Maeve took the initiative to move away, just as she'd taken the initiative to welcome the kiss, and he dropped his hands away.

The night air felt cooler than it had only minutes before. A chill ran across her shoulders and down her arms.

Was he thinking of his beloved wife? Perhaps he compared the way she'd made him feel. Maeve couldn't bear to fall short of his memories.

Something leaped in the water beyond the side of the ship, bringing them out of their reverie. Maeve turned toward the sound. "It's late," she said finally.

"Will you please let me walk you to your cabin?"

"Yes, of course."

He took her hand and led her toward the ladder. She led the way along the narrow companionway. "Rest well, Maeve."

"And you."

Even with all the troubles she'd had at home, Maeve had never had as much trouble sleeping as she had aboard the *Annie McGee*. Her problem was Flynn Gallagher, of course.

Chapter Twenty-Seven

Maeve had let herself fall in love with the handsome doctor. Even though she'd known from the beginning that she wasn't the sort a man like him could love, the inevitable had happened. From only the few mentions he'd made of his wife, it was obvious the woman had a similar background to his and had come from a well-to-do family.

Johanna had probably gone all the way through a fancy school and had read stacks and stacks of books, about which the two of them conversed at length. Most likely, Johanna had been able to entertain guests with ease and knew all about fashion and good manners. She'd been the perfect wife for a man of his position.

No wonder he'd had to bury those feelings so deeply. Losing one's true love had to be the worst heartache of all.

As she would soon learn.

Considering Maeve had known from the first time she'd met him that they were not destined to become a couple, she questioned her wisdom in letting her feelings rule. There was a proverb that said wisdom was better than rubies. Another said, "Happy is the man who findeth wisdom." She wanted to be wise. She wasn't a foolish girl.

Though she did act impetuously, it was true. She spoke before thinking and acted on instinct. It must only stand to reason then that she would fall in love headfirst and only recognize her mistake in retrospect.

She wanted to be loved by Flynn. She wanted him to care for her as deeply as he had his wife. She wanted him to want her for his wife.

What would a wise person do right now?

Sleep, of course, but she was finding that impossible.

There were only a few days until the *Annie McGee* docked in Boston Harbor. She rerouted her thoughts. She was a strong person. She could capture those wayward musings. Would she see any of the passengers who had come aboard that first week after they'd departed Ireland? The ones who'd fled the *Wellington* after a frightening fire on deck? Perhaps one of them might recognize her.

More likely they'd recognize Flynn.

Where would Captain and Mrs. Conley settle down? Maeve imagined all the years they'd been married, all the years Martha had traveled the ocean with her husband because she hadn't wanted to be apart from him. Even if she'd had a house and remained behind, she would have been lonely with him at sea.

Maeve's thoughts traveled to her mother and Laird O'Malley. Her whole life she'd believed her parents enjoyed a fairy-tale love. Now she questioned if it had been as perfect as she'd imagined. It could still be true. Apparently, her mother had chosen between two men, if the letter was a true indication, and had chosen Jack Murphy for a good reason. Love?

Praying for wisdom and sleep, she closed her eyes.

Only a few more days.

* * *

Flynn deliberately grew standoffish, placing much-needed distance between himself and Maeve. She made him look at too many things. She forced him to look inside himself.

All his past months of service she called self-punishment. What was he punishing himself for? She'd pegged it: he'd blamed himself for living when Johanna and Jonathon had died. He never even got sick.

In those early days he'd wished he'd died. Living was too painful. Remembering them was torture. It hadn't taken long until the house tormented him with memories.

He'd sold it.

People tried to comfort him, talk about his wife and child.

He'd fled from them.

His father assured him the practice would be a comfort, that family would help him come to terms with his devastating losses.

He'd quit and gone to England.

Instead of practicing medicine he'd taken up a cause that consumed his thoughts, his time, his energy. He'd lost himself in research.

He'd lost himself.

Maeve Murphy, with her unassuming grace and unaffected generosity had made a crack in the wall of his fortress. And then she'd planted her dainty foot in that crevice and brought the whole thing crashing down around him.

She made something happen that he'd deliberately protected against: he'd felt pain.

But along with pain, he felt other things.

Baby Grace inspired the same tender, protective

feelings Sean had brought about—the same feelings he thought he'd lost. Watching the trio of Murphys care for her resurrected stirrings of compassion.

The love between Maeve and her sisters made him admire them and long for something similar…long to be a part of it. They made him feel longing.

Maeve's unwavering faith in God both shamed and motivated him. Something came into play that hadn't been active for a long time—hope. If she could have that peace of mind and spirit, maybe he could, too.

When Maeve spoke of his work, he felt accomplishment. When he taught her something and she used the knowledge effectively, he experienced pride. When he learned from her—lessons like the most simple and basic principles of love—he felt humility.

Sorting through all that, he came to a hard-fought conclusion: as much as all that confused and pained him—as long as it had been—he liked feeling.

Feeling made him feel human.

Captain Conley passed the news that they would sail into Boston Harbor in two days. The relief that swept through the passengers was tangible. People sang and played union pipes on deck at all hours of the day. They hadn't had any illnesses or accidents for two days, so Maeve helped Flynn take inventory of the remaining supplies and wrap glass bottles for storage.

"We have most everything accomplished here," he told her. "Go join your sisters and friends and enjoy the day. If I need you, I'll send for you."

Kathleen was about and walking, and she and Estelle stopped by their fireplace. Bridget was helping the Atwaters pack, but Nora and Maeve were seated with Grace on her crate.

"We've brought each of you a little parting gift." Estelle opened the brocade bag she carried. "There are two bars for each of you—Bridget, too."

Maeve accepted the paper-wrapped rectangles. The scent reached her nose, and she knew immediately what lay within the wrap. "Face soap? Oh, ladies, this is so generous."

She placed a bar right under her nose and inhaled the lovely coconut fragrance.

"Thank you," Nora said. "Bridget will be grateful, as well."

"We just wanted you to know how much we appreciated your generosity."

Kathleen had been silent throughout the exchange. Her mother glanced at her expectantly. Finally, the dark-haired young woman looked at Maeve. "Perhaps when you visit Boston, you will come for tea."

"It will be nice to have so many friends in Boston," Maeve replied.

Once they'd moved on, Nora held the soap to her nose. "I shall save mine for special occasions."

"Not I." Maeve grinned. "I'm going to use it every day until it's gone." She folded all the bars together and tucked them in their basket. "My fingers are still sore from the last of our sewing. I don't know how Aideen does it day in and day out."

"She doesn't prick herself every few minutes."

Maeve chuckled. "At least all the finishing touches are done and the dresses are ready. I'm going to feel like a princess."

The afternoon passed uneventfully. Bridget had taken it upon herself to invite Judd Norton to join them that night, so the cowboy sat at their fire and shared their lobscouse. "No offense to your fine cookin' ladies, but

I am sorely missin' roast and ham. Even a buffalo steak would be a nice change right about now. The first place I go when we land will be to a restaurant with meat and gravy on the menu."

"I've seen drawings of buffalo," Aideen told him.

A visitor paused, taking them all by surprise. It was the gentleman who sat at his easel and painted each day. "Good evening, ladies. Gentleman. I hope I'm not intruding."

"Not at all. Please join us."

"I won't be staying, thank you. I simply wanted to present this to you."

He turned the canvas around so they could see what he'd painted. Maeve's heart stopped.

It was a likeness of her and her two sisters in profile. He'd painted them in stair-step fashion, with the sky and the ocean meeting in the background, and the three of them looking out across the vast Atlantic with wistful expressions.

Her heart beat again. Maeve studied the detail he'd given their hair, the turn of each mouth and the depth of their eyes. He'd captured how she felt about their voyage so instinctively and with such passion. In each face in the painting could be seen anticipation, uncertainty...hope.

A tear edged from the outer corner of her eye and she wiped it away. "It's absolutely breathtaking. I can feel the life in these people. In *us*."

Nora drew her gaze away to focus on the artist. "How did you do this? We never posed for you. At least I didn't."

"Neither did I."

"You were here every day, and you are fascinating subjects. And I have a knack for remembering details."

"An uncanny knack," Bridget agreed.

Maeve experienced regret. "We have nothing to offer you."

"There's nothing I need. If you enjoy it, that will be gift enough for me."

He was tall, so Maeve had difficulty giving him a hug, but he leaned forward to accommodate her.

"Oh, my goodness," she said when he was gone. "What an incredible gift."

"We shall hang it in the cottage." Bridget couldn't stop admiring the painting.

The instruments had all tuned up again, and men, women and children gathered to sing and dance. Bridget tugged Nora's hand and beckoned Maeve and Aideen. "Let's join them!"

Cuddling Grace, Nora followed, and their little group joined the bigger gathering. It was a lively tune, and the sisters joined the singing. "'As I got down to Turra market, Turra market for to fee. I fell in with a wealthy farmer, the barnyards of Delgaty. A linten addie toorin addie, linten addie toorin ae. Linten lowrin lowrin lowrin, the barnyards of Delgaty.'"

Judd grinned at the nonsensical lyrics, but he tapped his foot and clapped.

"'He promised me the one best horse that e'er I set my eyes upon. When I got to the barnyards, there was nothing there but skin and bone.'"

Maeve spotted the McCorkle boys with Mrs. Fitzwilliam, and they appeared to be having a jolly time. The brothers had all put on weight and looked clean and healthy. She hoped she got to see what became of them.

Her gaze found Flynn. He stood beside Margret Madigan and her children, and he was holding the baby in the crook of his arm.

Aideen laughed and clapped and finally grabbed

Judd's hand and pulled him toward the throng of foot-stomping dancers.

"I don't know how to dance a jig," he balked.

"There's nothing to it. You just move your feet."

Maeve had to laugh, because he looked so out of place among the immigrants in his hat and fancy boots.

Seeing Flynn disturbed her. As much as she wanted to put him out of her mind, he was always there. She leaned into Nora. "I have to check on something."

Quickly, she moved away from the crowd of merrymakers, pausing only to check that their fire had died down to glowing embers, and moved along to the far end of the ship, where she could be alone.

The stars had chosen this night to mockingly shine brightly and wink in the vast sky. It should have been the best night of the trip. She wanted to experience closure. She wanted to move forward into this new life with no regrets.

Help me, Lord.

"Maeve?"

His voice startled her. She turned. "Did you finish the packing?"

Flynn stood close and rested one hand on the side. "I don't want to talk about packing or patients, Maeve."

"Oh. All right. Is something else on your mind?"

"Aye. The same thing that's been on my mind ever since this voyage began."

"What's that?"

"You."

"I didn't mean to trouble ye."

"Trouble me is all you've done. Challenged me. Frightened me. I don't believe you've spared me a thing."

"Whatever have I done?" His words disturbed her now.

"You're just you, and that's enough. More than

enough. You made me look at myself. You're perceptive, and you never missed a chance to point our my self-defeating actions."

Maeve winced. "Mother always did say I had a tendency to lay things out in plain sight. I'm sorry if I overstepped. I meant no offense."

"Your plain truths were just what I needed. I was running away. From myself, from things I was too cowardly to deal with. I thought if I kept busy enough I'd never have to face things that were painful. It doesn't work that way."

"And now you can talk about your wife and son," she supplied.

"Yes. And say their names. I hadn't even spoken their names in years, Maeve."

"You will always have the memories of your time together."

"And I've let them go. Released them into God's care. I know they've been there all along, but on my part, I wasn't letting go. It seemed a betrayal."

"I understand."

"I realized something else, too. For me death was always defeat. Death meant I hadn't been successful at my job. But I've been able to accept that death is a natural part of life, as odd as that sounds."

"It doesn't sound odd at all."

"You're satisfied your loved ones are in a good place, waiting for you. Our years here on earth are but a blink of an eye to God. We'll join them soon. Death isn't the end of life, but the beginning of life eternal. That gives me comfort."

Maeve blinked back the sting of tears. "As it does me."

"I'm finished with this shipboard life. I need a purpose again. I'm ready to move on."

"Meaning you won't be sailing again soon?"

"I hope not to sail for a long time. I want a home. A family."

Her stomach lurched. He had told her he wasn't interested in Kathleen.

"What's your deepest desire, Maeve?"

She'd only recently admitted it to herself. The wish was still fragile. "Not so different from everyone else's, I expect."

"Won't you tell me?"

She shook her head.

"Tell me," he coaxed.

She took a deep breath. She'd made a fool of herself before, what was once more? "I want to be loved. Wholeheartedly. Unselfishly. I want a love that knows no boundaries. A love that age only deepens. And I want it while I'm young."

"Your wish is easy to fulfill. In fact, it's already done."

In the background the music and gaiety was a contrast to their serious conversation. "How can that be?"

He reached for her hands. She hadn't realized how chilled hers were until the warmth and strength of his captured them.

"Because I already love you. I fell in love with you when you saved Sean's life and insisted he let you scrub him and wash his hair. I fell in love with the way your brogue is exaggerated when you're arguing a point or when you're put out. I love your bravery and the way you challenge my thinking. I love how you do what's right—what comes straight from your heart—without compromise or question."

Maeve was listening, but her mind was catching up with her ears.

"I love how your hair curls around your ears when you've tried so hard to tame it. I love the twinkle in your eyes when you're amused. I love that you sing a little off-key."

"I don't."

"You do, but it's endearing. I love how you can talk to anyone and how you really, really care about them. I love how real you are, Maeve. How touchingly, beautifully real you are. You don't possess a single affected trait. Not one.

"My hair's too red."

"It's the perfect color to me."

"I'm too small."

"You're the perfect size for me."

She took a breath and released it. "I'm a poor farm girl with one good dress, and it was a gift I haven't even worn yet."

"There's only one thing that could be a problem."

"What is it?"

"I'll not ask you to marry me if you don't think you could love me in return. I wouldn't want—"

She reached up and placed her fingertips over his lips.

"I don't foresee a problem, Dr. Gallagher. But before I say it, I have one more question."

"Amssmms-bfft."

She removed her fingers from his lips. "What?"

"Ask anything you like."

"Are you able to love me as much as you loved Johanna?"

"I don't deny I loved her. But God and I had a long talk. I actually listened this time. I released her and Jonathon. I will always remember them and love them, but I'm still alive and I want to live the rest of my life loving you. I promise I'll make you a good husband, and you'll never want for anything."

"I don't want to be spoiled."

"It could never happen."

"Do you think you might stop talking long enough to kiss me and see if this still feels right?"

Flynn scooped her against him. She wrapped arms around his neck so tightly her toes lifted off the ground. She kissed him back.

And it still felt right.

Epilogue

Maeve felt like a princess in her taffeta day dress. Aideen had been right about the exquisite French silk plaid in shades of orange, yellow, green and blue being striking on her small frame. Even her underclothing was made of quality fabric and lay smooth beneath the dress. Since her headpiece had become a wedding veil, Mrs. Kennedy had added a ruffled piece of ecru lace to her tiny hat accented with yellow silk flowers made to look like wild iris. The hat smartly covered one side of Maeve's forehead.

Martha Conley had done the honors of placing the hat and veil upon Maeve's head, because tradition called for a happily married woman to do that task.

Maeve wasn't much for superstition, but she loved the traditions of her homeland. The fact that sun shone on her now was thought by some to bring good fortune. She preferred to believe God had brought a bright day to assure her He was present and blessing their union.

Her sisters took her breath away in their new dresses, as well. Bridget's emerald-green sateen showed off her lovely hair and sparkling eyes. Nora stood regally tall and elegant in vivid blue linen. Grace wore a gown fashioned from one of Flynn's embroidered white shirts and trimmed with lace and pink ribbon. Nora had even managed to get a tiny bow to stay in her wispy auburn hair.

Nearly every passenger had gathered on the foredeck to witness the occasion. Maeve's gaze took in the Atwaters, Goldie McHugh with her husband and children, as well as Kathleen and her mother. She gave Mrs. Fitzwilliam and the McCorkle brothers a warm smile.

"You're the most beautiful woman ever to cross the Atlantic." Flynn's voice made gooseflesh rise on her arms. His dark eyes made a million promises, and her heart swelled.

The captain stood before them, looking resplendent in a dark blue uniform with his beard neatly trimmed and his hair cut. Beside him Martha dabbed her eyes. "I'm so pleased that the last wedding the cap'n performs is yours."

Gulls and pelicans flew overhead in profusion. The *Annie McGee* now sailed only a few miles from Boston Harbor, the entire coastline in view. Butterflies set up a wild flutter in Maeve's stomach.

She reached for Flynn's hand.

"Are you ready?" he asked.

She turned and looked up into his handsome face, and everything else faded into the background. This was the most important day of her life. The day that united her with Flynn Gallagher for life, a day they would tell their children about…a day to rejoice and be glad in.

"I'm ready."

* * * * *

Dear Reader,

I'm excited about this new miniseries, *Irish Brides,* and honored to kick it off with *The Wedding Journey.* The series starts toward the end of the Irish potato famine, 1845–1852, when a million people died and a million others immigrated. At this time, nearly all the land was owned by rich English families and overseen by agents or middlemen. The tenants were powerless, penniless and lived on potatoes and water. It's no wonder why so many dreamed of a new life and the possibility of owning their own land.

In *The Wedding Journey,* you'll see how the ship-owners took advantage of the fleeing Irish by selling passage on overcrowded and unsanitary ships, where thousands upon thousands died at sea. One of the best things about what I do as an author is my ability to create characters who deal with the worst conditions history can throw at them and survive. Meet the Murphy sisters, three young ladies determined to leave their lives of poverty and forge new lives in the land of the free and the home of the brave.

I believe you'll be inspired by their stories of courage and their discoveries of love.

Best to you,

Cheryl St. John

Questions for Discussion

1. Much to her sister's chagrin, Maeve repeats a saying she learned from her mother. A lot of us find ourselves repeating things we learned from our parents and grandparents. Some sentiments are helpful and others aren't. Can you quote something one of your parents used to say?

2. Maeve and her sisters find themselves starting over in a brave move to a new land. Life changes are always difficult. Has there been a time in your life when you felt as though you were starting over? How did you handle it?

3. Maeve has seen so many friends and family die that at first she doesn't trust herself to nurse injured and sick people on the ship. It's human nature to be wary of reliving unpleasant things from our past. What would you say to encourage an obviously capable person who's insecure about her abilities?

4. Nora tells Maeve that working as the doctor's assistant is a divine opportunity. Have you ever reached a point when you knew a particular breakthrough was no coincidence, but was part of God's plan? Did that knowledge give you confidence?

5. We've all met someone like Kathleen or Mrs. Fitzwilliam, who seem to think it's their lot in life to appear richer, prettier, more refined or smarter than the rest of the population. It's often difficult to remember that their own insecurities have shaped

them. If you've been able to put yourself in the shoes of a disagreeable person and find compassion, can you share how your perspective helped the situation?

6. Maeve and her sisters are thankful for little things, like a can of peaches or a particularly beautiful rainbow. We are often so caught up in our daily routine that we don't take time to reflect on our blessings. We must develop an attitude of gratitude in order to take the focus off our problems. Make a list of ten things that you are thankful for. Is there something on that list you can share or give away to another? Perhaps you can write a note of thanks to two or three people.

7. The Murphy sisters, though busy with their own positions aboard ship, were perfectly happy to take on the responsibility of caring for an abandoned newborn. Flynn was impressed by their selflessness. Do you know someone who is always willing to help out, even if it requires taking on what we might see as a burden? How do you suppose some people seem to do it all and others can barely find their way through their own day?

8. There were men and women in history, like Flynn, whose hard work and dogged lobbying created standards for ships, jails, schools, hospitals and the like, saving lives and creating better conditions for future generations. How much responsibility do you feel to continue the legacy of great leadership by involvement in your community and government?

9. When thinking about their uncertain future, one of the characters quotes Matthew 6:28: "Which of you by taking thought can add one cubit unto his stature?" The Bible tells us over sixty times to fear not. Do you have any verses that help you overcome fear? What does Psalm 18:2 mean to you?

10. Maeve chose to forgive Kathleen for her rude behavior, and even prayed for her, with deep compassion. Everyone has had an opportunity when they could either nurture an offense or recognize the source of the other person's venomous actions and let it go. If you can recall a time you forgave an offense, how did that change your feelings about the person?

11. Mrs. Fitzwilliam and Maeve share the experience of seeing a person who looks like a loved one they lost and, for a moment, forgetting it couldn't be that person. Has that ever happened to you?

12. We often pray for guidance or help, but then pick the burdens right back up and carry them. What do Psalm 18:2 and Proverbs 3:5 say about putting our trust in God? Does faith in God mean we don't have to do anything on our own?

13. When the women friends observe Dr. Gallagher holding the newborn, they grow silent. Maeve thinks of the moment as too pure and beautiful to spoil with words. Are there times you've been reduced to pure appreciation and felt that words were unnecessary?

14. Maeve is deeply moved by witnessing a crime and then a gruesome punishment. What sort of things do you find disturbing about the condition of people's hearts and the lack of respect for life or even other people's property? What needs to change in our society?

15. Flynn challenges Maeve's thinking, but nothing can move her unshakable faith. What is the difference?

16. Denial is an unhealthy way to deal with hurt and grief, but most of us do it in some form. Flynn couldn't allow himself to think about his wife or child or even say their names. If there's something in your past that you're unable to release, would this be a good time to ask for God's help and comfort? He has promised to take our burdens and give us peace.

INSPIRATIONAL

Love Inspired.
HISTORICAL

celebrating
15
YEARS

COMING NEXT MONTH
AVAILABLE MAY 8, 2012

MISTAKEN BRIDE
Irish Brides
Renee Ryan

HOMEFRONT HERO
Allie Pleiter

THE HOMESTEADER'S SWEETHEART
Lacy Williams

THE MARSHAL'S PROMISE
Rhonda Gibson

REQUEST YOUR FREE BOOKS!

2 FREE INSPIRATIONAL NOVELS
PLUS 2
FREE
MYSTERY GIFTS

HISTORICAL

INSPIRATIONAL HISTORICAL ROMANCE

YES! Please send me 2 FREE Love Inspired® Historical novels and my 2 FREE mystery gifts (gifts are worth about $10). After receiving them, if I don't wish to receive any more books, I can return the shipping statement marked "cancel". If I don't cancel, I will receive 4 brand-new novels every month and be billed just $4.49 per book in the U.S. or $4.99 per book in Canada. That's a saving of at least 22% off the cover price. It's quite a bargain! Shipping and handling is just 50¢ per book in the U.S. and 75¢ per book in Canada.* I understand that accepting the 2 free books and gifts places me under no obligation to buy anything. I can always return a shipment and cancel at any time. Even if I never buy another book, the two free books and gifts are mine to keep forever.

102/302 IDN FEHF

Name	(PLEASE PRINT)	
Address		Apt. #
City	State/Prov.	Zip/Postal Code

Signature (if under 18, a parent or guardian must sign)

Mail to the **Reader Service:**
IN U.S.A.: P.O. Box 1867, Buffalo, NY 14240-1867
IN CANADA: P.O. Box 609, Fort Erie, Ontario L2A 5X3

Not valid for current subscribers to Love Inspired Historical books.

Want to try two free books from another series?
Call 1-800-873-8635 or visit www.ReaderService.com.

* Terms and prices subject to change without notice. Prices do not include applicable taxes. Sales tax applicable in N.Y. Canadian residents will be charged applicable taxes. Offer not valid in Quebec. This offer is limited to one order per household. All orders subject to credit approval. Credit or debit balances in a customer's account(s) may be offset by any other outstanding balance owed by or to the customer. Please allow 4 to 6 weeks for delivery. Offer available while quantities last.

Your Privacy—The Reader Service is committed to protecting your privacy. Our Privacy Policy is available online at www.ReaderService.com or upon request from the Reader Service.

We make a portion of our mailing list available to reputable third parties that offer products we believe may interest you. If you prefer that we not exchange your name with third parties, or if you wish to clarify or modify your communication preferences, please visit us at www.ReaderService.com/consumerchoice or write to us at Reader Service Preference Service, P.O. Box 9062, Buffalo, NY 14269. Include your complete name and address.

LIH11B

When Brooke McKaslin returns to Montana on family business, she has no intention of forming any new relationships, especially with a man like Liam Knightly. But things don't always go according to plan....

Here's a sneak peek at MONTANA HOMECOMING by Jillian Hart.

"What's your story?" Brooke asked.

"Which story do you want to know?"

"Why adding a dog to your life has been your biggest commitment to date."

"How many relationships do you know that have stood the test of time?" Oscar rushed up to him, panting hard, his prize clamped between his teeth. Liam scrubbed the dog's head.

"Ooh, tough question." She wrestled with that one herself. "My parents are divorced. My father has divorced twice. The twins' mother has been in and out of marriages."

"My parents are divorced, too. Although they both live in Washington, D.C."

"The lawyers?"

"Both workaholics. Both are Type A."

"Things you inherited?"

"Mostly." He tugged his keys from his pocket, the parking lot nearer now. "Maybe I inherited the bad marriage gene."

"I know the feeling."

"That's why you're still single?"

"One reason." The truth sat on the tip of her tongue, ready to be told. What was she doing? She swallowed hard, holding back the words. What was it about Liam that made her guards weaken? She'd nearly opened up to him. She shook her head. No way did she know him enough to trust him. "It's my opinion men cause destruction and ruin wherever they go."

"Funny, that's my opinion about women." His slow grin made her heart skip a beat.

Good thing her heart wasn't in charge. She was. And she wasn't going to let his stunning smile weaken her defenses any further. Time to shore them up. She hiked her chin and steeled her spine.

"I know that's not fair." Liam winked. "But that's how it feels."

So hard to ignore that wink. She let it bounce off her, unaffected. She'd gotten as close to him as she was going to. Best to remember she worked for him, she was leaving as soon as the trial was over and the last thing she wanted was a man to complicate things. She had a life again. No way was she going to mess that up.

You'll love the rest of MONTANA HOMECOMING, from one of your favorite authors, Jillian Hart, available May 2012 from Love Inspired®.

SHLIEXP0512